THE BANISHED

THE
BANISHED

RON GABRIEL

GRAMERCY
FICTION

This is a work of fiction. Any references to historical events, real people, or real places are used fictitiously. Other names, characters, places and organizations portrayed in this novel are either products of the author's imagination or used fictitiously.

Interior design by Ron Gabriel
Edited by Julia Houston

Library of Congress Control Number: 2019915443

ISBN: 978-0-9979449-2-1 (paperback)
ISBN: 978-0-9979449-3-8 (ebook)

The Banished

Published by Gramercy Fiction

www.rongabriel.nyc

FOR MAURICIO

CONTENTS

PART ONE
ILLUMINATION

ONE

TRAVIS TRAILED HIS PARENTS UP the ancient stone steps, ill at ease and wary of the spell they'd crafted to empower him without killing a soul.

They crossed the columned foyer where grim murals overwhelmed the facade. Steely demons with horns, bat-like wings, and cloven hooves coaxed naïfs toward a hidden crevice where flames consumed the doomed. Travis was tempted to touch the anguished faces.

"Spookier than I imagined," he said. "The same Devil as our own."

"Superstition persists for good reason," Monica answered. "Times are scary, and the fearful cling to crutches. Tonight you must use it against them to test what you've learned."

Travis followed his parents into the monastery. Thick oak planks creaked shut on rusted hinges, and they waited for their eyes to adjust. Dying light struggled to enter through narrow stained-glass windows. Candles flickered within the main chamber; the room was packed with congregants standing side-by-side and chanting in low, rapid voices that chilled Travis as he listened. The

3

unsettling sound echoed from the vaulted ceiling in all directions.

He took tentative steps forward and surveyed the room. There were no seats, and the stone walls were bare save for several paintings of Christ and assorted saints with severe, almost hostile expressions as if daring the faithful to look away. A modest altar along the back wall butted against a maroon velvet curtain drawn over a vestibule.

Congregants were tightly ensconced in the oval-shaped area of the main chamber. Black hooded robes shielded their engrossed faces as they bowed and prayed. The insistent chant cycled on and on with such vehemence in perfect unison, an urgent sibilance that seemed a supernatural rite of its own.

Their chant sounds sinister, Travis silently transferred to his mother. *Unnerving. Diabolical.* For the first time he could imagine mortals as monsters capable of exacting their own brand of terror. He shrunk within the robe he'd donned to blend in.

Don't be deceived. They scare themselves within this theater of their own making. It fuels their superstition and intensifies prayers. Find your confidence.

Travis took his mother's hand, and she led the way through the crowd to the rear of the main chamber.

"The night before my birthday," Travis said aloud. "I can do it."

Victor smiled at his son, nodded, and stepped away. *You will do it.*

His parents maneuvered two congregants between them. Everyone in the room seemed to ebb and flow as a single unit, pressed together, focused on the chant, mesmerized by the spectacle of the sheer number of souls stuffed within the chamber and the otherworldly sound of the ancient verse. The sun had dipped below the trees, and the windows went dark. Candles suspended from cast iron chandeliers struggled against a draft and threw wavering shadows.

Travis rubbed his right arm against the back of a man standing beside him and bent to whisper in his ear, exactly as he'd practiced. Travis mimicked the orthodox chant until he switched to the rite of witches. His test subject gave him a wary look. They locked eyes. The man shifted his focus back to the center of the room and joined Travis in unison.

It worked. I did one, Travis transferred to his parents.

He repeated the process with the congregant to his left and then stepped defiantly deeper into the crowd. Soon they were his. He checked on his parents, who were surrounded on his right flank, and listened as the witches' rite took hold.

Nothing's happening, Travis transferred.

Wait for the fear to start, Monica answered. *They need to sense that something's amiss.*

Congregants on the other side of the chamber began to raise their voices as the unified buzz of the underlying orthodox chant became garbled and diluted.

Again Travis moved forward, pressed against the faithful, and whispered to convert them. Voices reciting the verse forced by the spell began to overcome the faltering and increasingly desperate exclamations of those focused on the original chant. They looked up from the floor and gasped at the vacant stares of their fellow worshipers as the prayer session went amok.

Move to the other side, Victor transferred.

Travis wove across the chamber, got into position, and focused on the handful of congregants who shuddered with horror, silent, eyes darting, unable to fathom what force of evil had overtaken the monastery.

I feel something, Travis transferred. He began to channel the power generated by their fear toward himself and his parents.

Slowly, deliberately, Monica transferred. *We're getting it. You're doing it perfectly.*

Travis took his time with those who until now had escaped. They were the most potent. He fixed one with a gaze and consumed the panic that pulsated outward. The gentleness of his touch belied the sinister forces at play. He whispered until the others joined him one by one.

The monastery powers it? Travis transferred.

Yes. A clash of forces, Victor answered. *Desecration. Our ancestors discovered the catalyst. It's economical. No one is harmed. The coven kills to achieve the same result.*

With all of the faithful turned, the trio of witches fed on the rush of energy that crackled within them. Echoes from the rite reverberated within the chamber.

I can't breathe, Travis transferred.

Relax and focus, Monica answered. *It's more than you've ever absorbed.*

They allowed the chant to buzz on like a swarm of angry bees until they'd filled reserves, feeling refreshed and heady as if awaking from hibernation. Monica and Victor were convinced Travis had mastered the tactic and could repeat it whenever he needed to refuel.

Victor stood in front of the velvet curtain and extended his palms.

"It is finished. You may go. You will recall nothing curious until the next time you hear our whispers."

The family slipped into the crowd, and the chanting abruptly stopped.

Congregants made their way to the foyer, and the monastery emptied. The priest went to the vestibule and reappeared with a stepstool and snuffer to extinguish the candles. When he'd finished, Travis and his parents followed him out as the last of the congregants dispersed.

They took several steps away from the entrance and removed their hoods. Only soft light from the moon illuminated the cobblestones of the square.

"I'm jittery," Travis said. "I feel so strange. Electric inside."

"It's your first time at high power," his father said. "Test it." He pointed to the steeple of a clock tower. "The weathercock. Spin it."

"I don't know how."

Victor frowned at his son and pointed again. The boy focused, nudged thick raven hair from his gaze, and slowly the weathervane turned as if the wind had shifted.

Again, Victor transferred. *Faster.*

Travis took a deep breath with eyes wide, forehead crinkled, and neck craned skyward. He felt a vibration rise from the pit of his stomach, up the back of his neck, and out through his forehead, centered exactly between his eyes.

Victor doubled over and groaned. When he stood, blood streamed from his nostrils.

Monica gasped and Travis ran to his father. "I'm sorry. I didn't mean it."

"You bolted me."

"I got confused. You were in my head."

"A misfire. You need to focus." Victor held a handkerchief to his nose and raised his eyebrows. "I'm OK. Forget it. We'll work on it tomorrow. Back to the weathercock."

Travis took a step forward and closed his eyes. The weathervane made fitful rotations before it began to spin as if enduring a twister. He collapsed on his back and spread out his arms as he caught his breath. "I feel drained out, no energy to move."

"Bolts eat lots of fuel. It proves you absorbed plenty. You're at a high level," Victor said as he helped his son to his feet, "or you couldn't shoot them at all. But you need to train."

"They told me our spells are weak. Only a kill gives power."

Victor shook his head. "You needn't heed the ignorant. They don't understand our magic."

"They're envious because we innovate," Monica said. "The hardliners fear us. Their tactics are crude and outdated."

Travis looked at his father's bloodied handkerchief. "I made a mistake."

"On the contrary. You've outdone yourself on the eve of your fifteenth year." Monica stared into his gray-green eyes, and pressed both palms against his cheeks. "We bore witness for the coven. We are most proud."

"You will master more weapons," Victor said as he joined them. "High training's just begun."

"Why are we different?"

"The magic of our ancestors is elevated. One day the coven will covet our techniques." Victor's smile and deep-set charcoal eyes beamed at Travis even as he shielded his nose. "You will lead it forward."

TWO

THE COVEN HAD SECRETLY infiltrated the fabric of daily life in Bucharest even before Prince Vlad Dracula took up residence in 1459 to escape the isolation of Transylvania. Travis' parents were the privileged progeny of bloodlines that could be traced back centuries.

A taste for making their own rules emerged from an early age. They'd partnered during telepathic drills long before others had considered the tactic. Though nothing they'd studied encouraged it, the pair forged a connection that enhanced their potency whenever they teamed up. Coven elders bolstered innovation and curiosity by treating it as bullion.

Monica and Victor shared a desire to put what they'd uncovered within manuscripts into practice on unsuspecting townspeople. As they explored the markets among an uneasy mix of peasants and uppity Victorian-era shoppers in formal attire, the pair outwardly appeared as a young lady and gentleman from proper 1870s families even as they stalked their prey.

Monica selected exactly whom she wanted to control and

signaled her partner. They trailed a rotund man with a black top hat and a trench coat that failed to conceal the droop of his trousers as he perused offerings and stopped in front of the wooden cart of a cheese vendor. The man haggled for a taste of Bryndza cheese. The merchant shrugged and produced a piece of bread and spread a sample on it. The man took a piggish bite. Victor clumsily yet carefully bumped him from behind, causing him to drop the rest.

"Stupid boy," the man snarled.

"Sorry, sir," Victor said as he bent to recover the morsel from the muddy road. "Be careful. The cheese. It's rancid. Can't you smell it?"

The man spat out what he'd chewed. Victor discreetly scooped up the paste, pushed it into a small bottle, and passed it to Monica. Often the trickiest part was devising a way to get organic matter such as hair, sweat, blood, spittle, urine, or flakes of skin from their selected target. The residues were necessary catalysts for any given spell.

"Get away from here," the merchant snapped at Victor. "This is the finest cheese."

"I'm sorry. My mistake," Victor said as he and Monica stepped backward and disappeared into the crowd. They huddled together, shook the bottle to combine the paste with the resins and botanicals they'd prepared, and recited an incantation exactly as they'd been taught.

A few moments later, they returned to the cheese cart and found the man pressuring the merchant for a fresh sample. Monica gently rubbed the bottle against the small of the man's back. Victor reached up to rest his hand on the man's shoulder.

"Let me pay for it," Victor said as he rubbed against him. "Don't touch me," the man said and tried to shake off Victor's arm.

Victor resisted and dug in with his fingertips even as the man's demeanor changed. He turned to acknowledge Monica and then studied Victor for a moment before he spoke.

"Would you like anything?" the man asked.

A smile formed on Victor's lips to create dimples above his square jaw. "Yes, please," Victor said and motioned to the merchant. "Whatever he recommends."

The man ordered from the vendor, who looked with suspicion at the students as he prepared two parcels. The man paid and handed the cheese to Monica. She placed it into a bag she wore over her shoulder along with the bottle.

"Something else?" the man asked.

"Yes," Monica answered. "Candles, bread, and sausage. We've got quite a list."

Follow us, Victor transferred to the man. He nodded, turned from the cheese cart, and moved quickly to keep step with the pair. *Don't falter.*

Do you feel it? Victor transferred to Monica. *The rush? The infusion of energy?*

I could mount a stallion with no stirrups. Her long, straight black hair shifted as she ran, revealing a smirk and hazel eyes wide with excitement.

They made it to the bread cart and waited for the man to join them at the front of the line.

Two loaves bundled separately, Monica directed. He ordered from the vendor, paid, and handed the gift to Monica.

Meet us at the butcher shop, Victor transferred. *Hurry, lard ass.*

The teenagers smiled mischievously as they darted from the counter and disappeared into the crowd. *Let him struggle to keep up*, Victor transferred to Monica, who nodded and laughed as they jostled against shoppers and wove past horse-drawn carriages.

They joined the queue in the front of the butcher shop and ordered when their turn came. The worker asked them to pay just as the man arrived, sweating and breathless, at the counter.

"Our father will pay," Monica said and nudged the man forward.

The worker took the money and handed over bundles of sausage and lamb.

Next, candles, Monica transferred as they backed away from the counter and rushed outside. *What's taking so long?* They waited a moment for their benefactor to find them. As the threesome turned the corner, a regal woman with arms folded stepped from the crowd and planted herself in front of the students.

"Release him," the woman said. Golden hair framed a beauty both weathered and ethereal, and shimmered in the sunlight over the high collar of an ebony gown.

"Of course, Elisabeta," Victor answered.

The pair turned to face the rotund man and murmured softly.

He studied their faces with a quizzical look. "Who in hell are you? What's happened?" With an air of annoyance and confusion, he backed away and disappeared into the crowd.

"You've gone too far, as I've come to expect," Elisabeta said. "We will meet with your parents. Everyone together. You've left me no choice."

The students nodded with their eyes averted. Elisabeta was a coven supreme who enforced codes of conduct. Episodes in the field that might risk exposure of the coven were forbidden, and witches sought to avoid the shame of her displeasure.

"The cheese vendor," Elisabeta said. "He was suspicious. These are dangerous times. Changes are afoot. Even the telephone frightens. People are superstitious, and strange behavior is suspect. You could be branded troublemakers."

"The fat man will remember nothing," Monica said.

"But the cheese vendor witnessed his transformation and generosity. The butcher inside thinks the man is your father. These people might know each other. They talk. You need to consider what can spin off from your actions."

"We're sorry," Victor said. "Please don't tell on us."

"I must. They need to know about your pairing up and recalcitrant dispositions. Perhaps they can confront what is unfolding."

By the time they returned to the coven, Monica and Victor's parents had already been alerted and a chamber cleared for the seven of them to meet. Elisabeta explained the indiscretions she'd observed in the market, though she made her greater motive clear:

"As an elder, I must ensure the health and longevity of the coven. When a pair emerges with no bloodline or intimate link yet instinctively operates more powerfully combined than singly, the coven must take note. We must nurture the interaction and guide them so the rush of excitement does not cloud their discretion. There is every reason to expect their synergy to someday engender gifted offspring, at the appropriate time."

For two families from bloodlines of powerful witches, the news was welcome, even cause for celebration. That their handsome progeny appeared destined to one day court and produce a powerful heir elevated their own status.

With the overt approval of Elisabeta and a blessing from their families, Monica and Victor spent more time together with no cause to hide their mystic connection. At the age of twenty, they had a son, Travis. They enjoyed privileged status as the parents of a newborn from the bloodlines of high-level witches and put aside all experimentations in favor of bonding with their heir.

In keeping with common practice, the most powerful families maintained private volumes of spells that had been honed and recorded by their ancestors, rooted in black magic devised by disciples of the Devil. The private spells could only be performed by direct descendants, who sometimes took decades to advance the magic before passing it on to their heirs.

As soon as he was old enough to amuse himself, Travis accompanied his parents to practice sessions. He played next to them while they studied manuscripts spread out on the wide-plank table. Other times he chased animated objects or mixed exotic ingredients into bottles to create smoke, foams, and intense swings in color and temperature.

As he learned to read Romanian, they introduced him to the volumes of handwritten ancestral spells that would one day be his. Travis inherited his parents' curiosity and talent, to the delight of coven elders and tutors. Like all worthy parents, Monica and Victor felt an innate urgency to offer tools that would secure his future safety and happiness.

It wasn't surprising, then, when a poisoning befouled their oasis, and the pair panicked.

Soon after his twelfth birthday, Travis took the family dog, Dragos, for his nighttime walk. It was raining, so he let the dog off the leash while he took cover under a tree. Dragos detected a scent, tore off, and bounded back several minutes later, panting and dripping.

"Where did you go?" Travis wondered aloud as he secured Dragos and hurried inside the coven walls. "You usually hate the rain."

Travis toweled Dragos off in the main room of the house and left him to sleep on a tuffet. The young witch wished his parents good night and went up to his room.

A drizzle pattered, and Travis thought he heard whimpers in the night as he dreamed and tossed, but the distant thunder was soothing, and the window was drafty.

When he awoke, he thought of the nocturnal cries and sought to dismiss them. He scurried downstairs to check on Dragos, but pools of vomit and feces surrounded the dog's body on the floor. He stroked his pet, but was repelled by the cold stiffness. He shrieked and called out to his parents. They scrambled to his side.

"I heard him in the night, crying. I thought it was a dream."

"How could you know?" Monica asked and hugged him.

"I didn't check. I could have helped. I could have saved him."

"It's not your fault."

"He ate something," Victor said. "They use poison in the streets for rats."

"I never said goodbye."

"We will get another dog," his parents said, almost in unison.

"No." Travis pulled away and slunk to his room.

Monica and Victor cleaned up the mess, and then went to check on their son.

"Do you want to help me bury him?" Victor asked.

Travis didn't answer and pretended to sleep. His parents left and closed his door.

A few hours later, Victor collected the dog's things and dug a grave for Dragos under the tree in their garden.

Observing their son's pain was a new and unwelcome experience for the pair, and they took action. Monica found a spell marked with an encircled black star in a family volume. The star indicated it delved into a restricted genre that conjured life from death.

In the unnerving hush of the evening that capped the unsettling day, Monica brought the spell to her husband's attention. He advised they sleep on it before formulating any schemes. They tucked Travis into bed without a hint of what they were considering. After breakfast the next morning, with their usual quiet accord, they came to the same conclusion. They kept quiet until Travis left for school.

"It's impossible to resist," Victor said.

"We've never attempted a star," Monica said.

"I think we can handle it."

"Our skills are solid. We understand the logic."

"The body is fresh. Easy to dig up."

"I'll wash him before Travis returns from his lessons."

Victor went to the garden, and Monica soon joined him under the tree with a metal washtub. He dug carefully to undo the previous day's work. When he got deep enough, he kneeled and used his hands to clear dirt away from Dragos' body. Monica helped brush debris from the fur, placed him in the tub, and brought him inside.

When she finished washing the dog, she laid his body on a blanket to allow him to dry. Victor joined her to develop the incantation. They agreed on the changes they would make, given the central spell was composed to allow adaptation depending on what or who had died. They added a page of their own to competently record the experiment.

"How long will it last?" Victor asked.

"We can stop when we wish." She pointed to the text. "If something goes wrong."

In the early afternoon, Travis came home from classes and found his parents sitting quietly on the floor beside the cleaned body of Dragos. The mood in the room was somber, and he immediately became alarmed.

"What's happening?" Travis asked.

"We've prepared a spell," Monica answered.

"To help him?"

"Yes," Victor said. "To wake him, for a little while."

"Long enough to say goodbye," Monica said.

Travis nodded and sat down next to his parents with his legs folded under him. He was dubious but wanted to see if

Dragos would come back. The allure of his parents' magic overpowered his reservations.

Monica and Victor moved closer to Dragos, and gently massaged his body from head to tail as they recited their incantation. Travis stared as his parents chanted softly from the old book lying next to them. He carefully watched for any sign of movement from Dragos and held his breath when his parents stopped speaking and removed their hands from the dog. The room fell silent except for the *tick* following each swing of the pendulum of a large wooden clock in the corner.

Travis gasped when Dragos began to stir with a tiny tremor in his legs. Slowly, the dog started to paddle, as if he were trying to swim. He opened his eyes and raised his head off the floor. His gaze was confused and expressionless through dark, discolored pupils.

"He looks strange," Travis said between rapid breaths. "I don't like it."

Dragos struggled to his feet and lurched about, his legs buckling. Travis slid toward him on the floor, scooped him up, and held him close. Dragos trembled, and Travis looked warily at his parents.

"Just soothe him," Monica said. "Say goodbye."

Travis petted Dragos carefully and firmly, pressing the dog against his chest. He still felt cold.

"Shh," Travis whispered. "I'm sorry. I'm sorry."

He kissed Dragos on top of the head above his eyes.

Travis felt a vibration stir within Dragos' core that swelled into a menacing growl. The dog bared his teeth and snapped at Travis' face. Travis flinched and pushed the dog away.

But Dragos lunged at the side of Travis' neck in a savage, snarling outburst. Travis screamed and jumped to his feet. He dropped Dragos and cowered behind his parents.

Dragos kept low to the ground, ears back, livid and aggressive. He faced off against Victor, ready to pounce, his growl guttural.

"Make him stop!"

Monica spread her fingers in front of the dog's face and whispered a few syllables. Victor joined a second refrain. Dragos yelped and dropped to the floor.

Victor sprung to his feet and grabbed Travis. "He's bleeding."

Monica rushed behind and hugged them.

Travis began to sob quietly. "I didn't like it."

"I'm so sorry," Monica said. "We didn't know what to expect. It was the first time."

"Just an experiment," Victor said. "A long shot, to give you a chance to say goodbye. The poison wasn't your fault. There was nothing we could do for Dragos. Except try this."

"He hates me now," Travis whispered.

"Of course not," Monica said.

Travis wiped his eyes and went with Monica to the sink to clean the bite and dress it.

"Come down to the garden when you're ready," Victor said.

Travis nodded, and Victor gathered up Dragos in the blanket and headed outside. A short while later, Travis and Monica joined him under the tree. Blood from the bite had already begun to soak through a spot on the bandage on Travis' neck. Victor carefully placed Dragos in the hole and reburied him. When he finished, they sat together for a while near the small grave.

"He didn't mean it," Monica said and gently raised Travis' chin with her finger.

"It wasn't really him," Travis whispered. "And he wasn't happy."

THREE

THE BITE FROM DRAGOS had left a small scar on Travis' neck, and it would be two years before he opened himself to another pet. Lucian, a close friend of Monica and Victor, lived nearby and often let Travis play with his friendly Carpathian Sheepdog. The day arrived when Lucian appeared with a puppy from the shepherd's first litter, weaned and ready for adoption. Travis was seduced and his parents relieved. They named him Luca to honor the family friend.

Travis bonded with Luca for several weeks without incident. But the first excursion outside the coven walls revealed an additional scar left by Dragos. Travis obsessed over Luca's whereabouts, terrified the puppy might ingest poison. He resisted Luca's every pause to sniff the curbs or lick the bark of trees. Despite a short, strong leash and repeated attempts to reason with him, his parents were unable to assuage Travis' fears, which grew excessive and irrational as time passed.

Desperate for a trick that might calm Travis, Monica requested a bone from the worker in front, Dorin, who made clear without any cue from Monica that he was in control of the business and all significant orders. If she wanted just a bone, she would have to go to the back room where his father was stationed.

Monica found an old man hunched over a chopping block in the shadowy light of two oil lamps. He quietly introduced himself as Bogdan and explained without any cue from Monica that he'd been ordered by his son to remain in back, near the ice box, out of sight. He was the founder of the shop and missed contact with customers.

Monica politely told Bogdan about the accidental poisoning of Dragos and requested a bone for Luca that might discourage him from foraging about the streets. Bogdan was happy to produce a puppy's dream bone. Monica thanked him profusely, paid Dorin in the front, and joined Travis outside.

"Luca won't want anything else," Monica told Travis as she unwrapped the bone and Luca's tail whipped as he leapt for it.

Travis beamed and seemed to relax as they made their way home with Luca's attention fixed on his treat. "It's working."

Buoyed by the success of her plan, Monica made frequent visits to the butcher. She grew to despise Dorin, who viewed himself as powerful and irresistible and made no secret of his attraction to her despite knowing she was married. That he was handsome made it worse. He never wore a jacket, and left one or two shirt buttons open on top.

"Got a big one today," Dorin said.

"Same as always. Bogdan always takes care of me."

"Mine is thicker and longer."

"I'd like to pay, please."

"You'll be in no rush when I take care of you."

"Bogdan does just fine."

That he kept his father in the back room like a neglected servant angered her. Bogdan often shared that he felt discarded and powerless, a stranger trapped within the bowels of the shop he'd created himself from scratch. He couldn't stand up for himself against his strapping son, who diminished Bogdan's contributions from the chopping block.

"He's waiting for me to die," Bogdan told Monica one afternoon. "He'll take it all anyway. He can't wait for me to disappear. He lives across town but keeps me here."

Monica sat with him and sensed the seed of a scheme. She saw the arrogance and callousness of Dorin as an evil she could somehow put to use, something to feed from. Many of the incantations she'd studied had advanced her technique, but learning exactly how to absorb energy to replenish reserves of power had proven elusive. The conjuring of Dragos had produced no fuel.

Monica knew a spell needed to generate fear and confusion to bestow power in turn. The strongest witches had found ways to harness the energy needed to advance. No one would teach it. Those in control kept power to themselves and would never disclose the secret behind their ascent. That much she'd figured out about many elders on the council.

In the evenings after Travis was in bed, Monica discussed her visits to the butcher with Victor, who agreed Dorin would be a worthy target. In his own studies, Victor had discovered that potent fuel could be drawn from victims who at first exhibited high degrees of lust, greed, arrogance, or cruelty.

The rapid conversion of swagger to cowering fear catalyzed the power that could be absorbed.

"I have a plan," Monica announced one evening.

"To humiliate Dorin? Put his father in front. Make Dorin chop."

She considered it. "I think I'll wait for Bogdan to die."

Victor looked up from his book.

"He sleeps in a room behind the chopping block," she continued. "When he passes, there will be an opportunity, a chance to test on a human."

"Conjuring is restricted," Victor said. "We could get caught."

"I'd rather beg forgiveness than ask permission. It's the only way to advance. We've plateaued. We've got to create better tools for Travis."

"Control of townspeople works."

"It isn't enough. Power rises from fear."

"Or from kills, the traditional way." Victor closed the thick leather cover of his book, and prodded it over a knot on a tabletop. "We're going to exploit the monastery."

"That's not the only path our ancestors left us."

"They were visionaries."

"And resourceful. They worked with those already dead."

"But the coven stopped them." Victor rubbed his trimmed beard.

"Most elders can't do it, so they restricted it. They fear conjurings." Monica perused her volume and settled on a spell with a circled black star. "These are the most powerful tools we've got. Forget the dictates of some elders; the hardliners haven't the foresight or ability to try anything new."

"The coven used to allow conjurings."

"My grandmother got too strong. That's my theory."

"It's not fair to us. The spells we've inherited."

Monica nudged a long strand of raven hair behind her ear as she raised her eyebrows and locked eyes with Victor. "It's time to advance what's ours by birthright. All we need is a corpse."

"How could you know when he dies?"

"When he falls ill, I'll ask to be his caretaker. Dorin won't object. Less work for him."

Over the weeks to come, Monica stopped by the butcher shop every few days, sometimes for bones for Luca, other times for meats, but always to gain access to Bogdan, who grew to depend on her visits.

She suffered through conversations with Dorin, but secretly worked to ensnare him as she collected fragments of organic matter in a bottle: paper from parcels he'd handled and soiled with grease from his fingers or a smear of blood from a small knife cut; strands of hair on the counter or on his shirt; sweat from his forehead or neck that Monica sometimes flirtatiously wiped away with a handkerchief; and saliva from a bite of bread or cheese that Monica fed him by hand.

Bogdan slowly deteriorated and some days never left his bed. Dorin allowed Monica to visit his father and dispatched her to the back room, happily freed from any care giving. But he always preened until he was sure Monica was enthralled by his virility before dismissing her.

"I'm worried about your father," Monica said. "He's getting worse."

"He's just old."

"How can I help? You have so much to do. Here, you missed a spot." She dabbed at his thick lower lip with her kerchief and tucked it away.

"You can keep me company."

"Bogdan needs it more."

"I give him what he needs. I'm a people pleaser. I'll show you." Dorin folded thick arms across his chest, leaned over the counter, and puckered his lips.

"I'd like to see him, if you please."

Dorin huffed and put his hands on his hips. "Always such a rush. Go on back. You'll see there's nothing anyone can do."

Monica made her way to the rear of the premises and sat on the bed next to Bogdan. She encouraged him to rage against his son, who so obviously did so little to help him.

"Do you have enough to eat?" she asked.

"He leaves me a plate on the chopping block." Bogdan spoke slowly between coughs. A quilt was pulled up just below the neck of his nightshirt. "I never know when."

"He doesn't knock? What about the dishes?"

"I pile them on the floor. Roaches come. In the night, a mouse."

"You have to do something."

"If I could, I'd stick him," Bogdan said. "Watch him bleed out."

"He's your son, the only family you've got."

"Ungrateful. A disgrace. Inheriting everything. Not a care for me. Look at this room."

"What if you could make him pay after you're gone?"

"How? What do you mean?" He caught himself drooling and struggled to sit up.

"A sweet revenge to teach him a lesson. Scare him into remorse or madness."

"Tell me more."

"Make him beg for life."

"Why not now?"

"So much more fun after you've passed," the witch said.

"Imagine his shock."

Bogdan chuckled, which led to another coughing spell. "If only it could be."

When Monica next visited at the end of the week, she toyed with Dorin at the front counter as usual. After a few minutes, he casually informed her his father was dead. His demeanor was so nonchalant she thought she'd misheard. When she asked for clarification, Dorin explained that his father had passed in the night and was still in his bed awaiting the coroner, who was expected by day's end to transport the body to the city morgue. Monica asked if she could see Bogdan to pay her respects. Dorin nodded and returned to his work.

Monica made her way to the back, crept past the chopping block, and quietly opened the door to Bogdan's room. Stale urine and rot stained the air. She sat on the bed and touched the man's face. His skin was cold, gray, and rigid; his expression was pained, and his tongue was caught between his teeth; his eyelids were half open.

Come to the butcher now, Monica transferred to Victor. *Bring Travis.*

She propped up the pillows and tried to arrange Bodgan's

body to appear less contorted. She lifted the blanket and discovered his nightshirt and sheets were soiled from an overturned bedpan that apparently had gone unattended for days. It seemed he had been without food or water or human contact in his final hours, and Monica seethed at Dorin's neglect. She heard voices coming from the front of the shop, and soon Victor appeared in the doorway with the manuscript from Monica's parents under his arm. Travis looked warily about the room and covered his nose.

"And Dorin?"

"The bottle you prepared," Victor said. "He waved me through without a second look."

"Is he still under your control?"

"No."

"Good. I want him raw."

Victor opened the book and laid it on the bed. They stood on both sides of the old man's body and placed their hands on his face and hair, massaging the cold flesh with their fingertips. Travis watched awestruck from his post against the wall as his parents read the incantation aloud a few times before reciting it from memory with closed eyes. Several minutes passed before Bogdan began to stir, first with a twitch of his shoulders and then with a spasm of his neck that flung his head against the pillow.

The witches continued the chant but withdrew their hands as Bogdan bent his arms and struggled to sit up; darkened orbs in his sockets shifted wildly from side to side atop his grimace. His jaw opened widely and closed several times as if he were trying to speak, but no words came, only a low gurgle from the depths of his throat.

"Bogdan?" Monica asked. "Can you hear me?"

Bogdan grunted and seemed to study her face as she moved closer. His groan quieted as she spoke.

"It's time for revenge. Dorin did this to you. Do you remember?"

Bogdan hoisted himself to a sitting position. He nodded his head slowly. "Dorin," he said in a deep voice. His expression morphed into a malevolent sneer; the gurgle returned through bared teeth. Travis gasped and moved toward the door.

His parents watched their handiwork with amazement as Bogdan leaned forward and pushed the covers away with wild but effective thrusts of his arms. Travis saw the filth of his nightshirt and covered his eyes as Bogdan pushed his legs over the side of the bed and steadied himself.

Monica opened the door and motioned to Bogdan. "The butcher block."

Bogdan walked unsteadily with arms outstretched as he made his way out of the room. His nightshirt was askew because dried fluids stuck the fabric to the small of his back. He hobbled to the butcher block and with an approving nod from Monica took hold of a carving knife.

"I'll guide you," she said.

Bogdan grunted and gripped the knife tightly as he took steps forward. Travis scurried out of his way.

Victor and Monica passed in front of Travis, quietly unlatched the door that led to the front of the store, and listened as it creaked open while they waited for Bogdan to approach.

When he made his way past them, a guttural sound like

the growl of an enraged cat emerged from Bogdan's throat, chilling even Monica and Victor as they kept themselves hidden and watched as Bogdan lurched toward Dorin behind the counter.

When Dorin turned toward the sound and spied his father, he gasped. A stench filled the store as Bogdan drew closer with steps that grew steady as he hoisted the knife.

"No!" Dorin shouted. "It's not possible! You're dead. I was certain."

"You left me to die."

"There was nothing more to do."

"Liar." Bogdan slashed the air with the blade as he continued forward.

"The energy," Monica said to Victor. "It's flowing from Dorin."

"Yes. I feel it too. Incredible."

Travis watched transfixed as his parents opened their arms with upraised palms, like rods absorbing bolts, as power streamed into them while Bogdan closed in on Dorin.

"Stop!" Dorin shouted between rapid gulps for air. "Get away from me!"

He wheezed and backed away from his father, but he found himself trapped against the wall next to the windowsill. Bogdan slashed with the knife and forced Dorin to cower with his back sliding down until his buttocks hit the floor. He sobbed and struggled to shield himself from the attack. He glanced between his fingers and screamed as Bogdan towered over him.

An evil laughter filled the room as Bogdan appeared fully cogent and triumphant with legs planted firmly, knife held to

Dorin's throat, and his ungrateful son reduced to quivering in front of him.

"Do not kill him," Monica commanded. "Already you've gained your revenge."

The front door to the butcher shop burst open. Elisabeta sailed in and slammed her fist on the counter with enough force to belie her elegance. Travis scurried behind his father.

"Stop!" Elisabeta shouted, sternly focused on Monica and Victor, who still quaked from the rush of power.

They terminated the spell, and Bogdan dropped to the floor. Dorin continued to sob as his father's body collapsed upon him with the filth of the nightshirt in his lap.

"You know it is forbidden," Elisabeta said.

"We had to experiment," Monica said. "An exceptional opportunity to explore."

"Conjurings draw the interest of the Devil. The reanimated are difficult to control. There are more efficient means to empowerment."

"We will learn the controls," Victor said.

"It is safer to kill."

"Our best ancestral spells mandate use of the dead. What are we to do?" Victor asked.

"We can advance the technique for the coven," Monica added. "Do not reject it out of habit because we are outnumbered."

"The larger issue is disregard for rules," Elisabeta said. "And indoctrinating your son. You will both appear before the council tonight for a formal reprimand."

"We are on the cusp of something new without a trail of bodies," Monica said.

"Save it for tonight. You've got a mess to clean up. Watch for customers."

With a look of disgust, Elisabeta turned and left the butcher shop.

Travis panted in the corner.

"What's happening?" Dorin asked from a fetal position on the floor next to Bogdan's body. "Who was that? What's wrong with my father?"

"He's dead," Victor said and moved behind the counter. "Shut up and control yourself."

Dorin craned his neck and slowly made his way to his feet.

"Look at me," Victor commanded, and Dorin immediately complied.

You will return your father's body to his room. Clean him properly to be received by the coroner. Then get back to work. You will remember nothing of his attack or of our presence here.

Dorin nodded. He bent to grasp Bogdan's body by the armpits, turned him around, and slowly dragged his father away.

"Whatever trouble we face, I don't care," Monica said. "I've never felt so *aware.*"

"Elisabeta knows we've discovered it. An alternative means of advancement. The elders want to stop us and use dictates to keep us down. Hardliners lack any urge to evolve; their own ancestral spells empower them through murder. Fueling from fear alone is superior. I'm convinced of it. Bogdan was already dead, and put to good use. Dorin lives to charm another day. And yet we are empowered as if we'd slaughtered him."

"We'll stress our goal is to develop an alternative to kills for the betterment of the coven. No corpses lingering as clues, and we get to use our best tools. They'll understand."

"How did she know?" Victor wondered.

"The transference. Elders can monitor restricted spells. It's the only explanation. Next time, we'll find a way around it." Monica looked at Travis' stricken face. "Don't worry. Elisabeta can be reasoned with. The elders will come around. They'll see the value of our work."

"This is worse than Dragos," Travis said. "Scarier."

"But through it we've learned and gained strength," Monica said. "A witch must rise or wither. Power must be taken to survive. You are young, and it's all scary. I remember. You'll gain confidence when you master your own test on the eve of your fifteenth year. You will shock the coven. They will witness your infusion of power."

"They told me I must kill. That's the only way to grow strong."

"There's another way," Victor said. "We're forging a new technique to use in a monastery. Something just for you. No one will die, and no one will remember."

They listened as Dorin drew water into a bucket and watched from the doorway as he removed Bogdan's soiled nightshirt and underclothes and washed him on the floor near the chopping block. The bedding lay in a pile along the wall, on top of the abandoned dishes.

"I'd like to make Dorin suffer," Monica said. "But it's more work for us."

"Killing *is* easier," Victor said. "The hardliners have a point."

"Dorin is lucky we're enlightened."

"Can we still get bones?" Travis asked.

After that, he hated the butcher shop and would only return for Luca.

FOUR

AT THE MEETING WITH the council, Monica and Victor received a reprimand and a reminder that spells within certain realms were restricted, regardless of witches' access from family manuscripts. Common within the coven were ancestral spells that relied on kills because methods had been perfected over centuries. Accidents were easy to craft and a mighty power surge always followed. Conjurings were untested and unpredictable, some elders warned, and a second infraction would be dealt with most harshly.

"Mysterious deaths in ancient times were commonplace," Victor argued. "The world is changing. We need new ways to refuel. It is foolhardy to leave mortals clues to trace."

"Our spells are unorthodox, but no one has to die," Monica added. "Old methods are wasteful, and the family left behind is motivated to assign blame."

"Coven disciples toiled to ensure our survival over centuries," Radu, the principal hardliner and enforcer of discipline, declared. "Nothing can match the power from a kill."

"Our method surpasses it," Victor countered. "Desecration

catalyzes power spun from fear. It's a diabolical twist. An innovation. The founding disciples would approve."

"The secret lies in our ancestral spell," Monica said. "We can perfect it and share it."

Some members of the council seemed impressed; others, mostly hardliners, scoffed. "Corpses pose little danger. We disguise them. Conjurings aren't so easily hidden," Radu said.

For months following the meeting, Monica and Victor acted as exemplary models in the coven. The couple discovered the power they'd absorbed from Dorin had broadened their perceptions, as if they were suddenly fluent in new and foreign tongues. A clarity of thought took hold of them both with an expanded ability to recall long-forgotten incantations. They now understood important footnotes in manuscripts that had seemed extraneous.

Travis soon discovered the imperative to master weapons after his trial in the monastery. Markus, the son of a hardliner, challenged him after test results of all the fifteen-year-olds were announced near November's end.

"Think you're too good for us?" Markus needled Travis on the cobblestones of the central courtyard after tutoring sessions had ended.

"No. You have your spells. We have ours."

"You're the only one who hasn't killed. You're soft. You weaken the whole class."

"Not all magic works the same. Don't be ignorant."

Markus pushed Travis from behind and he stumbled down stone block stairs into a narrow alleyway. He rolled to his back and pushed with his legs to slide away as he craned his neck to watch Markus march toward him. Six classmates followed.

"Let's see whose magic is better," Markus said.

A loose cobblestone the size of fist sailed over the heads of the students and grazed Travis' cheek as it smashed against the footpath next to his head. The young witches chuckled.

"Stop it! It's not funny." Travis leapt to his feet and backed away.

"Defend yourself," Markus taunted. "If your magic grants enough power."

Travis had little knowledge of weapons beyond the nerve bolt he'd accidentally shot at his father. He tried to take a backward step, but found himself immobilized.

"What's wrong?" Markus asked. "Can't run away?"

Travis' heart raced as he strained to move, but could only watch as Markus drew closer. Another cobblestone sailed from the courtyard and struck Travis in the stomach. He groaned and was terrified to find himself helpless to move his limbs or torso. His eyes darted, desperate to detect the next attack.

"The magic of the majority is stronger. It's in witches' blood from ancient times. You've studied the disciples. Your family is misguided and had better learn quickly. The coven needs strength to survive among humans. You infect us with weakness."

A broken wooden shutter struck Travis and he closed his eyes. He felt a stirring grow in his gut and rise up his spine. He forced it with all his strength through the witch eye on his forehead, and heard Markus shriek. Travis felt the lock on his limbs release, and he trudged toward Markus, who was doubled over with pain and gasping for breath.

"We are not weak," Travis said. "Let us try new ways. We're *all* witches."

Markus looked up with wild eyes and gripped his nose to contain streams of blood. His classmates cleared the stairs, and Travis forced himself with all the confidence he could muster up to the courtyard without looking back.

He was exhausted from the energy spent on the nerve bolt, and cautiously navigated footpaths to his parents' stone villa nestled within the coven walls. The sitting room was empty when he entered, so Travis called out, and his parents came running.

Monica saw scratches on his face. "Travis? What happened? Are you OK?"

"Markus attacked me in the courtyard. I'm the only one who didn't kill." Travis held back tears. "I'm so sick of everyone treating me as lesser. Why are we so different?"

His parents hugged him.

"What did he do to you?" Victor asked.

"First, he froze me. Then came stones and wood. Why can't I do it?"

"We have different defenses. You've only unlocked one."

"I bolted him to escape."

"Good. And you will develop more weapons. It takes skill and high power. You've only just begun. I will teach you telekinesis. You have the ability. Remember the weathercock."

"I'm so tired. What's wrong?"

"Fighting burns through energy," Monica said. "You need to grow stronger, with reserves to carry you. For now, just rest. I'll draw a bath."

"Tonight we'll refuel in the monastery." Victor hoisted

Travis over his thick shoulders like a sack of kindling, and carried his spindly son toward the back of the house.

In early winter while Luca dozed on a blanket and Victor and Travis quietly studied at the table, Monica uncovered a passage in a manuscript that she'd previously disregarded. It outlined ways to temporarily evade the ever-watchful intuition of the elders. After the appearance of Elisabeta in the butcher shop, she knew it would one day prove useful. The primary method, she learned, was to transfer all thoughts to a third party, someone not performing the incantation, who would serve as a decoy.

"There's a way around the elders," she announced to the table.

Victor and Travis looked over.

"Communicate with Travis on one level while the incantation spins on another. We can do it now. Our abilities have grown. Dual planes. Travis will be the key to deflect our focus."

"It's too soon to risk it," Victor said. "The elders won't be amused."

"There's a reality we must face. Our ancestors gave us unique tools. It's our duty to advance what they began. The touch of desecration is original and economical. Fright is temporary; killings are not."

No one responded; then Travis closed his book.

"Why does power come from fear and death?" the boy asked. "Why not anything good?"

"We are witches of black magic, descendants from disciples of the Devil. Our essence feeds on darkness, not light. We may temper our methods to suit our motives, but we cannot glean power from good."

"Good is better?" Travis asked.

"Often there is little difference. They meet in the middle. Extremes are rare and repugnant to both sides."

"I want to help. I'm almost sixteen. Old enough."

"Yes, my son," Monica said. "You are ready. You've proved it in the monastery."

In the weeks that followed, the pair practiced transferring thoughts and whole pointless conversations to Travis while they performed telekinetic acts on a higher plane. Shattered vases confirmed their newfound ability to operate on multiple levels.

"Is it wrong to disguise a spell?" Travis asked Monica after a decoy practice session.

"No. It's arbitrary and unfair that the elders restrict them."

"I'm worried."

"About what?"

"Elisabeta."

"Don't be. She already caught us once, and everything turned out OK."

"Maybe next time she won't find out?"

"With you, I hope not. The coven thinks we're mavericks. But we aim to be enlightened. One day they'll catch up."

Victor taught his son to use weapons. Travis started with a cast iron candlestick, suspended it over a table, and in time hurled it at wine bottles lined up by the hearth. He learned to control the stirring that revved up nerve bolts before he fired them, and practiced on rats he stalked and still blamed for Dragos' death. The family refueled once a week, because spells and weapons burned power reserves. He was the only one of his peers who had yet to kill, but his magical prowess exceeded theirs, and he'd beaten Markus, so he trusted his parents' methods.

One sunny afternoon with Luca in tow, Monica led Victor and Travis to a quiet neighborhood of Bucharest, a twenty-minute walk from the city center. They climbed an embankment and arrived at a high, grassy ridge overlooking a pit containing bodies of cholera victims awaiting proper burial. No one spoke while they surveyed the grim spectacle.

"We'll select three," Monica said finally. "Conjure them as we did Bogdan."

"The grave is foul," Victor said. "Do we dare?"

"It's a resource perfect for our work: abandoned, plentiful."

"What is your plan?" Travis asked.

"To use those already dead to spawn fear," Monica answered. "We'll present our findings to the coven. Win over the skeptics."

"How will it go?" Victor asked.

"Our three emissaries revisit the families they left behind."

"And then what?"

"They disappear as if they'd never happened, nothing more than horror that dissipates with the dawn. They are forgotten by loved ones like a nightmare come daybreak."

"But we absorb the power that spins in the dark."

"Exactly."

Travis listened with wonder and eyed the contorted corpses.

"We wait for the vernal equinox," Monica said.

Luca grew restless, and they turned from the pit to return to the coven.

FIVE

AFTER WEEKS OF PREPARATION, it was time to set Monica's scheme into motion.

They'd practiced transferring conversational decoys to Travis while simultaneously honing the restricted spell on a plane hidden from Elisabeta. They bolstered the lessons learned from Bogdan's awakening with an incantation intended to direct and wield control over the corpses from the pit.

Monica and Victor understood their plan was risky, but the imperative to advance their work outweighed prudence. They needed to prove their hypothesis. Harnessing fear was safer for the coven than murder. Clues could be erased. And results would be potent.

In the afternoon, Monica, Victor, and Travis left Luca with food and water to last until morning, and Lucian agreed to walk him. They transcribed their newly crafted incantation to a single page, packed provisions, and ventured to the cholera pit. They placed their bundles below a tree in an adjacent field.

While Travis waited in the shade, Monica and Victor

43

began the grim work of examining corpses to find the least decomposed.

As the sun began to set, Victor and Monica pulled three bodies to a grassy rise near the tree. Travis watched as he transmitted the gibberish his parents passed him as they straddled each corpse and chanted while massaging their limbs, hair, and face. They stopped the incantation with the first spasms and backed away.

Travis could scarcely maintain his composure as vapor rose from each body and slowly congealed into rippling, translucent doppelgangers that hovered a while before seeping back inside. Each body quivered, then pitched forward, then floated upright with incongruous fluidity. A low growl rose from deep within, a warning, as dark eyes pierced through swollen sockets.

Travis crouched behind his parents, shaking. His contribution to the scheme as a decoy was complete, and he marveled at his parents' work. They quieted the snarls and established command over their drifting envoys with outstretched arms.

"Reclaim your earthly presence," Monica told them. "Return to your homes. Revisit your families. Implore them to receive you. If they refuse, convince them. Rage against the injustice of your fate. The hours ahead will be short and precious, ended at first light, a momentary respite from an eternity of tedium you've already tasted. You must savor this gift of vitality. At nightfall we act."

The ghouls glared at the trio of witches, hostile and confused as they came to a wavering suspension above the grass.

They look mean, much worse than Dragos, Travis transferred. *Don't let them close.*

They won't harm you. The spell is specific, Victor answered. *You are irrelevant to them. Summon your courage. We need you.*

When darkness settled in, the ghouls teetered toward the village square with an otherworldly smoothness punctuated by jolts as if repelled by a magnet. They navigated the ancient, winding maze of streets amid an unsettling chorus of snarls, and one by one veered toward their former homes.

Travis followed his assigned specter, which traversed the main street with a clear destination obviously in mind. Travis trailed from a distance, still frightened and ducking behind wooden carts parked for the night whenever pedestrians drew near.

Travis watched as a man emerged from a shop with a parcel, not far ahead. The ghoul seemed to fixate on him and gained ground. The man realized something unearthly lingered just beside him and ran. The specter chased him with outstretched arms, growled, and grabbed his shirt. The man screamed and dropped his package as he tried to break free. The ghoul overpowered him, pulled him close, and squeezed his neck while the man shrieked and flailed wildly. Fingers like claws lashed out with nails grown long after death and scratched his face. The man sobbed as he was helpless to stop a hand from entering his jacket and tearing at his chest through the front of his shirt. Buttons popped, and filth from the grave mixed with blood.

He's killing a man! Travis transferred to his parents.

All at once the specter lost interest, dropped his victim, and marched toward home.

As bystanders gaped from the street and hidden nooks along the way, Travis stole into the shadows away from gas lamps. A few people ran to the victim on the ground, who attempted to speak as he clutched at the wounds that bloodied his shirt. A woman spied the specter and screamed at the sight of its wavering silhouette as it mysteriously floated while other shouts and shrieks reverberated in the distance as the other two emissaries wrought havoc of their own.

From the moment of the attack upon the man until just before dawn, Monica and Victor absorbed an aura of power as it steadily infused them, fueled by the terror that gripped the streets. Townspeople hid or ran for cover, frantic, as they watched the ghouls glide with a menacing smoothness, shoes scarcely grazing the cobblestones. Bystanders unable to escape or foolish enough to interfere were scratched or bitten. Moans and screams punctuated the night as each of the three emissaries stalked their homesteads.

His neighbors recognize him, Travis transferred, as he continued to trail his specter, and he realized he was trembling. *They watch from doorways. I hear whispers.*

The conjured man, eerily wavering in the gaslight that flickered against masonry, came to linger outside a cottage window and tapped, waited, and then tapped again. Travis heard screams from within and ducked behind a tree.

"Daddy?" children's voices called out from inside. "Daddy's in the window."

Travis watched as the door cracked open and a woman took halting steps outside.

"Ivan? My God! Is it you?"

The ghoul glided into the light of the entryway. The woman reached out to touch his face and recoiled. Her dead husband, somehow risen, pushed her hand aside and stormed in.

"No!" she screamed as he marched toward four children huddled on the floor.

She leapt in front of the intruder, spread her arms, and waved them to block him, but her eldest son was snatched up and dragged from the room and onto the front lawn. The woman bolted out and jumped on his back while the children's screams pierced the darkness.

He's killing a boy! Travis transferred. *Shaking him like a rag. Do something!*

The woman fought savagely against bites and scratches and managed to wrest her stricken son from the attacker. They made it back inside and slammed and locked the door.

Travis watched the specter lurk outside. He pounded on the hardwood, gave up, and hovered in front of a window on the side of the house where his family huddled inside. The ghoul shattered the pane with a few sharp jabs, and shoved his head into the room.

"Don't leave me," a deep, otherworldly voice implored. "I am alone. Far away. Empty."

"Get away from here! My God. Help us!" Travis heard his wife shriek.

The conjured man pounded at the adjacent pane to widen the opening. He cleared away shards and then smashed another.

Travis hid under a hedge and watched as the back door

of the cottage creaked open. Two of the children climbed on their mother's back, and two clung to her legs. She slowly removed her hand from the mouth of her injured son, and motioned to him to remain quiet. They crept further, looked toward the intruder, and then made their way as quickly and silently as they could into the street.

Run! Please get away. Now's your chance.

The boy stumbled, but his sister grabbed his hand and dragged him until he regained his footing. They whimpered and chased their mother, who had already turned a corner.

The ghoul shimmied though the window with an incongruous grace. Travis waited and heard a roar. The former master of the house hovered beyond the back door, bellowed a second time, and then bolted after his family.

Travis sprang to his feet and followed. A mix of urgent pleas for help, shrieks of the children, and deep-throated moans of their father coursed through the darkness.

He's chasing them, Travis transferred. *He's awful. Please stop him!*

Come find us. Quickly! Monica answered. *On the main street, toward the clearing. We need to get away.*

Travis felt his mother's alarm and dropped his pursuit of the family to rejoin his parents. When he found them, he was struck by their wide-eyed jitters. *What's wrong?*

Too much to absorb, Monica answered. *The fear spirals like a geyser.*

Are you OK?

Yes. We've proven it works. Stronger than we expected.

It went too far. I saw horrible things. A boy younger than me. A whole family chased.

Spells work in steps. We will refine it, narrow its focus.

With the light of dawn, the trio fled to the tree near the cholera grave to watch for their emissaries, who magically reclaimed their places in the pit. What they hadn't planned on were the mobs armed with pitchforks, torches, and knives who took to the streets, desperate to punish and expose whatever dark force had stricken them overnight.

Townspeople directly attacked by the ghouls remembered nothing, but there were witnesses and strange, lingering injuries to explain. The blasé shrugs and blankness of victims dumfounded and enraged their neighbors who had watched events unfold.

The witches' optimistic and energized state gave way to trepidation as the fury gained strength. The trio retreated to the coven. Safely inside the stone walls, they still considered the night a success: a difficult spell had been mastered, great power surged through them without kills, and they were prepared to report the findings to the elders as a new tactic for the coven.

But the neighborhood's ordeal had been traumatic and impossible to rationalize. By midday, citizens stormed the streets and filled the monasteries. They vowed to fight the supernatural forces, and anyone suspicious would pay with their lives.

The violent atmosphere poisoned all of Bucharest. It didn't take long for the coven to assign Monica and Victor the blame for putting it at risk. Elisabeta had caught them with Bogdan just months ago, and they had been clearly warned to refrain from conjuring. A line had been crossed. Ancient rules established to ensure the safety of the coven had been ignored.

In the evening, Elisabeta knocked at their door and questioned Monica and Victor directly. They knew it was pointless to lie to a supreme member of the council.

"It was a ten-hour experiment," Monica said. "A test."

"Why did you shield us from your 'experiment?'"

"We knew permission would be denied."

"Yet you proceeded nonetheless?"

"We had to test our hypothesis. We've unlocked a new direction. Great power generated from fear alone. No unnecessary deaths."

"Can't you see you've speared a hornet's nest?"

"It was a first attempt. The spell needs refinement. Witnesses and injuries must be taken into account. Next time will be perfect."

"There won't be a next time. You've gone too far. The coven's at risk."

"That's a lie," Victor interjected. "The coven's safe. The townspeople are superstitious. They believe the Devil himself sent the ghouls. They will soon move to the next distraction. Perhaps one of the coven's endless, mysterious murders that keep the city on edge."

"The risk is real."

"It's an exaggeration spread by hardliners who want to hold power," Victor continued.

"You're not above the laws."

"They are used to keep us down. In time, our methods will prove worthy."

"You were already warned in the butcher shop."

"We've just begun to make it work. The ancestral spell may take generations."

"Please make an exception," Monica said.

"I cannot," Elisabeta said. "The hardliners of the council want to set an example."

"You attended our wedding," Monica whispered. "You brought us together."

With proof of a breach of conduct, the elders convened the next day and narrowly ruled to banish the family from the coven. They were granted twenty-four hours to pack and ordered to leave their valuables behind. Travis went numb. He left Luca with Lucian and said goodbye.

In a weakened state, severed from communal energy, the family was transported to a stone cottage far south of Bucharest until they could petition another coven or devise a plan of their own.

But any time to strategize was short lived. Within days, Elisabeta and four elders pounded on the cottage door in the dead of night. Travis watched from a wooden cot in front of the hearth as they broke the latch and roused his parents from the small room in the back. He listened to his parents' rapid-fire explanations and promises of penance. They swore to share valuable secrets and to stay away from the dead.

Travis cowered in fear as his parents were pulled from the room, bound with rope, and dragged outside. Two elders with torches led the way into the forest.

The coven enforcer, Radu, stayed behind and pointed at Travis. He looked hugely muscled to the boy, bigger than his father, and tucked tight trousers into black boots. With a malicious grin that seemed to span the width his square jaw, he stalked Travis around the room with a thick leather belt that whistled as he swung it.

"You're not getting off as easy as some others may like," Radu said.

Travis screamed when the strap lashed his back twice in rapid succession, and he scurried under the table. Radu kicked beneath it and forced Travis to flee across the room. A large log from the hearth wobbled skyward, then sailed at Travis, who dove to avoid it as it crashed and sprayed fragments of masonry into his hair.

A shriek from Monica in the darkness caused Radu to pause. Travis' heart pounded.

"We're not finished. Your mother beckons. It's her turn. I'll be back for you."

Travis froze for a moment then ran to the window, but everyone had disappeared in the darkness. He crept to the door and scrambled through the woods, following cries and voices that grew louder as he approached the edge of a clearing.

Travis stooped behind a tree and watched as his parents were bound to truncated tree trunks and hoisted to a standing position, encircled by brush, limbs, and timber. An elder lowered a torch in five points around them. The flames took several minutes to grow and unite into a single blaze. Monica and Victor's pleas for mercy were met with scorn. Elisabeta stood by quietly, resolute and expressionless. As smoke started to rise, Travis felt an impulse to run into the open. An instinct clearly dictated that his parents wanted him to see them.

The flames grew stronger, and instead of screaming his parents stared at him as he emerged and began to chant loudly. He felt a surge within, an illumination. A tingling sensation in the front of his forehead grew stronger even as the flames climbed higher, engulfing the larger branches and completely encircling his parents. Smoke and flame spread and expanded until it was difficult to see details. Monica and Victor continued with the fevered incantation even as they writhed, straining the ropes that bound them tightly to the beams at the center of the inferno. The blaze pierced the darkness, casting long shadows that danced along the thick tree cover that bordered the clearing on all sides. The elders stood dispassionately as they observed the spectacle. Radu turned away and glowered at the orphan.

Travis focused on the anguished voices of his parents until their chanting abruptly ceased, and the flames raged up the central beams. Travis choked back tears as he caught glimpses of skeletal char protruding above the blaze in the wind.

The other witches swiveled to face him. Travis knew instinctively he needed to feign weakness. He let the tears come and covered his eyes with one hand even as the illumination he felt expanded, and a sense of calm and confidence overcame him despite his predicament. He looked between his fingers and watched as the elders conferred. The frenetic inferno danced behind them as the first light of dawn streaked the sky. An argument broke out. Travis feared he would be dragged to the pyre to join his parents.

A few moments later, Elisabeta approached him.

"For what reason should we spare your life?" she asked.

Travis composed himself and dropped his hands to his sides.

"I am just sixteen and didn't do the spell."

"And would you not one day seek revenge?"

"Of course, he would," Radu interjected. "Wipe him out now as the shit stain he remains."

Elisabeta sneered at Radu, and then turned to face Travis. "We assume you might."

"I would not."

"For what reason?" Elisabeta asked.

Travis felt the illumination take control. His words—not his own, he would later conclude—came without effort.

"My parents violated a sacred pact to keep the coven safe. They sought to advance their theory without considering it. The pyre is formal punishment according to the laws of the coven to which we are sworn. There is nothing to avenge. It is a simple matter of justice."

"Perhaps not so simple. They believed their work would one day benefit the coven. That it would offer a means of power without kills. Punishment was swift and forced upon them. Without trial, without mercy."

"We outnumber their defenders on the council," Radu shouted. "It matters not that the ruling was close. They lost the vote. They lost the right to trial. Restrictions must be enforced."

"Matters are seldom so self-evident," Elisabeta responded.

"A reluctance to kill will weaken us," Radu continued. "It destroys our essence. The original elders were disciples of the Devil. We are all their descendants. We needn't apologize or soften our ways for upstarts who believe they know better."

An instinct told Travis to allow words to emerge from his mouth.

"But their experiments should not be a crime. As you

no doubt discovered yourselves, as elders, growth requires risk. My parents cannot rightfully be blamed for attempting to advance themselves simply because our ancestral spells differ from your own."

"You believe the law is baseless?" Elisabeta asked.

"You see? He is tainted," Radu shouted.

"The blame lies with recklessness, the risk of exposure they thrust upon the coven due to a lack of foresight and restraint. That alone broke the law of the coven. The experiment was ambitious and needed more time to perfect. This my parents did recognize and thus accepted banishment without resistance. It cannot be denied they were, in the end, compliant."

"You are well spoken for a youth," Elisabeta asserted. "So what shall become of you?"

Travis paused a moment. "A return to the coven?"

"That is impossible," Radu said. "We need to slay him. Out of mercy, of course. He will languish here and die slowly. Miserably. Repast for wolves or vampires."

Travis studied the faces of each of the five and tried to assess their intentions. Elisabeta held a finger aloft, and the others followed her closer toward the fire, convening in a circle with their backs toward Travis. The sky continued to brighten with tones of purple and persimmon, blending with hues of flame that had reduced to dance on embers. The bodies of Monica and Victor formed blackened lumps fused to beams that now leaned precariously forward.

Travis was unsure how much time had passed when finally the elders broke formation and walked toward him.

"You will continue your studies in Transylvania," Elisabeta

said. "We have an outpost and will make the necessary arrangements. Return immediately to the cottage. Gather your belongings and whatever food you can carry. We will send a carriage."

Travis nodded and tore into the woods.

When he reached the cottage, he yanked the door open and slammed it behind him. He tried to lock it, but the frame had been ripped from the wall. He collapsed on his cot by the hearth and sobbed, quietly at first, but then in bursts that left him gasping for air.

He wasn't sure how long he lay with his face buried in a small blanket that served as a pillow, but an intense stirring began to tingle.

Get up! Collect your senses. Gather your things. There's no time to waste.

He leapt from the cot and raced to the alcove next to the sink in the kitchen. Inside was a bundle with clothes he'd yet to unpack following their flight from Bucharest. He grabbed the few items he'd worn and hung on hooks and stuffed them into the canvas bag. *What else? What else?* he asked himself and considered what food he might scavenge from the kitchen and how much he would be allowed to carry.

He then remembered what should have been obvious, the most important thing. His parents had sat him down the morning after their arrival and shown him a wooden trunk for valuables they'd quickly culled together before they'd fled. It was filled with their ancestral volumes and manuscripts and a satchel of bills and coins. They'd shown him the contents of the trunk and where they would hide it. In the event of trouble, they'd instructed him to keep it with him at all times and at all costs. Everything inside would one day be his. He would inherit the life-sustaining power released by the spells he alone could perform.

He rushed to the back of his parents' bedroom to find the trunk. They'd shown him the hiding place next to the wardrobe. He removed the loose floorboards and grasped one handle with both hands and hoisted it out of the shallow ditch his father had hastily dug out. He dragged it to the side of the wardrobe and hid it under a blanket.

Travis ran back to the kitchen and packed a bag with bread, cured beef, apples, and nuts.

Get a weapon.

He pulled open a drawer and grabbed two knives: one small, sharp, and easy to conceal, and a meat cleaver with a blade that broadened toward the handle.

He gathered everything he'd packed and returned to the bedroom to hide the knives under a pillow on his parents' bed next to the bundles.

He went back to the main room and scanned for things he might need. What was he forgetting? A coat. A bottle to refill from fountains. Scissors. Soap. A towel and blanket.

He continued to grab things until there was a pounding at the door. Travis' heart raced. He froze but knew he had no choice but to open it. He crept to the door.

Travis sighed audibly when he saw Lucian standing outside with a mid-level witch he recognized from the coven, Alexandra.

"I'm sorry this has come to pass," Lucian said as he stepped in and embraced him. "Let's not speak of what's happened. It's too raw, and now is not the time for remorse. You will find a way forward. Luca is fine. I'll care for him well. One day we will be together again."

"You know why we're here," Alexandra said as she forced her way inside and scanned the room. "Have you packed?"

"Yes," Travis said. "My bundles are on the bed."

"Let me see them."

Travis led her to the bedroom doorway and pointed.

"And valuables? Money? How do you expect to live?" Alexandra asked. "With magic?" She wiggled her fingers and laughed in a mocking way that unsettled Travis.

"I've got silver," Travis answered.

"You were instructed to leave anything of value with the coven before you moved," Alexandra asserted. "Where is it? There won't be a lot of room for possessions."

"It's just a little. In a bag." Travis pointed toward a shelf at the back of the room. "What else could we do? It's needed to live. Not an extravagance."

No one spoke for a moment.

"You can inspect for yourself," Travis said.

Alexandra entered the room. "And what's under the blanket?"

Travis walked out of the room to feign indifference as Alexandra went to the wardrobe. Lucian quickly intercepted him and whispered, "Forget Transylvania. It's a trap, a ruse to placate allies of your parents. Soon you will suffer an 'accident.' Friends on the council alerted me. You must escape before the carriage arrives." Lucian reached into his jacket pocket and pulled out an envelope. "Inside are instructions. It's a long journey."

Lucian grabbed Travis and stuffed the envelope inside

the front of his pants. He reached into his coat pocket and extracted a small felt bag tied with string.

"I want you to have this." Lucian shoved it into Travis' pocket. "It will cover your transport from here to Bratislava. Plus extra for food and sundry expenses."

"Thank you," Travis whispered.

"You know I loved your parents. They were destined to be elders, and I believe they deserved it. But now hardliners are emboldened. A threat to their own standing has passed. I am very sorry you are alone. But it is done. You've got to fend for yourself. It's what your parents need you to do."

"What's this?" Alexandra asked as she emerged from the bedroom.

"We need to brief him on transport to Transylvania," Lucian said. "What time to expect the carriage. How many bundles are allowed. The food he'll need for a three-day journey."

"He won't be needing much," Alexandra said, and turned to Travis. "Many want you dead. Your parents created quite a mess. Now begins the clean up."

"Do not listen to her," Lucian said.

"The council's attempt at fairness has created this opportunity."

"What do you mean?" Lucian asked, and Alexandra stared him down.

"They sent you along to balance things out." She swiveled, drew a dagger, and pointed it at Lucian. "But your counterweight is a hindrance to the clean-up operation."

Travis and Lucian stared at her in shock.

"Old fool. Radu sent me to rid the coven of your influence.

You've poisoned us with so-called wisdom and restraint for too long. Now you both shall rot."

With one quick motion, Alexandra stabbed Lucian cleanly below his larynx before he was able to react to the betrayal. He desperately clutched at his throat as blood sprayed out, and he collapsed on the floor. Travis gasped and jumped away.

"Now it's your turn," Alexandra said and pointed the bloodied dagger at Travis.

He backed away from the table.

"We knew valuables would be hidden so needed you to uncover the manuscripts. We will archive them, study them, and mimic what might be useful—decide for ourselves if there's anything worth exploring for the coven's future benefit. No need to waste resources on your rehabilitation in Transylvania. Your usefulness has expired."

She stabbed at Travis with a shriek, and he dodged the blade and ran to the bedroom.

He made his way backward and felt for the pillow behind him with his right hand and watched as Alexandra approached.

Again she stabbed at him, and he squirmed away, finding the handle of a knife as he whirled to the other side of the doorway. As Alexandra lunged toward him, he jumped aside and plunged the knife into her back. She screamed with surprise, pain, and rage and flailed desperately in an attempt to dislodge the blade. Travis darted toward the pillow to reach the other weapon.

Alexandra saw what he was doing and lunged again with her dagger, but Travis evaded the strike with only a graze and pressed for advantage. He thrust the meat cleaver with all of his strength into her ribs. She screamed and staggered toward the bed. Travis leaped out of her reach. Alexandra struggled but collapsed on the floor. Travis watched as blood drained from the wounds. He approached her body and prodded her shoulder with his foot. Was she really dead? He felt dazed with the adrenaline in his veins.

She attacked you. You had to defend yourself. The coven lied. You were perfect. Now go. Hurry!

Travis detected no sign of movement from Alexandra. He navigated his way out of the room around pools of blood and crossed to the table near Lucian's body. He pulled the envelope from his pants.

You must get to Giurgiu to the shipping docks on the Danube and book passage to Budapest. The river is the safest way, far from the dangers lurking in the Romanian woods between here and Hungary. A single vampire can easily overtake a carriage, and you cannot reenter Bucharest, even to catch a train. They will know.

Depart the docks in Budapest, and transfer to the rails. Book passage to Bratislava. Seek out Sorinah Petrascu. She is expecting you. Show this to the carriage driver. He will understand.

Travis studied the foreign name, district, and street address.

Sorinah watched over my son when I travelled. I knew her many years before she fled the coven. She's powerful. You will be her ward.

A jolt of panic hit Travis when he realized the coven would know something had gone wrong when Alexandra and Lucian didn't return by nightfall, or the carriage driver reported the carnage in the cottage.

He ran outside and pulled a wheeled work cart from behind the house to the front near the door and loaded it with his bundles of clothes and food. A small stuffed dog made from rags caught his eye as it lay on his cot by the hearth, Luca's toy. It had somehow survived the flight from Bucharest. His parents had given it to him to remember Dragos. He grabbed it, tossed it in the cart, and returned for the trunk. He bent and dragged it with both hands backwards across the floor, maneuvering past the bodies and leaving a smear of blood from the bedroom to the front door. He mustered the strength to hoist it up onto the back of the cart and covered everything with a blanket.

Gripping the two wooden poles protruding from the front, he pulled the cart and made his way down the dirt road toward the river port. He passed the clearing where the pyre still smoldered, now little more than a mound of ash and embers. He hurried past and vowed to avenge his parents for the coven's treachery. They would pay for sending an assassin. The plan to kill him once he'd uncovered anything of value from his parents invalidated any claim of moral superiority.

Focus. You aren't safe. They will hunt you. Faster.

Travis hoped he had taken Alexandra by enough surprise that she couldn't transfer her peril back to the coven. He quickened his pace.

In an hour he reached the outskirts of Giurgiu and was relieved by the signs of life around him. Travis made his way to the riverfront and paused alongside an empty barn. He reached into his pocket to take some money from the bag Lucian had given him and resumed his trek to the river boats.

He scanned a ramshackle array of depots in front of a row of piers as he advanced before he finally found a sign in cleanly painted letters, *Budapest.* His heart raced as he hurried to buy his ticket. The next boat would leave by nightfall, so he loaded his things behind the other cargo that awaited transport. He was famished, so he bought lunch while he waited and tried to blend in with travelers spread out on the river bank. He scanned the grounds for any sign of witches. He patted his coat pocket to feel for the knife.

A few hours later as dusk arrived and the riverboat pulled away from the dock, Travis collapsed on the cot above his storage bin for several hours. When he awoke, he left the compartment and walked to the outside deck to survey the view. Moonlight illuminated the river banks that butted against the thick growth of virgin forest on one side and mudflats and marshes on the other.

He was certain the coven had learned of his escape by now. He hated the feeling of being a fugitive, hunted by witches he had once idolized. Travis returned to his assigned cabin space. He pulled out a blanket and made a pillow of his jacket. Curled under the cover, Travis concentrated on the sound of the water and the gentle rocking of the waves that lulled him. He quietly thanked Lucian for devising his route of escape. He struggled to block out images of his parents burning on the pyre.

As he drifted between a lurid dream state and lucidity, the illumination came:

Connected we shall remain until you no longer need our protection. We did not squander our power on a curse upon the elders. We conjoined our spirits with yours to protect and expand your perceptions. Secrets will reveal themselves. Great power lies within the ancestral spells in your possession. They are yours alone to advance. Sleep well, dear Travis. We are with you.

SIX

ELISABETA CALLED AN EMERGENCY meeting of the council
of elders when the carriage that was to transport Travis to
Transylvania instead arrived empty in the coven's courtyard.

"Tell them exactly what you found," Elisabeta ordered the
driver.

"Bodies and a trail of blood," he said. "A man drained out
through a slit in his throat, blood on the floor, pooling near
the front door."

"And inside?"

"I followed the crimson smear from the front door to its
source the bedroom, thick and wet. A woman sprawled near
the door, next to the bed, stabbed with two knives: a meat
cleaver in her ribs, a dagger in her back."

"No one else? No sign of the passenger?"

"I called out in case he was hiding. Looked around
outside, but nothing. I didn't touch the bodies. Too much
blood. I raced back. I'm sorry I couldn't find him."

"You did right. You may return to the stables. Tend to the
horses and prepare for the search party. We will send for you
if there are any further questions."

The driver nodded and left the chamber.

"Did Alexandra attack Lucian?" an elder asked. "We had all agreed on Transylvania."

"It was Travis," Radu interjected. "I saw him. Alexandra transferred a final vision."

"You alliance with her is no secret," Elisabeta said. "What else do you know?"

"The orphan attacked her," Radu said. "I warned you about him. I made it clear he needed to burn along with his parents. Let's hunt him while we can. He won't get far."

"Alexandra pulled a dagger on Lucian!" the elder shouted. "We are linked; I saw his vision. She incited the carnage."

"That's rubbish," Radu said. "You can't prove it."

"And neither can you," Elisabeta said. "Divisions are killing us. Look at what's happened. We are left with deceit and the deaths of our own. Rivalries must be tempered. We are united by ancient rite."

"The council's ruling was flawed," Radu said.

"We agreed Travis would survive in exchange for his parents," Elisabeta said.

"It wasn't enough. He remains a danger."

"I'm aware of your position. I am also aware that Travis' safety in Transylvania wasn't assured."

"Justice would have been served."

"That is not your decision to make."

"I speak for all members loyal to the disciples."

"You'd best remember your station. You may be their de facto leader, but I outrank you and can snap your neck with a glance before you discern your head's turned backwards."

"Yes, Elisabeta." Radu lowered his gaze.

"What exactly is your objection to magic different from your own?"

"Weakness. Kills have been our province since time immortal. They make us strong."

"I suspect it's more than that." Elisabeta swiveled and addressed the room: "Mortals kill with abandon and yet strengthen their numbers in alliance with God. Killing is widespread and timeworn, devoid of its potency. We can do better. My eyes have opened. Desecrations channel the Devil and catalyze untapped resources."

"Conjurings have always been restricted," Radu said.

"Because few bloodline families used them. Coven majorities had no need for complications. Murders were common. Conjurings were complex. There was no incentive to learn the equivalent of a new language. We didn't know enough to question the edict or to encourage experiments. Curiosity was squashed. I believe it is time to evolve. I heard Monica and Victor, even after it was too late. There are paths we must explore."

"The fury of townspeople suggests otherwise."

"It was an early trial. They've shown the potential. A smaller scale and added controls would be different. Monica and Victor paid dearly for their failings."

"They put the coven at risk for their own advancement."

"So it was decided. And the pyre followed."

Radu folded his arms. "I want to focus on Travis."

"What do you propose?"

"Hunt him while the trail is fresh." Radu looked for support in the room.

Elisabeta also addressed the chamber. "He must be taken alive."

"And if he escapes?" Radu asked.

"It's not your concern."

Radu nodded to Elisabeta. "I will find him. He is a fugitive. With your permission, I will assemble the search teams."

"Send one to the cottage," Elisabeta said. "Bring back evidence."

Radu made for the door.

Elisabeta transferred, *I will be watching.*

SEVEN

TRAVIS SLEPT IN SPURTS in the berth of the riverboat as his journey wound northward toward Budapest. His nightmares began with flames that flickered to expose a murky sky filled with winged demons circling to attack. They dove and chased him as he ran for cover across an open field into the woods, but there was nowhere to hide, so they tore into him. He thrashed as he woke up until he recognized the ceiling of his nook, and groped for Luca's rag dog.

As the boat approached the Hungarian border, the river narrowed, and the vessel navigated past fallen trees and underwater tangles. Each time the boat slowed or stopped, Travis' heart would pound as he feared the delay was somehow the handiwork of witches who had tracked him. He would slide a wooden panel to peer out a peep hole in the hull to watch for danger then hide under his blanket until the boat started moving again.

When at last the riverboat neared Budapest, a worker advised Travis to stay on the river instead of the rails that Lucian had suggested in his message. It was easier to connect, and Lucian hadn't known about the heavy trunk.

But he would need to transfer to a smaller, slower boat to negotiate the Danube north of Hungary. Travis wasn't in a rush and actually had no idea how much time had passed on his journey.

Once they were docked, the worker directed Travis toward the depot he needed. Travis gathered some coins, purchased some goulash, and waited for his transfer. Once settled into his berth on the new riverboat, he pulled out the parchment and reread the name Lucian had written: *Sorinah Petrascu.* He studied the address. Could he find her? What would he say? What if she didn't want to help him or if she weren't even there? She might be dead too, or a trap. The coven may have been on to Lucian.

Travis put the paper aside and attempted to sleep through the overnight trip, but again the nightmares came. His dreams scrambled painful images: the shame and fear of flight by night with his parents from the coven to the south of Bucharest; the days they had spent struggling to survive alone in the woods, banished, his parents hoping for a reprieve only to face a death by rite of fire; his hope to be taken back, to be cared for, only to barely evade the mercenary sent by those who had promised to transfer him to Transylvania. And now he was adrift, fearful of discovery, alone, and wholly dependent on a single parchment with Sorinah's name and address in a distant city.

A thud rocked the boat, and Travis jumped up, slid open the window slab, and realized they'd docked at a busy river pier. He was grateful he'd managed to sleep. He looked around and spied a large sign mounted on the roof of a terminal on shore, *Bratislava.*

Within minutes he had disembarked with his belongings on a cart he pulled behind him on the planks of the exit ramp. He watched as other passengers followed a path from the riverbank toward carriages lined along a busy street that ran parallel with the Danube. He joined the line to hire one. When he found himself at the front, the haunches of a horse towered above his head as it strode in front of him. The driver extended his arm as Travis reached up with the parchment and pointed to the address. The driver nodded, got down from his seat, and loaded Travis' trunk and bundles into the back of the carriage. Travis climbed up, and a moment later with a crack of the driver's whip, the horse trotted down the cobblestone street.

Travis watched as glimpses of the river disappeared behind stone and brick buildings as the carriage entered the twisting, packed-dirt roadways that wove through the city. He lay back to view sloped, red rooftops and facades of vibrant colors as they carved through the city. He realized he was trembling.

In about twenty minutes, the driver slowed to enter a residential neighborhood. They continued for several blocks and turned onto a quiet side street, flanked on both sides by weathered stone, taupe houses with gas lamps that seemed to float upon elegant, wrought-iron fixtures affixed in front. Nestled between trees near the end of the street was a single masonry mansion with a red tile roof. Travis felt they'd entered an oasis—verdant, secluded, and tucked away deep inside the city.

The driver pulled in front of the mansion and pointed. Travis noted the street number carved in stone, and within moments his things had been placed neatly in front of the door. Travis handed the driver some coins and asked him to wait to ensure he wouldn't be stranded. The driver looked puzzled, smiled, replied in his native tongue, and prodded the horse onward.

Travis watched him pull away. His heart pounded as he stood on his toes to grasp the large iron knocker. He lifted it and let it drop with a solid *clank*. He waited and listened for any movement from within. He knocked twice more and thought he heard a sound. The door slowly opened, and Travis imagined he'd arrived at the manor of a queen. He'd never met one, but it was the best way he could describe the elegance and beauty of the woman who appeared. Rippling waves of thick, straight hair the color of burnt caramel cascaded down the full length of her back. She wore a silver ruffled dress with a maroon cape that shimmered as she stepped through the archway.

"My name is Travis." He held up the parchment and pointed to the name and address scribbled in ink as if it would guarantee admittance. "Lucian sent me."

"You are most welcome here," the woman answered in Romanian. "I am Sorinah. I've been expecting you."

"Thank you," Travis said. He smiled as engagingly as he could.

"You were to arrive sooner, no?"

"Yes, but I stayed on the river," Travis answered. "Do you know about me?"

"Lucian had shared some details," Sorinah said. "You are alone. I'm very sorry." She looked at Travis and then at his belongings. "Let's bring these to your room and get you settled."

Travis nodded and bent to gather some bundles, but Sorinah shook her index finger and pointed at the trunk. "I'll help you with this one first." She bent to grasp one of the handles and motioned to Travis to take the other end. She led them into the mansion and up the winding staircase to the first door on the right. A large mirror hung in the hallway outside the bedroom. Travis caught a glimpse of an unfamiliar young derelict with angular cheekbones and dusky eyes that peeked from behind a thick fringe of raven hair.

"This will be yours," Sorinah said as they entered and placed the trunk in a corner. "Bring up the rest of your bundles. I'll draw you a bath."

Sorinah pointed to a door across the bedroom, and Travis headed for the stairs.

"When you're refreshed and ready, come find me in the dining room," she called out. "You must be hungry. Follow the smells."

About an hour later, Travis was bathed and settled in his room. He studied his surroundings as he slowly wound down the staircase and marveled at the paintings, small sculptures of iron and stone, and elegant vases and ceramics that turned the parlor into a sort of museum with ornate candelabras perched on round side tables. A chandelier of glass and gold dangled from a long chain over the center of the room. Plush curtains adorned the windows and were held back by large, golden clasps.

A delicious smell beckoned from somewhere beyond an adjoining hallway, and he ambled down the corridor and found a room that flickered with candlelight. Sorinah sat at a long, rectangular table with a cast iron Dutch oven in the center, a baguette, wine, and place settings for two.

"Please eat," she said as she motioned for Travis to sit. "Beef stew." She stood and lifted the lid and served spoonfuls until his bowl was full. She pushed the bread close.

Travis tore into the spread and listened intently as Sorinah spoke.

"I lived in the coven for many years. I knew your parents and Lucian. My parents were visionaries, much like your own, empowered with gifts they were determined not to waste. Studies led them to question core commandments of the coven that forbade joining forces with outsiders. My parents found the edict outdated in a modern age that pitted humans with their far greater numbers against everything else. My parents sought to explore a partnership with a single vampire colony in their ancestral village within Transylvania where they'd lived before acceptance into the coven in Bucharest. They set out for Sibiu, knowing full well the journey was dangerous, and left me behind in Lucian's care. But my parents were double-crossed."

"Mine were too," Travis said. "Or at least, I was. My parents admitted they were wrong, and paid the price."

Sorinah pursed her lips, and then took a sip of wine.

"My parents transferred to me the details so I would know what had become of them. A few days after their arrival, with the best of intentions, they took control of a local who led them to the vampire master of the walled city. He entertained their visit and feigned interest until elders from the coven appeared from out of the shadows. My parents were accused of collusion by both the coven and the vampire master. They confirmed the treachery of the elders. The coven had opted to entrap them rather than justify why forming an alliance was forbidden. My parents were dragged to a central plaza and feasted upon by vampires under approving eyes. A fire was nurtured into an inferno while blood was drained from their necks. When their transference to me halted, I knew they were dead."

"My parents were burned too," Travis whispered. "What happened after?"

"Lucian was well-respected and made a case for my adoption. It was granted, but I knew I could never stay in a coven that would sacrifice my parents rather than question ancient rules. I shared only with Lucian what had transpired in Sibiu. I studied and grew stronger. He trained me and presented the ancestral spells of my parents that he'd kept safe. He was like a father. That's how I knew when he died as he fell with a slit throat. I saw where you stood by the hearth through his eyes. I had watched him compose the letter that brought you here. I had no way to know if you would survive Alexandra's attack or the long journey, but I remained ready to receive you. Your tutelage shall commence immediately. The blood in your veins is powerful and must not be wasted. Through it courses all that your parents bequeathed you."

"Thank you." Travis tried to hold back tears, but the traumas of the past week swept over him. "They speak to me, sometimes. I feel it."

Sorinah moved her chair closer and leaned toward him.

"Tell me." She took his hand.

"I watched when they died in the fire. They stared at me and chanted until their last moment. I felt something. A stirring inside. Sometimes it tells me what to do, an instinct. I call it *illumination*, especially when there's trouble like before Alexandra attacked."

"You are in possession of a great power. They passed it to you through their strength. Not many witches ever achieve their level. For that they were a threat to some within the coven. It makes you very special, very strong. Intense training will be necessary to unlock your full potential. You must advance the gifts you've been granted, or your parents will have died for nothing."

Travis focused intently on Sorinah. "How did you get away from Bucharest?"

"With Lucian's help, I grew strong and was never dependent on the united force of the coven. I feigned an obsession with my genealogy and discovering what had become of my parents. Permission was granted for travel to Sibiu to research my ancestral past. From there, it wasn't difficult to disappear. Lucian concocted a tale of capture by vampires, and my death was assumed. Perhaps it was even desired by the coven. I was an orphan of law-breaking parents. I left Romania and in my travels met a baron and his wife who required a resident cook and housekeeper. This was their home. They are no longer here because of an unfortunate accident. Sometimes survival depends on accidents, as you shall discover."

"I will not kill," Travis said. He put down his spoon. "My parents worked to avoid it."

"But you already have," Sorinah said softly.

"I didn't want to."

"It is always a matter of survival. Spells drain power

that must be replenished. Lucian died linking you to me. In unimaginable pain, your parents transferred illumination. It is your duty to strengthen yourself. You are the only one able to advance the bloodline spells. You will use that power to one day get revenge."

"Are we safe from the coven? Can they find us?"

"We can't know for certain, but with me you will be safe. This manor is protected. Forget the torment. Now you must rest and recover. You need time to heal. A new life awaits."

EIGHT

TRAVIS SPENT HIS FIRST months in Sorinah's mansion demonstrating his skill level, so that she could assess how his training would proceed. He understood the theory and structure of spells and how to search from a vast array of handwritten manuscripts the elements needed to complete any trial she concocted.

Travis latched onto Sorinah as the lifeline she was. She told him the events that had brought them together—including the plight of her parents, her escape from the coven, the sacrifice of Travis' parents, and the murder of Lucian—fed her conclusion that his tutelage was the byproduct of fate. Their destinies were intertwined. Two witches orphaned by the coven and united to grow strong, join forces, and avenge the betrayal of their parents.

Travis took Sorinah through the contents of his parents' trunk. Silver and currency from Romania went into a basement vault, while texts and manuscript were shelved in his bedroom. Travis showed her the precision with which Monica and Victor had recorded specific processes, conditions, and revisions for their spells and incantations.

It was clear their level of expertise had allowed them to significantly advance the bloodline spells. Now they were left to Travis alone to perfect and perform.

But first would come days, years, and decades of practice: harnessing energy and executing the painstaking rituals required to incrementally increase power. The depth of Travis' talent quickly became apparent to Sorinah. They became linked at his first lesson.

My parents guide me, Travis had transferred. *The illumination from the pyre. It's opened me to you.*

Trust what comes, Sorinah had answered. *They know me. They know Lucian. They know we are united in purpose. Linked by circumstance, I adopt you as my own.*

Sorinah taught Travis to integrate the illumination from his parents into a steady state of instinctual awareness, rather than a sudden flash of insight activated only during extreme states of alarm, danger, or desperation.

As he grew older he took on the chiseled, handsome features of his father, and muscles began to sculpt his frame following a regimen of resistance exercise and recurrent work on a stone garden wall constructed by hand. Sorinah instructed Travis to wield physical appearance as a weapon. While he might expect to live centuries, he could select the age he wished to outwardly present and use his body to seduce or overpower an adversary. For a physique worthy of eliciting fear or desire, she stressed he had to develop it along with his mind.

Travis learned that cruelty was required to advance; they'd been born into black magic. Witches who refused to cause harm remained weak or withered away in a mortal's lifetime.

Power would advance from domination, fear, confusion, abuse, physical violation, or death. Transgressions could be mixed or used singly. Cruelty was not personal, always circumstantial and necessary. Witches whose lifetimes had exceeded mortal limits would drop dead without it. In line with the beliefs of Travis' parents, Sorinah taught that killing was to be avoided because it was messy and left dangerous evidence. Witchcraft worked best when undetected, leaving victims bewildered and vulnerable and oblivious. Lingering confusion and dread served to propel the strength of the witch even after the spell had vanished.

The day arrived when Travis was ready for a test subject. His first practical application of physical illusion, Sorinah decided, would be upon her chambermaid, Petra. They searched out a spell they both agreed looked tempting, just as a recipe begs testing.

Travis practiced using Sorinah as a test subject, omitting organic matter that would catalyze the spell, but ironing out specifics of language. They awaited Petra's return following the death of her husband who'd struggled with a bronchial infection that descended into pneumonia.

It was late morning on a Tuesday when the knocker summoned Sorinah to the front door. She greeted her servant with a hug and broad smile as she opened the door.

"We've missed you, Petra," Sorinah said. "How are you doing? I'm sorry for your loss. Are you sure you're ready to work?"

"I'm OK. A change of scenery will do me good," Petra said. "I need to start a routine again, too much moping around. I'm afraid I've put on some weight."

Petra stepped inside and rested her coat over the curved walnut frame of a red velvet sofa.

"Perhaps that's a good sign. Your house dress still suits you," Sorinah said. "Things in here are a bit of a mess. We managed the best we could without you."

Travis entered the room and smiled. "Glad to see you back. We're very sorry. Let me hang your coat."

"Thank you," Petra said. "Most kind of you."

Travis scooped up the coat and disappeared down the hallway.

A few moments later, Sorinah received confirmation: *Hair, face powder, and flakes of scalp.*

"Can I get you some tea before you begin?" Sorinah asked Petra.

"That would be lovely," Petra said and took a seat.

It didn't take long for Sorinah to reappear in the main salon with a small tea tray, which she placed on a side table next to Petra.

"Take all the time you need," Sorinah said as she smiled, turned, and walked to the hallway to follow Travis. "We'll be in the study in back."

"I'll begin the bedrooms in just a moment," Petra called out.

When she finished the tea, Petra left the cup on the tray and walked to the broom closet below the stairway. She got some supplies and made her way upstairs.

In about twenty minutes, she had finished dusting and was sweeping the floor in Travis' bedroom when she thought she heard muffled coughing nearby. She paused to listen, but after a few moments' silence, she resumed her task. Minutes later, again came a cough, this time louder and strained. She was sure it came from inside the adjacent room. She trembled because it sounded eerily similar to an attack her husband had weeks before.

She crept toward the bathroom door, which was ajar. "Is someone there?" she asked as she gently pushed the door open and peered inside.

The room was empty. She shook her head and returned to her broom. When she bent to collect dirt in the dustpan, behind her arose a volley of loud, rasping coughs, interspersed with wheezing gasps for air. Petra screamed, "There's someone up here!" and ran from the room.

She scanned the parlor from the top of the stairs but didn't see Sorinah or Travis. The house fell silent. She strained to listen for the sound of the coughs or any movement but heard nothing.

Petra descended the stairs one by one, and when she reached the main salon, she was shocked to find Travis relaxed in a chair behind the staircase. He studied her as she approached.

"There's someone upstairs," Petra said, feigning calm as she pointed, but her shaking hand betrayed her. "In your bathroom, a coughing."

"That's impossible. There's no one here but us."

"But I heard it. Something horrible. Please come look."

"OK. Show me."

Petra led Travis to his bedroom and motioned toward the bathroom door.

"In there."

Travis pushed the door open and entered the bathroom.

He got down on the floor as if to look for someone hiding under the legs of the bathtub. "There's no one here. See for yourself."

Petra came forward and inspected the room. "How curious."

"Perhaps noises came from the street?" Travis asked. "Through the window?"

Petra nodded, unconvinced.

Travis left the bathroom and walked toward the bedroom door.

"Can I ask you a favor?" Travis pointed to a large horizontal mirror in the hallway. "It's dusty and smeared with fingerprints. Do you have time?"

"Of course."

"Thank you, Petra." Travis smiled and turned to descend the stairs.

Petra warily returned to her duties. When she'd finished the upstairs bedrooms without further incident, she thought perhaps she'd imagined the coughs. Maybe the sounds really had wafted in from outside.

She placed a small stepstool in front of the hallway mirror and began to swipe with a damp cleaning rag. Again, from behind her, unmistakably came the sound of tortured breaths and rattling coughs with unnerving intensity. Petra swung toward Travis' bedroom and peered within to no avail. She shook her head and swiveled toward the mirror, but instead of her own reflection, the image of her husband stared back at her. He was inches away and echoed her movements until she shrieked and fell back off the stepstool.

Her head hit the wall behind her as she pushed away from the mirror. She chanced a look upward, and her husband glared down at her, laughing maniacally between spasmodic bouts of coughing. He pointed at her as phlegm and spit escaped his mouth.

Petra watched in horror as he reached beyond the mirror's surface and his hand morphed into a clutching claw with fingers contracting and curling, inching ever closer. His arm extended across the width of the hallway. The claw sought to anchor on her throat.

Petra screamed and pushed with her legs along the wall until her back hit the wooden post of the banister. She pulled herself up and her armpit clutched the rail as she made her way down the stairs. She looked back in horror to find her husband still in the mirror, watching her. His menacing laughter echoed throughout the house.

"Help me!" Petra screamed and ran for the front door. She twisted the knob, but it was locked. She pounded on the door and wailed as she scanned for Travis.

He meandered from behind the staircase and frowned.

"Petra? What's come over you?"

"Look!" Petra shouted and pointed up at the mirror. The laughter continued unabated, and the image of her husband's reflection stared down at them.

"Look!" Petra screamed again.

"I don't see anything."

"My husband. In the mirror. Can't you hear him?"

"What?" Travis asked. He twisted and turned as he looked up the stairs. "There's no one there. Please calm down. You're frightening me."

Petra collapsed in front of the door and sobbed loudly. The laughing stopped.

"Perhaps it was too soon to work," Travis said as he helped Petra to her feet. "You still need rest." With his arm around her, he unlocked the door, and Petra pulled it open and ran out without looking back.

"Wait. Your coat!" Travis called out behind her. But she was gone.

Travis closed the door, and Sorinah stepped up behind him.

"I'll follow her with the coat," Sorinah said. "I don't think she'll be back anytime soon."

"Did I go too far?" Travis asked.

"A bit, perhaps," Sorinah said as she walked to the sofa and motioned for Travis to join her. "But it was a great first effort. Tell me what you feel."

"A rush inside, like my mind is wide open—expanded, exhilarated, euphoric. I want to do it again. I can still feel her thoughts. I know where she is. I could scare her right now if I wanted. I could follow her into her bedroom, wait until she closes the door. Do it just for fun."

"That won't be necessary," Sorinah said. "You've done enough, and very handily. First attempts sometimes lead nowhere, being too big a leap from books to broad daylight."

"I learned from my parents, but doing it on Petra was different, so much better."

"You will learn it's not a game. It isn't funny. But you are young, and the journey's begun. Remember this experiment."

Others in the community would later ascribe Petra's

distressing symptoms to normal, if extreme, manifestations of grief.

As Travis' training continued, Sorinah taught him to store the power that surged after he'd triggered the requisite fear and confusion. It was the only way to advance to a higher level, the only way to become elevated enough to handle the difficult ancestral spells his parents had crafted that were his alone to perform.

"You're old and strong enough to defend yourself. Have you discovered any weapons?" Sorinah asked in the days that followed Petra's ordeal. "Injured anyone?"

"Twice, I think." Travis closed his eyes to remember. "I call them bolts. Once I shot my father by mistake. And I disabled a coven bully. He froze me but I broke through to escape. Later I practiced on rats."

"Excellent. Nerve bolts. Most witches don't have them and cannot overcome a first strike."

"Why not?"

"The same as our spells, we are born with different weapons."

"Like what?"

"Nerve bolts attack the spine, and can kill. But bolts can be blocked by a strong witch. So you need other tools like telekinesis, shapeshifting, pyrokinesis, or immobilization."

"I can hurl things like candlesticks. How can I test for more?"

"We will find your arsenal. Witches must fight to grow strong and defend themselves. Humans succumb quite easily, if they don't stab or maim you first. Mortal wounds may not heal quickly enough to stop death."

"I remember a bad feeling after shooting my father, and especially the bully."

"Combat comes with a price. Weapons burn through power that must be acquired and stored. First from tests of fear, like on Petra. Then with painstaking mastery of ancestral spells. You must advance the work of your parents to generate and reserve enough power for a prolonged fight with a coven elder. That will be the goal of our training. To prepare you for revenge. To fuel you for combat."

One evening as they relaxed in the dining room after an intense day of catapulting plant pots filled with pebbles across the length of the garden behind the mansion, Sorinah reached for Travis' hand on top of the mahogany table.

"You must learn from the mistake of your parents," she told him. The words sent a chill through Travis in the shadows of flickering, muted light from the chandelier.

"What mistake? Breaking rules?"

"No, setting a spell into motion they couldn't control." She took a sip of wine. "Our survival over centuries depends upon our stealth. I survive today only because I was able to feign weakness and dependency for years while I secretly strengthened myself. You must always maintain an unerring self-assessment. Don't overestimate your station. I worked as a cook and housekeeper for the baron and his wife because I recognized my vulnerability. For the fifteen years I served them, I studied and practiced whenever I could and slowly stabilized my living situation as I adjusted to life outside the coven. Beyond the walls of this mansion I would have nothing, and I knew it. I lived in the room behind the kitchen, and from that humble base, I incrementally strengthened myself. The point came when I accepted that I would need to exact pain in order to advance, as your parents themselves noted in the manuscripts you study."

"Did you have your own ancestral spells?"

"Yes, different from yours. Classic. They rely on kills."

Travis nodded and again felt chills.

"But I acknowledged my limitations. The only raw materials I had to work with existed within this mansion. As a matter of survival, I would need the baron. I had full access to his sheets, soiled clothing, and dirtied dishes, all the necessary organic components. It was rather simple to control him, and then to seduce him. I maintained an outward appearance he coveted while his wife aged appropriately. It became a game to try to allow her to catch us, slowly enraging her, giving her only enough evidence to arouse suspicion and jealousy, which of course, created a power stream for my craft.

"When the baron drew up a legal document leaving me possession of the mansion in the event of their deaths, she became enraged. 'You have no right to your anger!' the baron shouted at her. 'We have no dependents. I'm the Baron, and you're barren.' I remember he yelled from the bedroom, yet I heard it from where I studied downstairs. His wife started to cry. He was drunk and burst out laughing at his own crude humor. It was after this incident that his wife began a plot to kill me. I sensed it immediately. But she unwittingly increased the potency of everything to unfold because of her hatred."

"You could feel her emotions?"

Sorinah took a few more sips. "Yes, an energy fueled by

her jealousy, confusion, and rage. She'd lived a life of outward piety and morality, but when faced with an obstacle that vexed her, she shrewdly and without hesitation chose a very dark path. There were other options at her disposal. I could have been fired, forced to leave the house on an exaggerated charge of ineptitude. But instead she wanted me dead. It was a delicious sort of corruption. She hadn't a shred of hard proof of infidelity; I hadn't allowed it. Yet suspicion alone was enough to turn a God-fearing pilgrim into an attempted murderess. What power I had amassed was amplified by her willingness to commit a cardinal sin against her religion and to flagrantly ignore the laws of her own church and supposed morality. And so I exaggerated my innocence. Each performance served to further infuriate her. It drove her to unwittingly reveal her resolve to commit murder and to concoct an incompetent scheme."

"How did you stop her?"

"From years of housekeeping, I was aware of the arsenic she'd always kept in the master bedroom in front of the mirror on her vanity. A drop or two smoothed on her face kept her complexion porcelain white. I noticed the day the bottle disappeared and set out to protect myself. I was in charge of the kitchen, so knew I could control the safety of the food I prepared. I suspected she would seek to poison a small personal item, perhaps a toothbrush. I vigilantly monitored my small bedroom and, sure enough, watched as later that afternoon she crept in, foolishly thinking she'd entered undetected.

"I waited outside and pretended to busy myself in the kitchen as she was leaving. 'Oh,' she told me. 'I was refreshing the water decanters and thought yours might also be running low.' She arrogantly walked past and placed an empty water pitcher in the sink. I could see the outline of a small bottle in the front pocket of her apron. Her treachery was obvious as she'd never offered to refill the decanters ever before. 'How kind of you,' I told her. I knew I would make her pay that evening because she'd played her hand but failed, and I didn't want to risk a second attempt.

"Throughout the afternoon I made of point of going about my duties with a glass of water, stopping to take choreographed sips. Of course, I had already emptied and cleaned the tainted decanter. I watched her eager look of surprise when I feigned a fainting spell at the top of the stairs. I offered a loud, verbal self-diagnosis of shortness of breath. I coughed like Petra's husband as I descended, leaning on the handrail. The satisfied look on her face filled me with rage. I steadied myself in a chair in the parlor and covered my face with my hand as I leaned over in pain.

"'What's the matter, my dear?' the baroness asked. She walked over and took my hand. I told her I felt exceedingly strange, that I suddenly needed to lie down, and that I would have to finish my duties later. 'Of course, my dear,' she said. 'You'll feel better after some rest.'

"I staggered across the room and grasped the archway for support as I attempted to make my way into the kitchen toward my bedroom on the other side. I looked back and savored the victorious smirk on her face. An infusion of power began to tingle because she'd so willingly attempted murder, perverting herself completely of her own volition. With some audible groans, I made my way to my bedroom and closed the door. I quietly waited hours for the baron to return home, and when he did, I listened as the baroness explained I had taken ill and was resting, so they would have to go out for dinner. I knew her plan was to return home afterward, check on me with the baron as witness, and discover my body dead in bed.

"When I heard the front door open after they'd dined, I immediately seized control of the baron. 'Why not draw up a bath and relax before bed? I want to join you,' I made him tell her. The baroness giggled with delight, so starved was she for his attention and so sure of the success of her plan, the benefits of which she was already enjoying. She went up the stairs to undress in the master bedroom, content to leave my body to stiffen in bed until morning. I heard some insistent knocks at the door, but ignored them as I lay under the covers. Minutes later I heard the baron's steps on the staircase and then creaks from the floor of the master bathroom. 'I tried Sorinah's door, but there was no answer. I knocked a second time, but still nothing,' the baron told her.

"I heard the baroness call him to the bathtub. 'She was so overcome with exhaustion. I'm sure she's fast asleep. We'll check on her in the morning,' I heard her tell him as I snuck out of my room. I crept up the stairs. I entered their chambers and watched them through the open door to their bathroom, crouching down behind the bed. The baron lay back against one side of the tub with the baroness against the other. She lifted a toe and moved it playfully and gently down his chest. The arrogant spectacle she made while thinking she was in control produced a surge of power. She gazed lasciviously and stroked him with the bottom of her foot for a while before taking him with her hand. He moaned and groped between her legs below the surface of the water.

"Electric lights had become more common, and a single tall floor lamp illuminated the bathroom with three bulbs. I forced the lamp to rock and then topple sideways, hitting the side of the bathtub and rolling to the floor. The room was shadowed with light rising from below the legs of the bathtub. The baroness screamed and stared in disbelief as I appeared in the doorway.

"'Get out! You're supposed to be dead!' she shrieked as she covered her breasts with her hands. I released the baron from control to relish and feed upon his energy.

"'What is this outrage?' he shouted and scrambled to lift his girth out of the tub. His arousal bobbed in front of him like a pregnant catfish suddenly plucked from the water. I hoisted the base of the lamp and thrust it directly into the tub between them, breaking the bulbs and electrifying the water. They both screamed and writhed in pain, limbs trembling as the current coursed through them. The baron's frantic attempt to escape the tub failed; his legs buckled beneath him. Soon they fell silent, bodies slumped forward, sinking.

"The absorption of energy from their deaths immediately filled me with an onslaught that left me breathless. I wasn't even sure what was happening. I collected myself and opened the window. I would later tell the narrative that I'd discovered them in the tub, victims of an unspeakable accident caused by the wind's overturning a decorative lamp while they bathed. In the throes of passion, they'd apparently never noticed the breeze or any potential for danger and were helpless to protect themselves until it was too late. The new technology was dangerous."

Travis stared at Sorinah wide-eyed.

"The importance of masking a nightmare under the veil of normalcy cannot be overstated. It's where your parents failed."

"I thought about it with Petra," Travis said. "Planned the coughs to make sense."

"And you succeeded," Sorinah said. "People believed she was simply overcome with grief and hallucinating. She came to believe so herself. Your parents would be proud. One day, you will be strong enough to avenge them."

She refilled her wine glass.

"How long does it take?"

"The process cannot be forced or rushed. You have great potential from your bloodline, the illumination from your parents, and the incantations that are yours alone. You have much to learn before advancing the work your parents already started. I will continue to challenge you to rise. Their sacrifice must be your motivation. Devise proper plans, perform spells well, develop weapons, and you will be ready. One day, we will return to Bucharest to exact our revenge, and we must be as fortified as possible. We owe our parents nothing less."

PART TWO

EXPERIMENTATION

NINE

TRAVIS FEARED THE diabolical power behind his parents' forbidden magic. He would never forget the night the three specters haunted Bucharest more than a century ago. Desecration itself was a potent link to the Devil, its genesis mysterious, without which results would be tepid. Despite the risks, powerful spells in the ancestral manuscript beckoned him. He needed to advance them, or he'd amount to nothing, squander his most potent resource, and wither away.

Defile?

He stopped reading and pondered the requirement. Even with his level of mastery, the challenge was vague and intimidating. How are such things measured? One could argue that his presence alone, a predator in a distant, unsuspecting town, might be sufficient.

He put down the manuscript. The strain of reading the Romanian text hand-stroked by his parents caused him fatigue that he knew could be remedied with additional light, but he preferred the atmospherics of candles. His gray-green eyes were fine. He was 150 years old, but the appearance he'd crafted said otherwise. He liked the sculpted musculature of his late thirties, and kept the charcoal stubble on his square jaw closely cropped. Humans had responded, then, and now, so he kept it going. It was a look that gave him confidence.

Travis leaned back in his chair and gazed across the expanse of the attic. The ceiling sloped steeply, and two dormer windows opened to intermittent, shrouded moonlight.

Travis walked to the closest window and savored the night air. Beyond the trees he could make out the glow from the house of the nearest neighbor, but everything else was shadowed and motionless. He surveyed the landscape of the location he'd chosen: a small Vermont town as old and secluded as could be found in the United States.

Finding the house hadn't been difficult. The Malloy place had sat on the market for years, not decrepit or abandoned, but constructed in the 1850s and restored and refurbished by consecutive owners. The Malloy family couldn't sell in 2011 because of the real estate crash and the rural school district. The family changed strategy and offered it as a long-term rental through an agent. Travis found the listing online, applied, took a look, and booked the house for a year.

The property, isolated in the woods in an isolated town in the corner of an isolated state, assured the privacy he required. The old farmhouse reminded him of small cottages in Romania, with wide-plank hardwood floors, exposed brick walls, and wooden ceiling beams made irregular and dark by time.

Travis hoped to return to Eastern Europe by mid-autumn, so he'd traveled lightly. Only one nonessential box of books waited on the floor. He chose a cozy corner of a full-floor attic as his office, a minimalistic cocoon where he set up a large oak desk, an ergonomic chair, and floor-to-ceiling shelves lined with books, ceramic and glass containers, and candles for lighting and heat sources for potions. Travis kept his most prized possessions on his desk: the bloodline spells and hand-written manuscripts passed down from his parents, dog-eared, some marked with circled stars.

Travis reached for his favorite manuscript on the far corner of his desk and reviewed techniques to produce a slave to assist him with day-to-day tasks in this unfamiliar land.

He planned to observe townspeople in groceries and retail shops, at the gym, and in random encounters to assess the talent pool. In the meantime, he would articulate the exacting requirements of the spell. The time had come to test the level of his station. Sorinah had made clear a fight against the coven could never be won without a great leap in power. What his parents started in the cholera death pit was his responsibility to finish.

TEN

SUMMERS RIPENED SLOWLY in Sussex, Vermont. It was mid-June, finally perfectly warm and not yet hot, with no extra layers required. Rachel, Mia, and Sophia finished lunch at an American bistro in the town center and sat at a table on an outdoor patio as they waited for the check. They appeared oblivious to the attention they attracted from customers seated nearby: a pretty, poised trio of brunettes, intimidating and inadvertently coquettish.

The waitress came over, smiling. She handed the check to Rachel.

"You girls graduate already?" she asked.

They nodded.

"Seen you around for a few years now. Hope you're not going to disappear."

"We'll meet up again for Thanksgiving," Rachel said. "Starting college in August."

"Always happens with my favorites," the waitress said. "Triple Trouble. What we used to call you. The nearby tables would fill with guys. Some kind of magic?" She looked over at scattered patrons who tried to make eye contact. "At least looks that way from where I'm standing. Don't study too hard." She smiled as she turned away. "Take your time with the check."

Travis flagged the waitress from the next table.

"If she only knew," Mia said. "I'm gay." She pointed to Rachel. "You're a serial monogamist." She shifted her eyes to Sophia. "You're trouble and don't even know it yet."

The routine of high school was quickly fading into a haze of summer and the unknown. They vowed to remain close but knew they stood on a precipice.

Mia considered herself proudly Latina, though her dual-citizenship Mexican parents found her Spanish increasingly sloppy. A few weeks before graduation, Mia had confided to the others that she might be a lesbian and had yet to tell anyone, especially not her parents.

"I remember how scared I was to tell you guys," Mia said. "But I dared. *Gracias a Dios.*"

She had yet to kiss another girl, she'd told them, but had known for years the feelings were emerging, especially after repeated lackluster romances with guys in school ranging from jocks to bookworms. Long, straight hair framed her angular face and thick, full lips.

"I'm sorry you had to hide," Rachel said. "Couldn't figure out why you were the single one. Sophia's the recluse."

"Biding my time until I'm out of here," Sophia said.

Like Mia, Sophia had plans to travel out of state for college in mid-August. She'd convinced her parents NYU would be her best option for a major in education. They'd argued she could learn to teach almost anywhere, which made Sophia fight harder.

"I can't wait to escape," she continued. "I have to get away from here." She smiled and the sun spotlit her freckles and russet curls. "You guys know how I keep a bag packed in the back of my closet. A promise to myself. I know there's bigger and better out there."

"There's gotta be something more," Rachel agreed. "I tried the formula, and it doesn't work."

"The formula? Oh right. You left Rick after you met James," Sophia said.

"*Claro.* You swing like a trapeze artist from one to the next," Mia said. "But it seems to work. You landed the football jock. You win."

"Don't be a bitch. There's more to me than that. You guys know it." Rachel folded her arms and undid a messy bun. Thick chestnut hair dropped in layers as she shook her head and playfully pulled in her cheeks to accentuate bulging cheekbones.

Rachel planned to move ten miles away to the University of Vermont to study marketing or fashion merchandising. Though she wouldn't be far, Rachel worried about transitioning since she'd spent most of her time with Sophia, Mia, and James and would soon be on her own. She hadn't exactly reached out to anyone else given the security of Triple Trouble and the commitments that came with dating a jock, like attending home games and smiling at random parties.

Rachel had thought about ending things with James for a few months but didn't dare to or to tell her best friends, who even now watched her.

James had long been the dominant force in their relationship, and she'd felt weak for having gone along with comfortable routines, such as meeting after practice and cheering robotically at games. But his sex appeal had been difficult to resist, as well as his popularity. Players and their girlfriends attracted adulation. It had initially felt fun and clichéd in a good way, like a classic experience everyone was supposed to have in high school. But now with graduation passed, she was going to college, and he wasn't. It bothered Rachel that they'd both been unable to talk about important matters. It signaled to her their relationship wasn't as solid as she'd thought. Maybe it had never been real.

A man approached the table.

"I'm sorry, but the waitress seems to have disappeared. I'm new in town and wondered how to find Maple Street Park?" the man asked.

"It's nearby. Turn right out of the parking lot, then right at the light. It's a mile, maybe two," Sophia said.

"Thank you so much." He turned toward the stairs to the parking lot. "Pardon the interruption."

The girls hesitated until he left.

"That was forward," Mia said. "Ever hear of GPS?"

"Do you think he just pulled the question out of his ass?" Sophia asked.

"That accent," Rachel said. "Definitely from away."

"Older, but hot," Sophia said. "Muscles. DILF."

"*Dios mio*," Mia said. "Watch out, New York."

Rachel reached for the check when the waitress appeared and calculated the tip. "Twenty each should do it," she said as she placed a bill on top and used a corner of the condiment tray against the breeze.

"I admit. I'm getting excited," Sophia said. "Neurotic too."

"About?" Mia asked as she looked up from her phone.

"I'm so sure I want to escape, but to what?"

"Be ready for anything," Rachel said.

"Bring it," Mia said. *"Andale."*

"What if I hate the big city, and the joke's on me?" Sophia asked. "I'll come crawling home, humbled and embarrassed and working at Wendy's."

"Wow. Self-doubt much?" Mia asked. "Trust yourself."

"Big changes are coming," Rachel said and leaned back in her chair with eyebrows raised and lips pursed. "Stay tuned."

"What do you mean?" Sophia asked.

"I'm breaking up with James. Just decided."

"Wait. What?" Mia asked. "When?"

"Tonight." Rachel stood up from the table. "I'll text you when it's over."

ELEVEN

DYLAN BAXTER DREADED his upcoming thirty-fifth birthday. The milestone invited self-assessment, and he wasn't sure he liked all facets of the reflection. By financial and physical measures he was, he supposed, doing OK. He owned a small house, held a steady job with a savings plan, and was, thankfully, considered handsome and able to pass as younger. His health was good except for some allergies, which seasonally became annoying because his job always took him outdoors.

But an inspection of his personal life bothered Dylan because it had become clear he couldn't hold onto anyone. He could initially attract prospects, even date for several months, but inevitably the type of woman he liked didn't stick around.

He blamed his work.

Dylan was Sussex' head groundskeeper. He managed a few workers he could dispatch as needed to maintain the firehouse, municipal office buildings, police station, cemeteries, several war memorials, and a large park with a picnic area, playground, tennis courts, and swimming pool.

He claimed work in the park as his own because it included the added benefit of an assigned locker in a changing room adjacent to the swimming pool. He also handled the cemeteries alone because the oldest ones were deserted and offered solitude. The newer ones posed the challenge of scheduling services, deliveries, and coordinating with funeral directors. The mix of duties went beyond riding a lawn mower, replacing flowers, and trimming grass along the fence.

Dylan had grown up in Sussex but didn't go to college because his grades were just average, and he had been more interested in working with his hands. He was athletic and liked the outdoors, so in high school he'd worked for a condo maintenance company that had taught him to manage property grounds. It paid well, and because nothing else was calling him, he'd stayed on for a few years after graduation.

In time he'd opened his own cleaning and maintenance company, anchored by a new large senior housing development. Guys he'd known through practice matches at the local Golden Gloves formed a solid pool of contract workers as his list of clients expanded to include a restaurant, an inn complex, and a sprawling suburban cascade of retail outlets. But clients dried up as they became more established and could handle grounds keeping themselves instead of farming it out.

Eventually he'd heard about a full-time position with the town. Stability and decent pay were appealing. The Town Selectmen liked the local boy and his qualifications and offered Dylan the job.

Now, two years into the position, he enjoyed a quality of life he wasn't sure he'd ever have attained with his own business. He regretted he only held a high school diploma and never felt quite good enough in New England, where it seemed everyone went to college. And as his latest birthday approached, he feared it was too late to do anything about it—not because his station in life wasn't comfortable but because the women he chased didn't seem to like a man whose income came from manual labor. Or maybe he was just plain dumb. He wasn't sure which.

Classy, young, and fancy women, the kind he set his sights on, went after professionals like techies, doctors, or entrepreneurs, he imagined. He wasn't sure if his attraction to ambitious, white collar women qualified as a fetish but recognized he was headed nowhere. And yet he knew next Friday at 6 p.m., right after work, he would be on the prowl at a popular happy hour.

Before showing up at the bar, Dylan would often sneak in a trip to the gym to pump his chest, shoulders, and arms to better fill out a polo shirt. He called it his pick-up workout.

His routine was to schedule himself at Maple Street Park on Fridays. Any tasks that might come up late in the day he immediately assigned to one of his crew. It was a perk of his position. If luck were with him, he could wrap up work at the park by 4 p.m., change out of his uniform, and hit the free weights just down the hall.

He didn't consider it vain to spend time on his body. Physical fitness was a source of pride and power that had morphed into a hobby. It was something all his own that he could steer and shape more than anything else in his life. It made him feel virile and gave him confidence to pursue women who otherwise would be out of his league.

He told himself these things, but also, in lonely times in his kitchen after a few beers, he acknowledged he felt his body was the only thing special about him. He didn't see a handsome face when he looked in the mirror. He only saw the reflection of a loser with a job to keep hidden until it became impossible to dodge questions.

This particular Friday went according to plan, and Dylan found himself in the weight room right on time. He did repetitions until he worked up a sweat and felt he looked pumped enough to grab some attention.

Dylan made his way back to the locker room. As he entered, he noticed a professional-looking guy about his age pulling on gym shorts. Khakis, socks, and a polo shirt were scattered around him. Dylan walked past the man, took off his shirt, and tossed it onto the bench in front of his locker. From the corner of his eye, it seemed to Dylan the man was watching.

What's up with him?

The man stood, fiddled with his waistband cord, and dug inside his gym bag.

Dylan swiveled to towel off and shot another glance at the man, whose head was covered as he pulled on a t-shirt.

He looks better than I do.

Dylan sat to open his locker. He tossed his t-shirt inside and pulled off his shorts. He stood and casually glanced behind his back. The man was standing with one foot on the bench as he tied his sneaker. Their eyes met. Dylan quickly looked away and turned back toward his locker. It still seemed the man was tuned in, observing. He felt it.

Why am I so tense?

Dylan finished undressing and placed his things in the locker.

Is he into me?

Dylan wrapped a towel around his waist and put on flip-flops. He grabbed a small bag of toiletries and closed the locker.

"Where do they keep towels?" the man asked.

Dylan paused before he answered, trying to place the man's accent. "Gotta bring your own," Dylan said as he turned.

"Next time," the man said. "Thanks."

Dylan nodded and headed to the showers. He soaped up carefully with the expectation he might find himself naked in a few hours. When he was through, he toweled off and headed to the sinks. He wiped steam from the mirror and rubbed some moisturizer onto his face. Wimpy, perhaps, he thought, but psychologically necessary. He scooped a dab of hair cream, rubbed it between his palms, and smoothed it through his hair.

As good as it's gonna get. Just go, already.

Dylan returned to his locker to get dressed. His polo shirt was on top, and he pulled it carefully over his hair. He bent to poke around for his briefs. Where were they hiding? Why did the locker seem oddly empty? His heart beat faster as he realized his briefs were gone, along with his t-shirt, shorts, and socks. Was it really possible? He pulled out his gym bag and dug around some more. Everything else seemed to be intact, including his car keys, cell phone, and wallet.

How could he have been so stupid? He'd never in the past bothered to lock his locker while showering. It had seemed unnecessarily vigilant. Now he felt oddly violated, singled out. He should have known better. That guy with the accent was obviously the crook. Some kind of pervert into men's sweaty gym stuff.

I'll hunt him down and kick his ass.

Dylan went commando, then studied his wallet; all cards and cash were untouched.

He stuffed his boots and work uniform into his gym bag, slammed the locker closed, and dashed out.

Never again. There was something about him. I knew it.

TWELVE

"CAN YOU TAKE A BREAK from texting and help me set the table?" Paula asked her daughter, Katherine, who sat on a barstool at the counter.

Katherine looked up from her phone. "In a sec. Are we three?"

"Yes. James'll be home by 6."

Paula turned toward the stove and checked the chicken. She liked to cook but wished she had more time to experiment instead of endlessly repeating her stable of old-reliables. A full-time job and two teenagers made it hard. Sometimes summoning the energy to cook after a day in the office was impossible, and she'd send James to Hanniford's.

Two years had passed since her divorce, time enough for feelings of stagnation and loneliness to take root. Paula had won custody of the kids. She'd made the case that she was stable and Aaron wasn't, and the judge had agreed, considering his temper tantrums on the high school athletic fields where he'd been a coach and extramarital encounters throughout town where he'd been a player. Meanwhile, Paula appraised property values for an insurance company.

She worried about James and blamed the family crisis for his decision to take a year off after graduation. Katherine was two years younger than her brother and had already proven herself with her class rank and PSAT scores. She wasn't nearly as devastated by the divorce as James, or at least she didn't show it.

Katherine finished her text, opened the cupboard, and gathered what she would need.

"Chicken again?" she asked as she arranged the silverware and napkins.

Paula turned from the stove to check if she were joking. "Last time 'til tomorrow. Promise."

They worked side-by-side without speaking until dinner was ready. The sound of a scratchy motor in the driveway still took them by surprise. Paula had given James a car a few weeks ago as a graduation present—used, but robust. He would need it, she'd reasoned, to make trips to visit Aaron and hopefully for a job soon. They heard the car door slam and waited until James appeared in the kitchen.

"Perfect timing," Paula said and motioned him toward her. James hugged them both, then excused himself to wash up. When he returned, honey soy chicken stir fry was on the table along with quinoa. Paula and Katherine waited for him to sit.

"How was the lake?" Paula asked.

"Fun. Most everyone showed up," James said. "But water's freezing."

"Rachel?" Paula asked.

"She didn't go. Not really her crowd. How was your day?"

"The way it should be this time of year, slow. It usually

stays that way until Labor Day. I think it's human nature. Everyone needs a break. Especially here where the summers are short."

They ate, and the kitchen grew quiet except for the hum of the refrigerator and the clack of cutlery on dishes.

"What about me?" Katherine asked after a moment. "Anyone care?"

"Let me guess," James said. "Nonstop texts and Insta?"

"Maybe. It's how I keep informed." Katherine smirked and flicked ombré bangs from her eyes. "It pays to have a spy network around town."

"For what?"

"Local intel. You didn't even know we've had a neighbor for months already."

"Where?" James asked.

"The Malloy house. My source is legit. There're lights on at night. I checked myself from my window upstairs."

"Took long enough to sell the place," James said. "No one wants to live out here in the middle of nowhere."

"I think it's a rental," Paula said. "We should introduce ourselves. Be neighborly. I'm surprised I haven't heard anything."

"How could you? You're kinda busy," James said. "It's not exactly next door."

"You're legit in your own world, Mom."

After dinner, James helped to clear the dishes and then pushed his chair back under the table.

"I'm gonna skip dessert because I gotta head out," he said. "Sorry to eat and run."

"Where to?" Paula asked.

"Meet up with Rachel."

"You should've invited her for dinner."

"She wants to talk. We need some privacy. She asked me to meet her at the park."

Katherine and Paula gave each other a playfully suspicious look.

"That can't be good," Katherine said.

"OK. See you when you get home," Paula said. She stood from the table, hugged him, then sat back and watched as he went back out to his car.

"That was quick," Katherine said.

"It's legit none of your business," Paula said with eyebrows raised.

"Don't even." Katherine shook her head and held back a smile as she served another spoonful of rice.

THIRTEEN

JAMES FELT BAD SKIPPING OUT, but Rachel took priority. It was odd she'd blown off the party. She'd said she'd already committed to lunch plans with Mia and Sophia, but they'd been invited to the lake too, and they always saw each other anyway, so the excuse didn't make sense.

James hated that he felt guilt, even now, while driving to see his girlfriend and leaving his mother and sister alone. Guilt followed him everywhere. The divorce still felt raw. James loved both his parents, but hated how his dad had left his mom stranded to run the household by herself. He was unable to make sense of how his father could have ditched them all for a girlfriend on the side. Why couldn't he control himself? The traits that had made Aaron a role model—athletic, adventurous, extroverted, handsome—over time had turned into a curse that had transformed him into a narcissist. Why hadn't his father recognized it before it was too late? And now James worried he weren't much different. On the football team, the same traits were highly prized.

He turned up the music as he drove. It was summer, after all, and the night was young with nothing to do the next day.

He needed an attitude adjustment. Maybe things weren't always so complicated. Maybe Rachel wanted to be alone so they could fool around outdoors. Maybe there would be something going on, like a bonfire party.

James parked his car and walked past the swimming pool and locker rooms toward the wooded area with benches and picnic tables scattered about. He spotted Rachel sitting on one and waved. She didn't seem to notice—texting, he guessed—and jogged toward her.

"Hey," he said as he approached. "Nice night."

Rachel stood, and James opened his arms for a hug. He leaned in to kiss, but she only grazed his cheek.

"We need to talk," she said.

"OK. How was your day?" He meant it as a joke.

Rachel didn't smile. "Mia and Sophia stopped by the store. We hung out and later went to lunch at the tavern. Sat outside."

"Wish you'd made it to the beach."

"I told you I wouldn't. Not really my crowd."

"Since when?"

"For a while now. That's what I want to talk about."

Rachel looked at James, folded her arms, and sat down. James watched her as he settled into a spot on the bench a few inches away.

"What about?" he asked.

"About us." There was silence as James swiveled toward her. "There's so much happening. So many changes. New directions." James watched helplessly as she paused a moment, and then whispered. "I need to take a break."

"Don't talk to *me* about changes," James said.

"I know. You've had it bad."

"Take a break like how?"

"Like break up."

"For real? Why didn't you say anything?"

"I'm saying something now." Rachel took his hand. "I'm moving to campus in about two months. Everything will be different. It's a natural time to assess things."

James closed his eyes.

Somewhere in the back of his mind, he'd feared this might happen even though he'd always pushed away doubts and flashing lights. Denying their existence had worked. Until now.

In a moment he opened his eyes and looked into Rachel's face.

"You don't have to say anything more."

"Of course I do."

"I know what's happening."

James focused on a star and spoke slowly and quietly.

"I'm not good enough for you. I'm taking a year off. You think I'm a loser. And maybe I am. But I miss my dad and feel bad for my mom. I'm not even sure where I want to be living or what I want to do. The last thing I need right now is to commit to four years of college with no idea of what kind of person I want to become. I doubt I could even get in."

Rachel's eyes teared up. "I don't think you're a loser."

"I think I'm a loser." He tugged at the gray t-shirt sleeves that couldn't hide his biceps.

"You're not."

"Football captain, and what did it get me? Girls? I know I didn't study enough. I'm just like my dad."

Rachel was silent for a moment.

"It's fine to take a year off. I'm not judging you. No one is," she said. "The breakup is about me and what I need to do for myself."

She put an arm around his shoulder. James stiffened, then exhaled. He leaned his head toward hers.

"It was great being with you," Rachel said. "Everyone loves you, and I got caught up in it. Just went along, basically as a sidekick."

"You felt that way?"

"Yes. Not an equal. Like I lost myself. Starting fresh in August is helping me figure things out. To take time for myself. Reset. I need to find *me* again."

"Wow. I never saw that."

"I didn't either, until now with college and moving and everything."

They sat quietly a bit longer.

"I don't want to work. I don't want to go to college. I don't want to live here. I don't want to live with my dad. I've never been so lost. You're smart to get away from me. You deserve better."

Rachel sat up straight, swiveled toward him, and looked him in the eye. "You'll figure things out. You also need time to yourself. Knowing you're lost is a huge step. Most people have no idea. Or won't admit it. I'll help you."

Rachel watched James' face. She'd never seen him look weak. "I promise." She poked at his spiky blond hair, and he smiled.

Clouds churned and dulled the moonlight on the walk back to their cars.

FOURTEEN

THE NEXT MORNING RACHEL fought with the lock on the door at Old Gold. She managed to get inside and clicked on the lights. What to do first? She wanted to take her mind off of James. He'd reacted differently from how she'd expected, and now she felt conflicted.

Stop second-guessing yourself.

She knew to her bones breaking up was the right thing to do. They'd already started moving away from each other. It was better at this point to research her roommate.

Focus on your job.

She read the note her boss had left on top of the jewelry case:

Hey Rachel. Check out the new arrivals I put out last night, including a flapper dress. Chunky shoes from the '80s, both men's and women's. AND rose gold jewelry inside the case. Very on-trend. Please mix up the display. Feels stodgy. Call with any problems. Thanks. See you around 4. MK

Pleased with her boss' show of trust, Rachel got to work, and soon had customers to greet. She helped them with size swaps near the changing room, and fiddled with the jewelry.

Just before lunchtime, Sophia and Mia showed up and found Rachel tagging dresses on a rack near the front of the store.

"Got your text," Sophia said.

"We're checking on you."

"Thanks. I'm fine," Rachel whispered. She motioned to customers exploring the rack behind them. "Let's move to the counter."

They walked to the back of the store, where Mia and Sophia moved chairs from the shoe area closer to the counter, and Rachel stood next to the register.

"And James?" Mia asked.

"He texted me earlier," Rachel said. "Seems OK. Took me by surprise."

"What about you?" Sophia asked.

"Relieved but feeling guilty. He's still kind of a mess after the divorce. Directionless. Now the breakup. I'm making things worse for him."

"His problems aren't your fault," Sophia said. "It's for the best. You know it."

"I thought it was a no-brainer. If he'd acted like a jerk, in a funny way I'd feel better."

Rachel folded both arms in front of herself and leaned back against the counter.

"In the beginning I loved the attention. Everyone thinks he's cool, and he is, but I got swept up in appearances. Like, I had to always act a certain way and be upbeat and bubbly for his bros and wanna-be followers. And girls, who obviously hoped we'd break up. Fake smiles. Loaded jokes. When news gets out, James will be fine. Lots of girls want him."

"Word's already out," Sophia said.

"You need to focus on what's ahead," Mia said. "Getting ready for college."

"I know. You're right," Rachel said. "We all do."

"Think you'll stay in touch with him?" Sophia asked.

"Of course. We're still friends," Rachel said. "I'm not dropping him completely just because we broke up. Not after last night. He's vulnerable."

No one spoke for a moment. Sophia's phone buzzed, and she tapped it before even looking at the screen.

"Got my housing assignment for first semester," Sophia said as she read. "Looks good, I think. At least I hope. East 10th Street in the Village."

"Go online and find out," Mia said. "I joined a chat group for incoming freshman. You should too. I think most schools have one. I'm already Skyping with EmmaFromAustin, who's super cool. We're in the same dorm. Really helps break the ice."

"Did you guys get your classes?" Sophia asked.

"All but one. Still waiting to hear on an alternate," Rachel answered. "You?"

"*Todo perfecto,*" Mia said. "Mount Holyoke's so civilized."

"Same," Sophia said. "Biggest worry was housing. Scary in the big city."

"Scary here too," Rachel said. "What will life be like by August?"

"We're each gonna have a roommate," Sophia said. "A total stranger. I can't even."

"Where's your dorm gonna be?" Mia asked.

"On campus, near the field house," Rachel answered.

"Gonna be fun."

"*Sí chicas,*" Mia said. "Fun for all of us. A whole new adventure."

Rachel stood tall and reached up with her hand out.

"Customers are behaving themselves. MK just got a new shipment. Let's model."

They smacked palms and marched toward the rack.

FIFTEEN

TRAVIS SWIRLED A SMALL Bellarmine jug he'd selected from the collection of bottles on an upper shelf. He set it on his desk and pulled a duffle bag from below. He studied the garments he'd plucked from Dylan's locker and looked over a favored manuscript.

Combine the target's organic residues promptly with the base mixture, his mother had written in the margin next to the spell. Travis wondered if too much time had passed during the drive from the town park to his home. But the nylon gym shorts felt damp. The cotton t-shirt and socks were fragrant and warm. He held a sharp pair of scissors.

Travis selected areas of sweaty fabric and whatever body hairs clung to it. He carefully stuffed small snippets though the mouth of the witch bottle, along with clippings from his briefs.

Travis closed his eyes to recall Dylan's striking face and striker's body. He would make a fine slave: physically strong, emotionally remote, locally astute, and free of complications. Travis recited the incantation as he gently shook the bottle and pushed in cork.

He felt duty-bound to innovate and advance Monica and Victor's vision, empowerment without kills. He bore no malice toward the host town and sympathized with the daily struggle faced by humans to survive. His life as a witch hadn't been so different. And soon, he hoped, his trials would be done and he could return to Europe, fully fueled for the fight ahead.

SIXTEEN

DYLAN'S GOLDEN GLOVES PRACTICE ended well before sunset, and he liked to cap it off with a swim. On the summer solstice, he drove to Maple Street Park and headed to the locker room. He changed into his swimsuit and sauntered outside. A few teenagers floated near the divider between the shallow and the deep ends. A family with two children splashed in the kiddy pool.

Dylan staked out a chair near the diving boards and plunged in. He swam a few laps, and then relaxed in the water to soothe a lucky punch from his sparring partner. When his fingertips began to wrinkle, he climbed out and toweled off before returning inside.

The locker room was empty. Dylan spread his towel on the bench and sat with his hair still dripping wet. He became aware of softly spoken words in another language—*Latin?*— coming from behind him.

Dylan turned and saw a robust figure in the doorway whom he recognized as the guy who'd stolen his gym gear the week before. The man held a jar and shook it gently like a rattle.

"I know what you did, scum." Dylan stood, turned, and took an aggressive step over the bench toward the man and clenched his fists. "You're going to pay."

"No," Travis said. "You're going to sit."

He stared at Dylan, steely and unfazed by the boxer's build and threatening stance.

Dylan felt a dizzying rush that forced him to the bench. He shook his head to try to clear it. He found himself transfixed by the voice of the man who continued to murmur words he couldn't understand, yet he could focus on nothing else.

Then resistance was no longer necessary. What was he fighting? Everything felt good. Dylan understood perfectly he had nothing to fear and what mattered most was gaining the man's approval and enjoying the process. The brawny figure in the doorway moved closer, and Dylan swiveled his body to face him directly, not wanting to look away. His thighs straddled the bench, and water continued to drip.

The man stopped directly in front of Dylan, knees almost touching, and spoke quietly.

"I'm Travis. We haven't been properly introduced. I'm sorry I took a few things from your locker. I've brought you replacements."

"I'm Dylan." They shook hands. "Don't worry about it."

Travis released his grip and gently rested his hand on top of Dylan's wet hair.

Can you follow with no words? Copy me.

He lifted his hand, raised it high, balled it into a fist, and watched as Dylan mimicked the movements.

Travis opened the palm of his left hand and placed it over his heart. Dylan followed: palm on chest, down to stomach, up to right shoulder. Travis stepped back from the bench and leaned against the lockers.

Very good.

Why can I hear you? Dylan asked.

We're connected. Call it magic.

Travis waited a moment and studied the energized look on Dylan's face.

"Retrieve your things," Travis said. "My truck's in the parking lot. You'll know the one. Trust your instincts. Look in the duffle bag on the front seat."

Dylan stood and pointed to his swimsuit. "Should I change first?"

"No need for modesty. You'll only be a minute."

Dylan nodded and left the locker room. He strode through the lobby of the complex barefoot and wet. He headed to the parking lot and realized pebbles on the pavement hurt the bottoms of his feet, exactly as he'd remembered from childhood visits. The pool had been solid concrete, painted bright blue with sloped sides and a deep end that descended to 16 feet for the high divers. It had since been renovated, leveled out, and padded with vinyl.

Dylan? Focus on your task. No daydreaming.

Dylan understood that he'd annoyed Travis. He had to do better. He scanned the vehicles in the parking lot and picked out a black, full-size pickup truck.

That's the one.

He walked to it, peered in the front window, spied a duffle bag, and tried the door handle. It was unlocked, so he entered and unzipped the bag. Inside he found a new package of medium briefs (Calvin Klein, his brand), a new pair of no-show socks, gym shorts, and a large t-shirt (all Under Armor, also his brand). He took the items, slammed the door, and returned to the changing room.

"Thanks for the new stuff," Dylan said as he approached Travis, who sat on the bench near Dylan's locker.

"Sorry for the inconvenience," Travis said. "It was a necessary step in a larger process."

Travis stood and gently squeezed Dylan's forearm at its midpoint.

"I'll be leaving now," Travis said. "Glad we met. We're going to be collaborators. I'll contact you when things move forward. Not a thing to remember until then."

From pressure against mesh lining, Dylan nonchalantly observed he was becoming erect and smacked Travis twice firmly on the chest. Travis relaxed his grip, smiled, and walked out.

Dylan turned to his locker and tossed the new garments inside. He kicked off his swimsuit, hid his arousal with the towel, and closed the locker door. He secured the padlock and tested it twice. He would never take a shower again without locking it. He'd learned his lesson.

It wasn't the safe town he'd always known.

There were strangers about.

SEVENTEEN

THE OLDEST CEMETERIES IN Sussex were ensconced behind wrought-iron fences and often discovered in unlikely places because they dated from before the Revolutionary War, long before the zoning, growth, and sprawl of modern times. Monuments to war heroes like Ethan Allen and wealthy shipping families shared space with the plots of the original British and French settlers with modest, rounded, rectangle slabs and etched writing long since covered by lichen.

Even the land had shifted over the centuries, creating steep mounds where streams that flowed after downpours had carved out and then washed away terrain that had once been flat. Old grave markers settled into the earth at awkward angles too heavy yet too delicate to be righted. Some cemeteries were essentially abandoned. Descendants of the deceased had themselves disappeared. Bloodlines ran out. Families moved away.

Only the upkeep of the grounds provided an illusion of life. Grass needed to be mowed and brush controlled to tame nature's relentless drive to reclaim the land and make it nothing more than a meadow pocked with forgotten crosses and stone slabs.

Dylan used only a push mower to cut the grass in the oldest cemeteries because spaces were too tight and the plots too unruly to fit a riding mower. On a hot July day, he completed the back half of the cemetery and paused on the dirt road that followed the fence around the sweeping expanse of gravestones. He turned the mower off, got a bottle of water from his backpack, and leaned against the iron railing to take a drink.

He became aware of the sound of a motor. He focused and realized the sound was drawing closer. Was it a truck? He hadn't asked for help from his crew. He watched as what looked like a forklift came into view as it turned a corner along the front edge of the fence. As it got closer, Dylan made out a metal post in front of the vehicle. Was it a tree planter? No one had told him that was on the agenda, and he didn't like surprises. The last thing this old cemetery needed was more leaves to rake.

The vehicle came forward and stopped in front of Dylan's lawn mower. The driver stepped out from behind the controls.

"Hey, Dylan," Travis said as he walked toward him and extended his hand.

Dylan took it, and they shook firmly. "I know you from somewhere."

Travis smiled, released his grip, and took a step back.

Dylan studied the handsome and brawny action hero who'd appeared from nowhere. How did he know him? Golden Gloves? From wherever it was, Dylan realized he had forgotten all about the man until just now. But why did Travis seem so familiar? It was like he had known him forever, and yet they'd only just reunited. A long-lost classmate?

"Are you a boxer?" Dylan asked.

"I just work out."

Dylan paused a moment. "Trying to figure out how I know you so well."

"We formed a bond," Travis said. "Surprising, I know. Happened very quickly."

Dylan looked puzzled, but not alarmed. "Wonder why?"

"I have that effect on people," Travis said, smiling.

Like this, Travis transferred wordlessly to Dylan. *You can hear me?*

Dylan smiled and nodded. *But how?*

"Your thoughts, your feelings transmit to me. And I communicate to you. Nothing intrusive. Purely instinctual. Life continues as usual until something I require takes precedence. You'll feel the calling. When we're apart, you'll remember nothing. You'll be free. I will take pains to avoid unnecessary disruption."

"Where are you from?" Dylan asked. "I hear the accent."

"Eastern Europe. Bucharest."

"What brings you here?"

"A work assignment. I need your help."

Travis started walking and called, "Follow me," as he turned. "More equipment is in the back of my truck."

Dylan walked alongside Travis to the main road in front where he was parked on the shoulder. Travis pointed to a large industrial leaf vacuum on a wheeled cart.

Help me with this. Travis lowered the rear door. Dylan nodded, mounted the truck, and together they lowered it down. *Back to the mower.* Dylan pulled the vacuum rig by the handle until they made their way to the rear of the cemetery. They left the equipment, and Travis guided Dylan up the hill away from the fence and into the gravestones.

"Your precision will be absolutely required," Travis said. "I have zero tolerance for sloppy work. No daydreaming. Do you understand the importance of what I'm saying?"

Dylan nodded and stared at Travis with rapt attention.

Travis pointed to the headstone he'd settled on and to the shape of the terrain of the grave itself. "You will examine each plot and assess each one's suitability."

Travis motioned to the grass below his feet from where he stood directly on top of the grave just below the headstone.

"If you were to dig down from here, you could expect to need a depth of about two meters—or, rather, six feet."

Travis took two steps down the slope of the mound and pointed to the same grave from the side. "But if you approach it from here, the depth to the casket within would be considerably less." Travis pointed toward the tree planter parked by the fence. "For example, using the auger to enter from here would take much less effort."

Dylan looked eager, yet confused. He studied the grave and shot looks at the tree planter.

You want me to dig? Dylan transferred. *Drill into the grave?*

Travis nodded with no expression.

"Several factors are very important," Travis continued. "You must remain undetected and hide your work. Always start with a circular piece of sod. You will save it to cover the hole at the end. The auger drills neatly, and the soil collects around the opening of the hole, so it is easy to shovel back in. Then replace the sod and stamp it down."

Travis looked closely at Dylan: *Are you following?*

Dylan nodded. *I think so. I need to hear the rest.*

"Again, precision is paramount. You need to drill carefully. Learn to feel exactly when the tip meets and then penetrates the casket. Only a small opening is needed, just enough to contain the vacuum hose. It is wide enough to pass along bones if necessary. Breakage is not problematic. Dirt and debris will not interfere with the end result. But finesse is required as you work. Care with handling the canister is critical. One bag per grave. Simple to remember. No exceptions."

Dylan, despite effort to appear enthusiastic and supportive, couldn't mask his unease. "I've never done this. I'm not sure I will be good at it."

Travis smiled, placed his hand on Dylan's shoulder, and urged him down the hill toward the equipment. "I'll show you everything."

They began training with the tree planter, and Dylan studied the levers of the control panel. He raised and lowered the auger, experimented with the speed of rotation, and played with the knobs that moved the tractor forward and backward.

They moved to the vacuum rig, and Travis showed Dylan how to install and change out the liners. They studied the controls for the propane engine that created suction. Dylan toyed with the equipment until Travis signaled and pointed up the hill.

"It's time to select a grave," Travis said. "Something dated between 1900 and 1950 with good vantage points."

Dylan nodded and followed him into the maze of headstones.

Travis stopped to read inscriptions as they passed and examined physical characteristics of the terrain. *This one.* Travis rested his hand on top of a gravestone. *Explain my selection.*

Dylan paused a moment and examined the grave site.

"The year's correct, and the drill can pierce at a good angle," Dylan said, pointing to the slope on the side of the grave. "And nobody can see from the road."

"And what if they did?" Travis asked.

Dylan shook his head. *I don't understand.*

"What if they caught you and questioned you?"

"Easy," Dylan said. "Drilling to plant a tree or dealing with a drainage problem."

"Good. Or exterminating rodents, moles, maybe," Travis said. "Don't forget you are in charge here. People aren't in a cemetery looking for trouble. Help them find their plot and return to cutting grass until they leave."

"It's rare that anyone comes."

"You've got to be prepared," Travis said and directed his attention to the headstone. "Now, let's see who we have here."

He touched the inscription as he read aloud:

In Loving Memory of
Beloved Daughter and Sister
CAROL STILTON
Laid to Eternal Rest
April 12, 1949
Aged 20 years
We will cherish and remember you always

"Eternity can be abridged," Travis said. "I'll show you what to do."

Travis and Dylan walked down the hill toward the equipment. When they reached the tree planter, Travis pointed to the controls.

You drive. You are in charge. I will stop you only to correct a mistake.

Dylan nodded. He mounted the tree planter and started the motor. It lurched forward with the auger rocking in front as Dylan got a feel for the controls. Travis walked behind and watched as the tractor advanced more smoothly. Dylan maneuvered up the hill to the grave they'd selected and stopped the tractor on stable ground below the slope of the grave mound.

Nicely done, Travis transferred. *Now, the vacuum. You need all the equipment in place before you begin.*

Dylan nodded and disappeared down the pathway. He returned minutes later, pulling the vacuum rig. He parked it behind the auger and looked at Travis. *Should I start?*

Aren't you forgetting something? Travis answered and folded his arms. *The sod.*

Dylan looked crestfallen. *I'm sorry. I won't forget again.*

He turned, jogged to his stash of equipment by the fence, and soon reappeared with a pitchfork and shovel. He eyed the width of the auger and pierced the grass with the shovel's tip. He continued to cut a circular patch of grass until he was able to remove it with a pitchfork and toss it next to the vacuum.

Travis nodded and pointed to the tree planter. Dylan took the controls and raised the auger high above the target he'd dug as if the drill bit were a tremendous spear positioned to pierce a bull's eye. He hit a switch, and the auger began to twist. Dylan slowly lowered it and began to dig.

Get a feel for the resistance and pressure. Be ready when the drill gets close. From there you must proceed delicately with just enough force to pierce and enter the chamber.

Dylan focused on the flow of earth out and around the hole. He continued to go deeper, the drill bit now almost completely obscured within the hole. A moment later, Dylan felt the tractor rock backward as the auger met resistance. Wary, he looked at Travis.

That's it. Back the blade out slightly. Increase the speed of rotation. And then force it forward again slowly.

Dylan watched the hole. He manipulated the auger up and down as the tractor rocked against the blockage. The tractor lurched forward, and the auger drove deeper.

"Excellent. Stop. You've pierced it," Travis said and raised his hand.

Dylan let the auger spin without forward pressure to clear the hole, and then withdrew it. He raised it and backed the tractor away from the grave. He looked at Travis.

The vacuum hose.

Dylan pulled the rig close to the opening and unwrapped the hose from around the canister. He kneeled next to the hole and fed the tube in with both hands.

Proceed gently and carefully as far as you can go, then pull back slightly.

Dylan extended his left arm within the hole to guide the hose until it buckled and went no further. He jiggered it a bit, stood, and switched the motor on. A sudden burst of debris rumbled into the tube and flowed into the canister. A sound like a large spill of popcorn kernels careening down the hose momentarily overcame the whir of the motor. Dylan crawled down and grasped the hose, rocking it to and fro, adjusting his moves to the reward of intermittent rushes of debris. When the noises slowed, Dylan looked up at Travis.

"Let's see what we've got," Travis said and switched the motor off. Dylan unfastened the latch to the lid of the canister and opened it. They both peered inside.

Travis picked up a branch and gently prodded the dirt and debris within the canister. He lifted a swatch of fabric on top of the stick and held it up.

Carol's dress.

He dug some more.

Her jaw bone.

On the tip of the stick he hoisted a thick necklace.

This will work.

"A good first dig," Travis said. "Cover the hole."

Travis sealed the canister while Dylan pulled the vacuum hose from the ground. A pile of dirt formed around the hole, and Dylan shoveled it in batches. He raked the grass, replaced the piece of sod, and stomped it down.

"Like nothing happened," Travis said. "Time to go."

They met at the side of the road in front of Travis' pickup truck. Dylan drove the tree planter up a metal ramp, followed with the vacuum rig, and closed the hatch.

Get your truck and follow.

A few minutes later, Dylan pulled up behind and tailed Travis as he drove toward his house several miles from the center of town. Dylan recalled the man's panther-like moves during the training. He wanted to please him. He didn't know where they were headed, only that he would follow him anywhere to provide himself.

He watched as Travis signaled and pulled onto a dirt road. They drove the heavily forested route until Travis turned onto a long, winding driveway that led to an old farmhouse with a steeply sloped roof and dormer windows. Travis pulled his truck around the back of the house, stepped out, and waited for Dylan.

"Welcome to my home," Travis said as Dylan walked toward him. "I'll help you unload."

Travis lowered the hatch and extended the ramps. They moved the equipment and left it alongside a small, weatherworn barn.

"Be very careful," Travis said as he opened the lid of the vacuum canister, lifted out the bag inside, and sealed it. Dylan watched as Travis opened the door of the barn and placed the bag on a large, wooden platform. From a shelf on the wall, he took a label and a black Sharpie marker and wrote, *Carol Stilton, April 12, 1949.*

"Always take a photo of the gravestone to get the details correct," Travis told Dylan as he tied the label to the bag. Travis ushered Dylan out of the barn and secured the latch.

"Pick up a trailer for your truck," Travis said, and they walked down the driveway. "Big enough for the equipment. I'll reimburse you."

"Should I come back?"

"No. Return to work."

"At the cemetery?"

"Yes. The lawn mower you abandoned," Travis answered. "You have to finish the front."

Dylan had more questions, but he didn't want to appear stupid in front of the man he was infatuated with without reservation and dismissed them.

He got into his truck and drove to Northern Tool to purchase a utility trailer on sale for $595. He attached it to his trailer hitch, drove to the cemetery, and parked on the dirt road along the back fence of the cemetery. He found the lawn mower exactly as he'd left it.

He checked the time on his phone. It was late. Where had the day gone? He was starving and attacked a sandwich from his backpack. If he didn't pick up the pace, he would be late for GG. And the weather was perfect for an evening swim.

EIGHTEEN

TRAVIS CLICKED ON THE LIGHTS and closed the creaky door to the shed against nightfall. He brought a notebook with the incantations he'd transcribed and tailored for the remains that awaited in the bag on the platform. He put on rubber gloves and opened it. He hated this part, though his parents had seemed to relish all aspects of conjurings. What was wrong with him?

Travis understood his family's bloodline spells were rooted in black magic. To ignore the fact was folly. He was born into it, and to shun it meant death. He closed his eyes and thought of the monastery and his trainings. *Find your confidence. You will do it.*

A continual means of empowerment was necessary to survive the centuries. He could choose to be neutral with limited power and therefore modest fuel requirements. But that possibility expired the day the coven burned his parents and tried to kill him. He was bound to take revenge and needed power reserves to enable weapons like nerve bolts.

His parents' spells had left him with the thorny work of desecration. They'd pinpointed conjurings as the strongest key.

It was messy and distasteful but, for now, he was stuck with it. Perhaps one day he could come up with something better.

Travis gently probed the top layer of debris in the bag. The dirt was loose, so he dug deeper with his fingers until he felt something. He pulled up a skull fragment and placed it on the platform. He continued to search until he'd assembled a collection of artifacts: bones large and small, a necklace with a pendant, a shoe sole, and fabric from a gown. The relics and essence satisfied the requirements of the spell, and Travis arranged them neatly on top of the debris.

He held his hands with palms down over the remains of Carol Stilton, recited the incantation in Romanian, and backed away. At first there was a flicker, an almost imperceptible stirring in the dirt that became vapor and rose from the bag. The girl wavered in and out of focus until she materialized, undulating, in front of Travis. She fixated on him with a pained grimace, eye sockets large and hollow, pupils burning as embers. Travis took the necklace from the bag and placed it around her neck. He continued to chant as she billowed above the platform with an agonized look and both hands grasping at the pendant as if it were too hot to touch.

Travis knew he was trembling, though he wasn't certain if out of fear, excitement, or dread of what was to come. The wraith's forlorn and frightened expression unsettled him. He remembered Dragos' tortured countenance, and the terror of the boy seized by his conjured father in Bucharest. Travis closed his eyes and murmured a phrase, and the girl vaporized in a fluid arc into the bag. Travis sealed it and collapsed on the floor.

Travis took deep breaths to collect himself. When he felt

ready, he left the shed, and went up to the attic. He closed his eyes and reached out to Sorinah, who was just rising in Bratislava.

"It's exhausting and intimidating," Travis transferred. "My first attempt with the spell."

I've been eager to hear, Sorinah answered. *I feel your angst. Tell me everything.*

"I collected remains. Sucked essence from a grave with a drill and vacuum."

Resourceful.

"I briefly conjured a girl from the residues and set the condition. But the spell's prerequisite is dastardly and I hate the dirty work of defiling corpses."

That's the key. The desecration component packs power. It's the additional twist that turbocharges fear yet allows you to spare the victim. Dark arts can only be so tepid.

Travis drank some water. "It would be easier to kill. I understand the point made by hardliners. But I am bound to the manuscripts of my parents."

The complexity yields the power you need for the fight that awaits.

"The girl looked tormented." Travis paused and closed his eyes. "Not what I expected."

There is little you can do to temper the process. We are witches. Focus on your progress.

"Dylan the local has the skills and experience I need to gather residues."

I watched him in the cemetery. He seems a good choice. And the larger plan?

"I need to keep things simple, contained, and focused."

That's an improvement. Your parents bedeviled an entire neighborhood.

"They intended to target only three households. But they forgot about witnesses and injuries. It has fallen to me to improve what they started."

How, exactly?

"One by one encounters in private to avoid scratches or broken bones or kills or memories. I'm still fine tuning the incantation and adding controls."

Think carefully, my Travis. It is your first attempt to master your parents' spell. Try to steer clear of complications. Mistakes are hard to correct.

"A century's passed. I can no longer hide behind an eternity of preparations. It's my duty to advance my parents' work or die trying."

This test in America is the culmination of decades of training. Do not lose focus on the goal: revenge on the coven. Only with mastery of the ancestral spell may you gain sufficient power to stand against the elders. We strike back in Bucharest when at last you are empowered.

Travis said goodbye to Sorinah and went to his desk. He opened the volume that contained the central spell and traced his mother's handwritten strokes with his finger. He found himself unable to concentrate. Something didn't feel right. The wraith's obvious distress gnawed at him. He feared the power of the spell and its dark secrets, but he could never share his doubts with Sorinah. She had conditioned him to be self-sufficient, an island. She'd taught him to seek nothing and no one except expertise. Now he wondered if his isolation and appetite for vengeance came at a much greater cost than he'd imagined.

NINETEEN

THE FIRST FRIDAY OF AUGUST, Rachel got to work at 9:30 a.m. with a venti cold brew, a shoulder bag, and the keys to Old Gold. She fumbled with the lock for a moment, as usual, because it seemed as if the key had to turn forever before the latch would give, and it seemed she always started in the wrong direction, but then she discovered she was right the first time and had to repeat. The lock and heavy metal door were annoying, and MK had agreed when Rachel complained in May, but replacing either or both would be a lavish expense with little to show for the effort, so they both agreed to suck it up.

Upon entering, Rachel immediately noticed furniture and departments had been moved around from when she had finished her shift two days ago. A small men's section, including accessories that had been lumped with in the women's, had been carved out in a back corner with its own signage. The jewelry case near the register had been moved to the front.

Rachel put the keys and her coffee down on top of the jewelry case and read the note MK had left her:

Surprise! Time to shake things up. Menswear is finally all together in a single section. Check out the retro track jackets. Tell your guys. Also, amazing pieces in jewelry. Stunning. Whole top shelf rocks. You gotta show the ladies when they come in. Everything's vintage. I want to keep it all for myself. But we've got to stay in business, right? Ha, ha. See you in the afternoon. Thanks. MK

Rachel took her things and the note to the register in back to set up for the day. She turned on the lights and looked over the new men's section.

Rachel unlocked the rear panel of the jewelry case and opened it. From the top shelf she took out several rings, two bracelets, and an assortment of necklaces. She held them up to the light and studied each piece so she could dream up hooks to use on customers.

Unique, quirky and cool. MK wasn't exaggerating. She arranged them within the case so they looked their best and were easy to reach.

By late morning customers began to enter, and Rachel created a new routine to greet them, escort them to the jewelry case, show off the men's section, and return to her perch by the register where she could monitor the store while checking her phone.

Classes at UVM would start in a few weeks, and Rachel was consumed with reviewing everything she could about her dormitory, class schedule, and roommate, whom she thoroughly investigated via social media. Her roommate's public persona looked great, but Rachel was wary.

We're a nation of self-promotion whores. The whole thing's conformist and sleazy.

Rachel herself cringed at her own polished posts, some of which were already embarrassingly dated yet difficult to delete without inviting unwanted attention. What shallow image had she been projecting? *Girlfriend of a high school football star. Reluctant selfie-queen. Member of a clique, though she would never admit it or use #tripletrouble.* No hint whatsoever of storm clouds gathering in posts with James until the breakup proved the portraits in paradise to be an exaggeration. There was no hint of the extreme anxiety she felt almost daily now just a few weeks before the start of her freshman year.

At home, she'd been channeling her nervous energy toward a productive purge of clothes and knick-knacks from childhood and toward piles along the walls in her bedroom of things that would make the cut to her dorm room.

Rachel had remained in touch with James just as she had promised, texting daily and meeting him at a party the past week. Rachel was surprised to find that since the breakup she'd felt much more comfortable mixing James with Mia and Sophia. It was as if the elimination of couple status had eased away a barrier.

Now, they were all single and equals. It felt more relaxed. However, when the topic of college inevitably emerged, James withdrew from conversations because the girls were all soon leaving and he wasn't. But it was impossible to contain their excitement, and it seemed to Rachel that James understood. Perhaps their enthusiasm would even prod him toward taking forward steps of his own, she hoped.

After lunchtime, Mia and Sophia appeared in Old Gold and as usual headed straight toward Rachel at the register.

"You moved things around," Mia said. "I like it. *Mucho mejor.*"

"MK did. The men's section is more of a thing. Cute jackets and retro t-shirts. And we're gonna push vintage jewelry, one-of-a-kind statement pieces."

Rachel walked to the front, and they followed.

"Take a look," she said as she unlocked the jewelry case and slid open the rear panel. "Fair prices. Top quality. Everything's super special, as good anything in Burlington or Montreal."

Mia and Sophia made no attempt to contain their enthusiasm as they reached inside and carefully examined anything that caught their eye. They tried on rings, bracelets, and necklaces, walking to the full-length mirror to scrutinize the head-to-toe look, then coming back to the case.

Mia held up a long and chunky metal chain with a pendant of a black-and-white photo of a woman's face. "This speaks to me."

"Looks kinda like Audrey Hepburn," Sophia said.

"Maybe the former owner," Mia said.

Rachel reached for the pendant and turned it around. "You can change the photo if you want. There's a clasp. Or just use the chain by itself. It's versatile."

"I like it as it is," Mia said. "*Misterioso.*"

Mia put on the necklace. Suspended over ample breasts, the pendant hung almost to her navel. "*Mira.* The chain can go long or doubled up."

Rachel and Sophia eyed it and nodded their approval.

"I'm taking this," Sophia announced a moment later and held out her wrist to flash a charm bracelet. "*With All My*

Heart," she read as she pointed to the writing etched into a bulbous, heart-shaped silver charm.

"Love it," Rachel said as she grabbed Sophia's wrist and inspected her discovery.

Mia and Sophia stared at Rachel as she considered her options.

"Get something you'll always keep," Mia said. "We'll be separated for a long time."

"A symbol, a memory," Sophia said. "Something that unites us."

Rachel smiled and pulled out a gold ring with an oval bloodstone.

"I had my eye on this," Rachel said and placed it on her second finger. "I think it's Victorian. Maybe an engagement ring."

"You've got to take it," Sophia said.

"Why haven't you pushed jewelry on us before?" Mia asked.

"MK's brainstorm to try something new," Rachel said. "We're gonna see how it goes."

"We need a selfie," Sophia said.

They leaned together over the glass case, and took different options and poses. *#lastshoppingspree* They took a moment to post on Instagram and waited for a few likes.

"What's going on with James?" Mia asked as she looked up from her phone.

"Visiting his dad this weekend in Massachusetts," Rachel said. "Hoping he gets his act together."

"He or his father?" Sophia asked. "Still no plan?"

"Taking the year off," Rachel said.

"Applications for next term start, like, now, *pendejo*," Mia said.

"Probably not gonna happen," Rachel said.

"You gotta help him pick out what to highlight," Mia said.

"You should help him," Sophia said. "You're the living, walking, perfect example."

"Excuse me, *puta*?" Mia raised her eyebrows and smirked as she flicked back her long, straight hair.

"National Honor Society, high SATs, letters in soccer and basketball, leadership, blah, blah blah." Sophia sniggered.

"We've all got that," Mia said.

"Plus the Mexican thing. In Vermont. A trump card. I'm just ordinary, with freckles."

"My dad dragged us here from Houston for work at the hospital. It wasn't my choice, and it isn't always easy. Not everyone likes Latinos. They make assumptions. Not everyone's nice."

"Did you write about the hard parts in your essay?" Rachel asked. "Maybe James can capture the inner torment of a football captain."

"I wrote about the isolation," Mia said. "And the people dumbfounded by my accent. Is it seriously that difficult? *Por favor.* But I left out the lesbian part. Latina is one label, and I don't need another."

"It's a joke it's still an issue," Sophia said. "So many labels."

"High school for me was 'don't ask, don't tell,'" Mia said. "That's why I only shared with you two. You were cool with it, *gracias a Dios.*"

"You had to tell us," Rachel said. "It'll be so much better in college."

"I'm still chatting with Emma, the one from Austin. She's gonna be in my dorm. It helps to know one person, but I'm still nervous."

"We're nervous too," Sophia said. "That's a given."

They continued to chat until a few customers requested help in the fitting room.

"Whoops, forgot about work," Rachel whispered as she left Sophia and Mia alone for a while. More customers entered, and it became clear Rachel would be hard-pressed to escape.

Mia and Sophia waved their goodbyes to Rachel, who smiled back, and they left the store.

Mia lived close enough to downtown to walk home, so she escorted Sophia to her car; they hugged, and Sophia drove off. After three blocks, the road crossed a set of train tracks that served as a shortcut to Mia's neighborhood. Trains were infrequent, so Mia walked in the center of the rails, quickening her pace for a cardio workout with careful strides over the imperfectly spaced railroad ties.

She thought about Emma. Video chats had become Mia's favorite cap to each day. When Emma had shared she was a lesbian and completely at ease, Mia thirsted for more. *How can she be so comfortable? Maybe because she is from a cool city, big enough not to care.*

When Mia got home, she quietly climbed the stairs to her bedroom and closed the door. She didn't feel like tracking down and then making chit-chat with her mother. There would be time for that at dinner when she could kill a few birds with one stone because her father and younger brother would be present as well.

Now, she had more important things to do: packing, organizing, and researching. There was plenty to study in advance of her arrival to Mount Holyoke, including the exploration of bike trail networks and bus schedules to Boston and New York. She could plan a trip to visit Sophia at NYU in the fall. *Reunion weekend in New York's going on the calendar.* She began to grasp that the freedom of moving away and growing up came with unexpected surprises.

When it was time for dinner, Mia spilled out some tidbits: a Latina social club on campus, a community center with lots of restaurants, a large and highly ranked freshman class. Mia's parents planned to settle her on campus two weeks from Saturday, and her brother would tag along so he could get a taste of college. Her mom promised to take her on a last-minute shopping trip. Mia apologized for dominating the table conversation, skipped dessert, and excused herself to get back to her laptop.

She went upstairs and locked the door. It was almost time for a video chat with Emma, and Mia didn't want her parents or brother walking in. She set up her MacBook Air on the bed and signed in so Emma would know she was available.

Mia surveyed her closet and took out pants, tops, and dresses she still liked and made rough piles on the floor along the wall below her window. She did the same with the t-shirts, sweaters, and shorts in her bureau and began to make a shopping list.

Mia stripped to her lace bra and panties and tried on whatever was on the floor; items that made the cut she folded into piles beside the bureau. She counted the number of pieces so she could compare her collections with what Emma planned to bring. She lay on the bed in front of the laptop, slathered on lotion, and busied herself with Instagram feeds until she could no longer resist calling Emma. It was after dark, and she'd delayed her favorite part of the day long enough. Emma's icon showed she was available, and Mia clicked to connect.

"Hey, I was about to try you," Emma said as her face appeared on Mia's screen. "You're later than usual."

"Working on a shopping list," Mia said. "Going with my mom Saturday. Are six jeans enough? How many are you bringing? I feel like a ten-year-old getting ready for camp."

"You need gray, black, and blue," Emma said. "What have you been wearing most? Skinny low-rise or high-waisted? Distressed or dark?"

They worked through Mia's list, counting items pile by pile until Mia felt satisfied she'd identified the weak spots. She remembered the necklace she'd purchased and held it up to the screen, the chain thick against delicate bra straps. She opened the round disc pendant.

"Check this out," Mia said. "Got it today."

"Amazing. Who's in the picture?"

"I'm guessing the original owner. She's retro-cute."

"Pair it with a cami, and you'll have a great outfit," Emma said. "Something for the Girls' Dance."

"What girls' dance?" Mia asked.

"First weekend. Orientation," Emma said. "I'll send you a link. Best way to meet people."

"I don't know if I'm ready."

"We'll go together."

"*Tengo miedo*. Nervous to meet you, too."

"Why? We've been chatting for weeks," Emma said. "Already friends."

"In person is different," Mia said. "What if it's awkward?"

"Impossible. Too late for that."

"I've never even kissed a girl."

"It's better than a boy. Smoother. Slower. Sexier."

Mia smiled. "You can't tell anyone."

"Tell them what?"

"I've never been with a girl."

"Of course, I wouldn't. It's nobody's business."

Mia heard something outside her bedroom window.

"That's odd," she said as she paused to listen. Yes, there it was again, a scratching sound.

"What?" Emma asked.

"A weird noise at the window."

"Just ignore it."

Mia stopped talking and strained to listen. "I guess it went away."

"Get a new top specifically for the dance. You'll feel more confident."

"I'll add it to the list," Mia said. *Girls' Dance top.* I'll leave that part out for my mom."

Again came a sound from outside. Mia frowned and looked toward the glass. Was it a squirrel in the rafters? Someone scraping paint off the side of the house?

"What's wrong?" Emma asked.

"*Coño.* That sound again. Annoying. I'm gonna check it out."

Mia got up from the bed and walked to the window. It was dark outside, so she turned off the bedroom light to see better and bent down. Wind rustled the leaves of an old oak not far from the window. A gust could've pushed a branch against the side of the house, or thrown some acorns, Mia guessed, and walked back to the bed and lay in front of the laptop.

"Sorry. I'm back," Mia said. "Probably the wind."

"Focus, Mia," Emma said. "This is more important. Are you going for flirty? Sophisticated? Tomboy? Intellectual? Bombshell? Butch? Biatch?"

"Wait. What?"

"At the dance," Emma said. "You have to consider the image you want to project."

"No idea. This is harder than I thought. *No puedo.*"

"And figure out your type." Emma laughed. "Whom do you want to attract? What turns you on? I bet you've never really considered it."

Another sound came from the window, this time different. Something was tapping on glass. Mia looked over and gasped when she noticed a shadow in the window that seemed darker than a cloud shrouding the moonlight.

"That's really weird," Mia said. "Something's not right."

"Where're you going?" Emma asked as Mia disappeared from the screen, leaving Emma's monitor focused on a pillow in the middle of the bed.

In the darkened room, Mia crept toward the window. She moved her face close to the glass and peered outside. A breeze shuffled the tree branches, but it was not nearly enough to force one to the window with a measured *tap, tap, tap.*

Just as she was ready to give up, Mia noticed a flicker of white by the fence in the backyard. She waited for moonlight to pierce cloud swirls and watched, fascinated, as a woman in a tattered gown materialized from vapor and seemed to ripple as she floated across the lawn, arms wafting as if in a belly dance or an attempt to balance. Patches of hair hung from her scalp in tangled disarray, and Mia froze as the white-clad figure drew closer and seemed to notice her in the window. Ghostly eyes burned within grotesquely swollen sockets, suspended within emptiness. The apparition seemed lost and disoriented, frantic yet on the brink of despair. Leathery skin constricted her skeletal, wraith-like limbs, and she raised a bony finger that trembled as it pointed at Mia even as she continued to drift inexorably toward the house.

"Someone's coming, something awful," Mia whispered loudly and stepped away from the window as the wraith grew closer. "What should I do?"

"I can't hear you," Emma said. "What's happening? Come to the screen."

Mia took backward steps toward the bed and shrieked when the figure, somehow, inexplicably, hovered outside the window and peered inside. Her fingernails tapped the pane. Mia watched in horror and disbelief as a hand passed through glass, and the wraith floated into the bedroom, arms outstretched, as if the walls of the house were nothing more than a suggestion.

Mia gasped and jumped away from the window.

"What's happening?" Emma shouted through the screen of the laptop.

"Don't fear me, Mia," the wraith whispered in an otherworldly tone as she took a step closer and extended an open palm, anguished eyes fixated on Mia's bosom.

"What do you want?" Mia whispered. "Get away from me!"

"Give me my locket," the wraith growled, as if each word required effort.

"What?" Mia asked through short, rapid breaths. "Who are you?"

"My name is Carol Stilton. Please help me." The wraith's jaw trembled, and her face contorted as gasping sobs began, but without tears. "I beg you."

"What's wrong? Why are you here?"

The wraith murmured quietly, as if to someone else, and lurched forward, swiping at the necklace. "Give it to me. Quickly. The locket. Save yourself!" Her sobs grew stronger.

Mia hyperventilated and fell backward on the bed, rocking the laptop as she clutched wildly for the locket at the base of her necklace.

"Stop playing games, Mia!" Emma shouted. "This isn't funny. What's happening?"

A loud pounding at the door added to the cacophony in the room as Mia's parents shouted from the hallway. "Open the door! Now, Mia! *¿Qué haces?*"

The interruption seemed to panic the wraith, and she grabbed the thick chain of the necklace, but Mia recoiled and fell off the bed. She gasped for air as she kicked against the mattress and tried to break free while pulling on the locket. The laptop rocked backward, screen facing up, and Emma shrieked as the pounding at the door continued.

"Take it," Mia managed to whisper. "It won't come off."

Mia grasped at the locket with both hands as the wraith hoisted her up from the floor by the chain and looped it over the closet doorknob. The bedroom door strained at the hinges. All at once, Mia's head lurched sideways, and she fell silent. The wraith pried away Mia's fingers, snapped the locket from the chain, and evaporated like vapor into the darkness.

Mia's father kicked the door in, splintering wood from the frame.

"The hell's happening?" he shouted as he and his wife rushed to Mia. "*Dios mío!* Help her! Get her down!"

"Call an ambulance!" Mia's mother shouted as they tried to revive their daughter. Mia's brother made the call while her parents moved her to the bed.

Emma shouted Mia's name, and her father grabbed the laptop.

"Who in hell are you?"

"Emma," she said through sobs.

"What's happening?"

"I don't know. Someone came in. Where's Mia?"

He jumped down to look under the bed and rifled through the closet. He raced to the window and scoured the yard.

"There's no one but you!" he shouted at the laptop. "You're in trouble, *puta.*"

The police and an ambulance soon arrived. They attempted to resuscitate Mia and rushed her to the hospital, but she wasn't breathing, and they weren't optimistic.

In the hours to come, Emma found herself the focus of intense scrutiny. She was shaken, unreliable, and unconvincing. Why was Mia wearing nothing but a bra and panties? Were they lesbians? Had she coerced Mia into experimenting with some sort of autoerotic asphyxiation and things went too far? Why did her version of things have no evidence to back it up?

There was no locket, though Emma swore she'd seen a photo inside the glass, and no intruder, though Emma swore she'd heard frightening voices.

Police studied the second-floor window and the towering oak just outside. They ordered backup to search the grounds.

Emma couldn't cry and couldn't sleep. She trembled and stared in disbelief at the computer screen for hours. But it became clear Mia wasn't coming back. So she shut it down.

TWENTY

"WAKE UP!" Travis transferred to Sorinah in Bratislava, who clicked on a lamp in the predawn darkness. "Something's gone horribly wrong."

I can sense your alarm. Tell me.

Travis paced the length of the attic loft. "I've killed someone. I lost control of the very first wraith. I thought Mia was alone, the test subject."

Slow down. Calm yourself.

"The computer was unexpected. I didn't consider it. A foolish oversight. If something was recorded, it's over. I understand how it all went bad for my parents. The spell is dangerous."

What about the computer?

"I only recognized the threat once inside the bedroom. The video camera was on. Mia was chatting. I tried to keep the wraith away from the screen. But the conjured girl had to speak and had to act. I thought there would be more time.

You could have guessed her family would rush to her aid.

"I didn't expect such screams from the computer. I expected Mia to remove the locket and to escape unharmed and confused and blank. But I couldn't operate freely. The door was about to burst down. It is a matter of luck the wraith vanished at all."

You must learn and improve. Luck goes both ways.

"Mia would be fine if the locket had come free faster. I panicked. I thought they would catch the wraith. It happened so fast. Mia died because her hands gripped the locket."

Why not just stop the whole thing? Call back the wraith yourself?

"The conjured girl would be caught on a circle of hell. Perhaps forever. I can sense where she's trapped until she breaks the cycle. Mia would remember the attack. The spell dictates the condition. It's beyond my control."

What condition?

"The wraith must retrieve the charm. The target must surrender it, or the wraith must forcibly take it. Only then is the memory cleared. Only then is the emissary free. Witnesses cut short the sequence."

You were forced to act. At least the wraith got out. So now what?

"It defies logic Mia would have killed herself. Yet her neck hung on the chain with no rational explanation. There will be suspicion, people on edge—like Bucharest."

It's not the same. Calm down. The damage is contained. It was a first attempt. Next time will be better. You must ensure your subjects are completely alone.

"I've diminished my parents' vision. Already I've killed. They were banished and burned for less, punished for unleashing chaos alone. No one died that night."

You misjudged the situation. Every detail must be

analyzed. That you know from our decades of training. This spell needs time to complete its cycle.

"Carol Stilton escaped hell, but Mia paid with her life. The blame is mine. It's not something I can undo. I felt the wraith's torment. I can't ignore it. My parents didn't know."

Advancement is a long, incremental process. Mistakes are inevitable. Use your remorse as motivation. Conjuring is difficult. Your eyes are opening to a bigger picture.

They said their goodbyes, and Travis descended to his bedroom. He undressed and stood in front of the mirror. He looked youthful, energized, and robust from the power he'd absorbed.

But he'd neglected to share an important observation with Sorinah; still smoldering was the intoxicating pleasure that followed Mia's kill.

It worried him. He was supposed to be superior to the hardliners. He'd thought his family's methods were elevated. Mia's death violated the entire thrust of the ancestral spell. And worse, deep inside, he could not deny the allure of the kill, the same as a hardliner.

TWENTY-ONE

THE COVEN HAD MODERNIZED over the course of a tumultuous century in Bucharest. No longer sequestered behind a series of gates and stone walls, witches infiltrated all sectors of the city. Most lived modestly to avoid attention. Supremes and elders mixed with the privileged class.

Elisabeta summoned Radu to her châteaux. She didn't like him, but was bound by edict to involve him. An aide escorted the enforcer to her door.

"It seems Travis has revealed his whereabouts," Elisabeta stated with no expression from where she stood in front of enormous beechwood bay windows.

"And so, an old case reopens." Radu raised his eyebrows and grinned. "The elusive, little orphan finally slips up."

"He's no longer little. He's managed a conjuring of his own, in America."

"How do you know?"

"We monitor desecration spells. If you'll recall, I caught his parents in a butcher shop conjuring the proprietor. It activates an alarm. He doesn't know, or he forgot." She studied Radu as they locked eyes.

"Excellent news." Radu's right foot twitched with nervous excitement. "Time doesn't pardon him. Rules must be enforced. He pays as a fugitive. He killed one of our own."

"Slow down. Let me refresh your memory. Alexandra acted of her own accord. Travis defended himself against her attack. That much was clear from the evidence. The slice in Lucian's throat came from her dagger. The council agreed Travis would be spared."

"I remember like it was yesterday. It stuck in my craw. His parents thought they were better than us. Alexandra was correct in taking action. The orphan remains a significant threat."

"You will bring him back to Bucharest unharmed. I'll be watching. Do not forget your allegiance to coven law, despite your traditionalist loyalties."

"Yes, Elisabeta." Radu stood at attention.

"He has grown powerful. Monitor his conjurings. You cannot stop them, and you might learn something. You are not his judge."

"I must have freedom to act. What strategies are permitted?"

"You may interfere with the outcome of his experiments."

"Nothing more?"

"You may employ your own weapons to capture him: pyrokinesis, immobilization, physical force. But only enough to convince his return. I recognize he's unlikely to submit easily."

"I'll leave by morning."

Elisabeta nodded and handed him an envelope. She turned toward the window.

"I have waited for this." Radu made for the door. "No one hides forever."

PART THREE

INTRUSION

TWENTY-TWO

PAULA WAS FREE FROM WORK on a summer Friday and considered ways to spend time with her kids. After breakfast, she suggested they could finally introduce themselves to the neighbor who had moved into the Malloy's farmhouse a few months ago. It was the friendly thing to do, and at the least, they would enjoy a hike on the way.

When her plan was met with blank stares, she amplified her case with the logic that if they didn't do it now, they probably never would because they'd all soon be too busy once September arrived. Even James, who had become unmoored, would need to start doing something—anything.

The siblings grudgingly agreed, though they had no burning desire to meet anyone new. It was obviously more important to their mother, who was lonely after the divorce, they reasoned, and so they agreed to tag along. She could bring the muffins from breakfast that she'd baked too many of as a welcome basket.

The property behind their house extended for several acres and was a playground, garden, and yard that morphed into an abundant meadow that abutted a forest owned by the town. A wide, overgrown pathway through the woods was a remnant of the stagecoach run that formerly linked the scattered farmhouses of the community. The stagecoach road, as they'd nicknamed it, began at the back edge of their property.

James and Katherine had spent many hours there as children, playing, creating hideouts, climbing trees, and exploring. The stagecoach road carved through the forest to the back edge of the property owned by their closest neighbor. It was the quickest route between the houses.

With muffin basket in hand, Paula led James and Katherine as they wandered the pathway. The trees overhead provided cooling shade from the late morning sun. Paula liked the idea of having a neighbor within walking distance again and privately hoped they would get along. It had been years since she'd last taken the stagecoach road to visit the Malloys. She had missed them when they'd moved away. She felt isolated sometimes and didn't like depending on a car just to see another human being.

"I can't stay for long," James announced, apropos of nothing, as they continued through the woods.

"No one said you had to," Paula said. "Just say hello."

"I've got the funeral in the afternoon," James continued. "And I still gotta pack."

"What time is the funeral?" Paula asked.

"At two," James said.

"Mia Rivera?" Katherine asked.

"Yes," James said.

"Everyone's talking about it," Katherine said.

"What happened?" Paula asked.

"No one knows," James said. "Looks like suicide."

"That's horrible," Paula answered.

"We were friends, through Rachel," James said. "Never thought she would do that."

"Shouldn't you postpone the visit to your father?" Paula asked. "To help Rachel?"

"I just want to get out of here," James said. "Creeps me out."

They wandered until the trees thinned to brambles and then became the neighbor's lawn. The family headed toward a shed behind the farmhouse that had once been a small barn for livestock. A winding driveway looped toward the front where a pickup truck was parked.

They walked up the steps to the main entrance. Paula felt nervous, pointed to the doorbell, and motioned to Katherine to press it. What if this were a mistake? The chimes resonated loudly in the stillness, and they stood for what seemed a long time before the door opened. A brawny man wearing a polo shirt and shorts, barefoot, opened the door and smiled.

He's handsome, Paula thought. *Late thirties? A good first impression.*

"Can I help you?" the man asked.

"I'm Katherine. We're neighbors, more or less."

"This is for you," Paula said as she stepped forward and lifted the muffin basket. "Sorry it took so long to say hello."

"What a nice surprise." He blushed and smiled broadly. "I'm Travis."

Paula liked that he seemed touched by the gesture. "From the second floor you can see our house in the distance," Paula said as she pointed toward the woods. "I used to be friends with the former owners."

"Oh, I know your house," Travis said. "Glad you stopped by. Please, come in."

He stepped back and held the door open.

James, the last to enter, extended his hand. "Nice to meet you."

"Let's head to the living room," Travis said as he led them forward. The visitors found places on the sofa and chairs. A large wooden table anchored the room. "You can put the muffins there for now. Would anyone like some coffee?"

"Just finished breakfast," Katherine said. "Too many muffins already. Mom overdid it."

"Can't really stay for long," James added.

Travis leaned against the dark wooden beams that framed the exposed-brick entryway. Paula tried not to assign importance to or interest in his level of fitness and focused on the table.

"What brings you here?" Paula asked, looking up. "I detect an accent."

"Oh, that," Travis said and smiled. "Trying to get rid of it."

"From where?"

"Eastern Europe."

"What brings you here?" Paula asked again.

"Studies and research."

"What kind?" Paula asked.

"Antiques, jewelry, collectibles," Travis said and paused a moment. "Early American craftsmen were trained in Europe or taught by old-world masters. Quality stuff."

"Sounds interesting," Paula said.

"I like finding hidden treasure," Travis said.

"Do you have a business?" Katherine asked.

"Some individual clients. An antiques dealer in Montreal. I'm on the lookout for venues."

"My friend works at a vintage store in the center of town," James said.

"I think I know the place." Travis walked to the table. "Thanks again for the muffins. They look decadent." Travis looked at Paula as he reached into the basket, grabbed one, took a bite, and then resumed his stance in the entryway.

"Why here?" Paula asked. "Why not a big city?"

"Not sure how long I will need to stay," Travis said. "Depends on my ability to learn and to make the most of things. Montreal, New York, or Boston would require a much larger investment on my part. For now, starting small makes sense."

"Do you have a fallback plan?" Paula asked. "If it doesn't work out?"

"Yes. I've only leased this place for a year. I can extend if necessary. But I do hope to return home before winter if I can prove myself worthy of return."

"Sounds like you're hard on yourself," Paula said. "What is the measure of worthy? Who gets to decide?" She couldn't stop herself from asking. Perhaps something was lost in translation. And for someone in his business, he didn't wear a single piece of jewelry that might offer a clue as to his marital status. Maybe he was gay.

"There's someone special back home," Travis said. "She's helping to gauge my progress. For now, things are still in flux."

Paula smiled politely. "I hope things go well for you."

"Thank you."

"I like your accent," Katherine added. "Legit from a movie."

Travis laughed. "I need more English lessons. Pronunciation."

"I could help you practice," Paula interjected.

Katherine rolled her eyes, and James stared at the floor.

"Do you think you have time?" Travis asked.

Paula looked at James and Katherine.

"Probably not. It would be tough. I'm raising kids on my own."

"Divorced?"

"Yes. But I got custody."

"Looks like you're doing well."

There was an awkward silence as Travis finished the muffin and no one jumped in with a response.

"Muffin was delicious," Travis said finally.

"Glad you tried one." Paula looked at her watch. "We should probably get going."

"Do you want to refresh your memory of the place?" Travis asked. "A tour?"

"Maybe another time."

"You can try over the weekend if you'd like. Saturday's pretty open."

"It might work. Afternoon?"

"Great."

Paula almost offered her number but feared looking overly enthusiastic. She went to Travis and shook his hand like a professional. James and Katherine followed. They said their goodbyes and circled around to the back of the house. They kept quiet until a safe distance away.

"That was cray," Katherine said.

"What was?" Paula asked.

"You legit threw yourself at him."

"Did not."

"*I can help you practice,*" James mimicked.

"It wasn't that bad," Paula said. "Besides, he's got someone in Europe."

"Guys like that cheat," Katherine said.

"Just look at Dad," James said. "You're gonna repeat the same mistakes."

"Settle down, everyone," Paula said.

"Maybe you deserve some fun," Katherine said. "He's hot. And you're bored."

"Calm down," Paula said. "I'll never leave the house again except for groceries and for work. I promise."

"Just teasing, Mom," James said. "You can do what you want. Can't wait to tell Dad tomorrow about the stud next door. He'll be so pissed."

"He has no right to an opinion," Katherine said. "I hope he gets jealous."

"Nothing happened," Paula said. "A basket of muffins happened."

They continued to banter as they walked the stagecoach road. When they reached home, Katherine and James helped Paula water the garden and pick whatever looked ripe.

After lunch, Paula waited for her son to appear in the suit he'd worn only once just two months ago for graduation. She kissed him goodbye.

"Will you be home in time for dinner?" Paula asked, and James nodded. "Give Rachel our best. Send our condolences. We want to respect the Rivera family's privacy. The last thing they need is to be overwhelmed by unwanted attention. A child's funeral is every mother's nightmare."

TWENTY-THREE

THE PARKING LOT AT THE FUNERAL home was packed, and James had trouble finding a spot. He entered the front doors and was intimidated by a crowd congregated in the central hallway. He wove through the visitors and peered into an elegant salon with chairs scattered about yet with no vacancies. The room itself was actually overflow space for an adjoining parlor with chairs set up in even rows facing Mia's casket.

James heard sobs as he shuffled through the first room and into the parlor trying to locate Rachel. He glanced at the casket but immediately looked away and scanned the rows of chairs. Rachel and Sophia got his attention, and he maneuvered toward them and what appeared to be an empty seat.

James gently touched Sophia's shoulder as he entered her row. She looked up and smiled weakly. "We saved one for you."

"Thanks," James said as they lightly embraced. "I'm so sorry."

He squeezed past her to take a seat on the other side

of Rachel, and put his arm around her. "I'm so sorry," he whispered, again.

Rachel nodded but didn't try to speak through tears. They sat silently until she regained control.

"I'm in shock," she whispered. "This can't be happening."

James nodded with his lips closed tightly. Some time passed.

"You should go see her," Rachel said and glanced toward the casket.

James lumbered out of his seat and joined the queue to view the casket. When it was his turn to kneel, he tried to make sense of the surreal sight in front of him. What had gone so wrong for Mia? How was this possible?

He felt dizzy even as he couldn't take his eyes off her face. In that exact instant, he felt as if the world had morphed into something twisted where nothing made sense and even innocuous people and things could not be trusted. He wasn't prepared for the jolt of seeing Mia laid out so graphically before him, cold and stiff and discolored and fake and dead. A bruise on her neck was covered by makeup and lace above the high collar of her dress. He reached out to touch her hand, and the texture felt morbid, not at all comforting. He stood, fumbled back to his seat, and shook his head to regain focus.

For how long he, Rachel, and Sophia sat together quietly, he didn't know.

At some point, Rachel leaned toward his ear and whispered, "Did you see her neck?"

"Yes. Unreal," James said. "They tried to cover it. But it didn't work."

"I can't believe she hanged herself," Rachel said. "Even by mistake."

"Do you want to take a break?" Sophia asked. "A change of scenery?"

Rachel and James nodded. They found three open chairs in a far corner of the adjoining room.

"I never saw her despair," Rachel said. "I feel so awful."

Sophia swiveled her chair to face James and Rachel with her back to the rest of the room.

"There was nothing to see," Sophia said. "We can't beat ourselves up. Mia wouldn't want that. We know who she was, and she wouldn't do this. None of it adds up. Something strange must have happened. Or Mia kept incredible secrets. I want to find out."

"You're right," Rachel said. "We've got to investigate. We owe that much to her."

James followed a winding pattern on the carpet and lost himself.

"I've been racking my brain and finally thought of something," Sophia continued.

"Tell us."

"We're not her only friends. Maybe she hid stuff from us. Remember she'd mentioned someone new, an incoming freshman to Mount Holyoke?"

"Yeah. Emma from Austin. It had a ring to it."

"Mia told me they were becoming close. Nightly video chats. She liked that Emma was out and happy and knew about things. She's more urban than us. I'm going to track her down on social. Maybe she knows something, a dark side Mia kept away from us."

"At least it's a start," Rachel said. "Keep me posted."

Sophia took Rachel's hand, and her charm bracelet dangled. She rotated her wrist to watch it. "Seems like forever ago," Sophia said. "So sad now. Tragic."

Rachel stared at the bracelet. "I had to give my ring back. MK made me."

Sophia looked troubled.

"She said it was too expensive for a discount. For now. I can ask again later if it doesn't sell." Rachel paused. "She picked these out for me instead." Rachel pulled back her chestnut hair to expose two gold clip-on earrings with ruby-red glass centers. "Costume jewelry. From the 1950s."

"It's not the same," Sophia said. "It's not what we shared together."

Rachel pursed her lips and stared at the chandelier. "I know. It's a copout. I took them to be nice."

"You have to get the ring. Explain things to MK. She'll understand."

"You're right. Especially now. The memory matters."

"Seriously. It's symbolic and important, our last photo together."

Rachel took off the earrings and clenched them. "I would have fought harder, but how could I have known?" She started to cry and spoke slowly, quietly. "I really don't want them. They can't just substitute."

James snapped out of his trance. Rachel reached out and grasped his hand.

"Please take these. Maybe your mom would like them? Or your sister? For free. They're fun to use for a party or special occasion."

She placed the earrings in his palm. James closed the fingers of one hand and wiped at her tears with the other.

"Sure thing," James said. "They'll love anything coming from you. They like you more than me."

They sat for a while, quietly.

"What are you guys doing later?" Rachel asked, sitting tall and composing herself.

"Gotta pack," James said. "Going to Massachusetts tomorrow for a week."

"Right. I forgot," Rachel said. "Your dad."

"I want to get out of here. Too weird. Too depressing."

"I just want to lie down," Sophia said.

"I'm afraid to be alone," Rachel said.

"Text me whenever you want," Sophia said.

They remained in the corner until the crowd in the room diminished.

"Do you want to go to the casket one last time?" Sophia asked.

"Sure," Rachel answered. They looked at James.

"I can't," he said and reentered the carpet pattern. "I'm not good with funerals or death, and I won't be at the church service or at the cemetery. I just have to go."

"We understand," Rachel said.

James hugged them.

"Good luck with everything. I'll be back in a week. Maybe this is just a dream, and we'll all wake up by then."

TWENTY-FOUR

OVERTIME WORK GYPPED DYLAN of a coveted evening swim at Maple Street Park. A sudden and unusual death demanded a quick and discreet burial. The plot had to be prepared for the next day. It was a Saturday morning service, top priority, no excuses. The stern tone from his usually laidback manager, especially on a Friday afternoon in summer, meant he needed to deliver exactly as instructed.

The intrusion on his time made him uneasy. What if Travis needed him? The rest of the day would be shot, and he would have to work the weekend. Dylan wanted to alert his mentor that he was slammed. He wanted to show courtesy and respect.

I have no choice but to prepare a grave for a morning burial. I'm very sorry.

Dylan knew the next instant that everything was fine. He was free from obligation. A deep sense of relief and satisfaction swept over him whenever he felt Travis' presence inside him. He flushed and became excited like a teenager with an unexplained, unwieldy, and unresolved boner in homeroom. With deep breaths, all tension dispersed. He refocused on work.

At the cemetery, Dylan oversaw the team that came to dig the plot with a backhoe. They took away the distracting pile of dirt that would cover the casket. Dylan lined the edges of the plot neatly with Astroturf, and the team pitched a canopy. Folding chairs were on order and would arrive for setup in the morning.

Dylan recognized the name on a tag on a wooden post identifying the plot. He'd read about the curious death of a pretty girl. It was presumed to be a suicide, but unanswered questions lingered. It seemed more likely a murder, and a strange voice was reportedly heard by an online witness, though no evidence could be found. The voice may have been the victim's own, some kind of game gone wrong. Specific details remained unreleased though it was initially reported the cause of death was hanging.

Who'd want to hang themselves at eighteen and about to leave for college, Dylan wondered? Especially a beautiful girl like that. He'd studied her photograph as if it would somehow provide an answer.

He suddenly felt grateful he'd reached his thirty-fifth birthday.

He made the setup around the gravesite as tidy and elegant as possible to help the girl's family. His work was important, he decided, even if no one else thought so.

TWENTY-FIVE

THE KITCHEN WAS QUIET as James got ready to leave. Katherine was already out with her friends, and his mother was at Hannaford's. James found the lunch Paula had packed for him along with a note. He wrote a note of his own for Katherine and left it on the kitchen table with the earrings Rachel had given him. They seemed more Katherine's speed than his mom's. He grabbed the lunch and the duffle bag he'd packed and was on the road to Massachusetts before 11 a.m.

Once a good distance beyond town limits and into less familiar scenery, James thanked himself for making the decision to leave despite a measure of guilt that he should rightfully be attending Mia's funeral.

He wasn't religious but considered himself spiritual, believing that an identical, universal force for good was at the core of all religions, whether devotees thought so or not. He couldn't envision himself sitting in Mia's church service listening to some sort of message of hope when there was none. Nothing could be said that would bring comfort or meaning. True believers probably thought Mia was already in Hell, anyway, considering the lesbian rumors and apparent suicide. *That* combination constituted an express ticket on a bullet train directly into the outstretched arms of Lucifer.

James knew he could have supported Rachel by joining her, but she had Sophia to rely on, and anyway, he and Rachel had broken up, and perhaps it was best for both of them to stand independently. He had problems of his own, no plan for the future while anyone smart sailed off to college. Was he stupid? He imagined so with a high school transcript of mostly Bs, with a few As, Cs, and Ds thrown in. A larger problem was that he had no passionate plan for the rest of his life. He'd lost his bearings.

He'd grown up idolizing his father's athleticism and cockiness. In pursuit of his father's approval, James had focused on sports over academics. The rush of winning tests of physical strength and skill and the adulation that followed had been an aphrodisiac with a bitter aftertaste because his biggest fan had revealed himself to be a narcissist. His role model had cheated on his mother and ultimately chosen to live alone over the responsibilities of fatherhood. The hurt it had caused his family rocked the value system James had constructed upon a foundation of enthusiastic cheers from his father, Aaron, the jock who wouldn't grow up.

Trying to process his pain and move on from his father's betrayal had proven much harder for James than for his sister. A lifetime of conditioning was difficult to ignore. Even now, as the GPS led him toward his father's house, James felt a familiar uneasiness and knew he would soon be seeking his father's approval. Each passing mile fueled the reincarnation of the eighth-grade football captain.

It was just past 2 p.m. when James pulled into the

driveway and stopped the car. Aaron immediately came out and greeted him with a wave. James stepped out from the driver's seat, and Aaron hugged him.

"Wow, nice car," Aaron said.

"Graduation present from Mom."

The look on Aaron's face indicted he'd only just now realized how far he'd been outdone.

"My bag's in the trunk," James said.

"I'll help you."

They walked to the back of car, and with a *click* the trunk opened.

"I've got this," James said. "Take a look up front."

Aaron went to the driver's side door and sat down. He felt the steering wheel and perused the control panel. "Looks great. Your mother did good."

"I love the new iPhone," James said pulling the door open wide. "Great gift."

"I'm glad," Aaron said as he stepped out. "How're things going?"

"Not so great," James said. "We'll talk later."

"You're looking good."

"You too. Still holding it together at forty-three."

"Takes work," Aaron said. "Trying to keep in shape. Coaching soccer this fall, then wrestling. Still gotta work out. Part of my job." Aaron led James inside. "Let's get you settled. You know which one's yours."

James made his way to the bedroom he'd made his own over the past year. "When you're ready, meet me out back," Aaron said and headed toward the kitchen.

James unpacked, changed to black nylon workout shorts,

and headed outdoors to a patio off the kitchen to find Aaron with his shirt off sitting in the sun next to a wooden table with an ice bucket filled with bottles of Bud Lite.

"You're shaving your chest now?" James asked.

"Trimmed. Not shaved," Aaron answered. "Women like it better."

"You have a girlfriend?"

"Some dates. Nothing serious."

"I broke up with Rachel," James said as he adjusted his chair and opened a beer. "Well, she dumped me."

"Ouch. Sorry. When'd that happen?"

"About a month ago."

"Wonder why?"

"Lots of changes happening. Everything's different since graduation. For starters, she's going to college, and I'm not." The sun blazed and James pulled off his tank top. He stretched his legs and leaned back in the lawn chair as he kicked off his Chuck Taylors. Bare feet felt good in the grass. Cicadas buzzed along with a lawnmower, not far away.

"You gotta make a plan. Get your head right."

"You helped fuck it up in the first place."

"Didn't want you to waste your talent. Not everyone's born athletic. It's a gift. Pushed you to persevere. Improve yourself. Master something you were good at."

"Leading to what?"

"A scholarship, maybe. Coaching jobs. Wasn't sure brains were gonna get you anywhere."

"Thanks, Dad." James took a swig. "Wasn't your degree in phys. ed?"

"Yes."

"Sounds dumb in today's world."

"Then study something else."

"My grades aren't the best."

"That's why I put your money on football. You were team captain for two years."

James paused a moment. The beer was beginning to do its job, and he wanted to shift the focus from himself. "Why couldn't you just control yourself?"

"I'm sorry. I can't change what happened," Aaron said, and took a deep drink. "Biggest mistake of my life."

"Then why'd you do it?"

"I don't know exactly why. I'm talking to a therapist."

James paused a moment, stunned. "That's cool. About the divorce?"

"There's more."

"Tell me."

Aaron considered his words, and took another drink. "Something inside makes me run."

"From what? I run too."

"A trapped feeling like panic sets in. Something I gotta escape from, no matter what. I don't like being tied down. Suffocated. When you get older, life speeds up and sex slows down, and you're left with cuddling. I'm not gonna talk about that. You're too young. But I'm not ready to give up and sit on the sidelines. I can't. Something won't let me. I gotta keep looking for what's next, or I'm irrelevant. Doesn't mean I don't love you and Katherine, even your mom."

"It hurts people," James said. "I looked up to you. I wanted to be you. Not anymore."

No one spoke, so James stood to adjust the umbrella.

"I don't blame you," Aaron said after James settled back into his lawn chair.

"You really ruined things."

"I'll make it up to you. I promise."

"Good luck with that."

They sat for a while and opened new beers. The lawnmower stopped.

"There's a lot of pressure these days," James said. "A girl from school just killed herself. I knew her. Best friends with Rachel."

"That's horrible."

"Was about to start college."

"I'm sorry. Suicide's a real tragedy. Hurts everyone."

He looked at his son and recognized pain. James stared at the bottle label, eyes glassy.

"What about your plans?" Aaron asked to change the subject. "A job or college. You've got to start something. Get a plan going."

"The best laid plans didn't help Mia."

"Who's Mia?"

"The girl who's dead."

"You can't think like that. You're in charge of your own life."

They continued to talk, tossed a football, and drank more beer until it was time to pick a place for dinner. For the first time ever, James realized as they played, Aaron had shared hidden feelings with him, a private side James hadn't considered before, a flaw somewhere deep.

For the first time since the divorce, James wondered if they might rebuild a relationship.

TWENTY-SIX

JAMES HAD ALREADY LEFT for Massachusetts, and Katherine had gone to the lake with a few friends who had offered to drive, so Paula found herself with free time after lunch. She busied herself in the kitchen but knew exactly what she wanted to do. It was simply a matter of getting the nerve and taking a walk.

Travis had said it was OK to visit in the afternoon. It would, in fact, be somewhat rude to ignore his invitation. Paula admitted she would never take a second walk to visit the new neighbor if he weren't so attractive. She felt a nervous excitement like she'd felt in college before deciding to flirt with trouble.

Luckily, she'd been motivated to work out after Aaron left and knew she was seen as a MILF because she'd overheard guys in the office and classmates of James and Katherine when she'd waited in the lobby to pick them up after school. She'd let her honey blonde hair grow long, and added highlights that got sunnier all summer.

Her suspicion was triggered by what Travis had said about another woman waiting back home. Paula didn't want to become attracted to someone already in a relationship or to become a homewrecker or to be used for entertainment while Travis was temporarily free to play. She'd already learned plenty from Aaron.

Paula calmed her nerves by telling herself that her intentions were neighborly, nothing more. She was taking a walk through the woods. The target happened to be a hunk living nearby, but no ulterior motive was necessary.

She checked the mirror briefly before setting out but refused to adjust or change what she'd already chosen to wear: tan L.L. Bean chino shorts with a blue gingham short-sleeve top. A friendly visit did not require fussiness. This time she wouldn't bring any kind of gift; she didn't want to appear overbearing.

She made her way down the stagecoach road. Late-summer light filtered through the trees and cast undulating shadows on the wild turf, pocked with ragweed, milkweed, and dandelions. She realized how much she'd missed taking walks after the Malloys had moved. Maybe she would share it with Travis? The pristine route between their properties might entice him to visit.

That's ridiculous; you barely know him, Paula thought as she emerged at the far end of Travis' backyard and headed to his house.

As she climbed the front steps, Paula realized her nervousness had returned, stronger than before. She took a deep breath and rang the doorbell. It didn't take long for Travis to appear. He smiled and extended his hand.

"Welcome, Paula. Glad you didn't forget."

"Is this OK for you?" Paula asked. Her nervousness melted away.

"Yes. Come in," Travis answered and showed her to the living room. They settled onto the couch. "Can I get you something?"

"No, thanks. I'm fine."

"Can I show you around?"

"If you'd like. I knew the previous owners. Years ago."

Travis led Paula to the kitchen and first floor bedrooms.

"My office is upstairs. The attic. We can check out your house from the window." They made their way through the T-shaped hallway linking the kitchen with the rest of the house. "I call it the attic, but it's really a loft with a bathroom, laundry, and office space in the far corner. It's cozy like an attic because of the sloped ceiling."

They creaked up steep hardwood stairs, and Travis led Paula to an open dormer window. He pointed toward her house on a hill beyond the woods. There were more trees than she'd remembered, and they'd filled out to frame the stagecoach road as a verdant glade between the properties.

Paula turned and surveyed the room to find neatly organized books and collectables lining floor-to-ceiling shelves. Travis explained he was an avid reader, and his interest in antiques and jewelry extended to old books and glassware.

Paula gripped the thick bannister as they returned to the living room and sat on the couch.

"Surprised you don't have more stuff around," Paula said. "Clutter. Antiques."

"I keep my possessions minimal," Travis said. "Not sure how long I'll be here, so no point in filling the place. Still figuring things out."

"If things go well, you'd stay?"

"If things go well, I'd leave. I need to learn and return. I know it sounds counterintuitive. Success would mean my work here was complete. A longer stay would mean failure and back to the drawing board."

"So your gain is our loss?"

"I'm afraid so."

"Would your spouse relocate with a longer stay?" Paula couldn't help herself. The timing seemed right, and she might not get another chance to ask.

"She's not my spouse," Travis answered. "She's someone special I've known for a long time. Like family. We're not romantically involved. That would be impossible."

Paula felt her pulse quicken but forced herself to concentrate and to remain objective and detached with no agenda.

"I didn't want to get into specifics in front of your kids," Travis said. "She's a mentor with a similar family history. It's unlikely she'd be inclined to move."

"Will you go back to her?"

"When the time is right, I must. We have unfinished business."

"Antiques? Jewelry?"

"Not exactly. That's merely a means to an end."

Paula found herself befuddled and unable to look away from Travis as he spoke. She watched the movement of his square jaw and the interplay of muscle and sky blue golf shirt. He rested his leg on the cushion between them, thighs defined and thick. *Stop it.*

"When did your marriage end?" Travis asked.

"About two years ago."

"That's fairly recent."

"Problems started before that."

"Like what?"

"Womanizing," Paula said and paused a moment. "I'm not looking to repeat the same mistake."

"We all learn from our mistakes," Travis said and nonchalantly shifted position, extending his arm along the back of the couch. "We all make them. Some are devastating."

"I should probably be going," Paula said.

Travis seemed to murmur something quietly, as if talking to himself.

"What was that?" Paula asked. "Sorry, your accent."

She felt a gentle wave. Why did she think it was time to go? She'd just arrived, what was the rush?

Paula shifted on the sofa cushion. The mood was warm, relaxed, and inviting. Did she dare let her guard down? Slowly, she tilted her head back until her hair brushed his arm. She felt him move closer, and she rested her head on the curve of his bicep.

"It's OK." Travis put his arm around her shoulder.

"We shouldn't do this."

"Maybe not. But do you want to?"

She smiled, exhaled, and could think of no reason to resist. What was she always so uptight about? It seemed the attraction was mutual. She should be happy.

Travis shifted toward Paula, leaned in close, and kissed her. She felt the stubble from his face brush her cheeks and bit gently on his thick lower lip. He pulled her tight against his chest and rolled onto his back on the couch so that Paula rested on top of him. He propped his arms behind his head and smiled playfully. Paula reached up and gripped his wrists, pretending to pin him down. They lay together kissing for a few moments, until Travis pulled his arms forward and maneuvered to a sitting position, swiveling Paula beside him.

"Don't want to get too carried away," Travis said.

"Of course. Didn't mean for anything to happen."

The witch smiled. Paula reached up and ran her fingers through his thick, raven hair. His gray-green eyes now seemed enormous, and drew her in. How could she have overlooked their depth and beauty?

"What's your friend's name back home?"

"Sorinah. Again. Nothing romantic." He leaned over and kissed Paula's forehead. "Would you like something to eat? A snack?"

"Maybe a glass of water."

Travis stood and led her to the kitchen, tailored European shorts flattering his broad frame and muscled buttocks. *Wow.* They both leaned against the countertop.

"Not sure what came over me," Paula said. "I'm not like this, ever."

"I'm impossible to resist. No other explanation," Travis said with a smirk. "And extremely modest."

"I've got to take things slow. The kids won't like it. I know them."

"I understand."

"They don't want a replacement for their father."

"We've only just kissed."

"They don't even want me to date."

"It's strange for kids to see their parents as sexual."

"They don't want me hurt. They saw me unhappy."

She took a drink of water.

"I should get going," Paula said.

"I'm glad you came over."

Paula walked to the back door off the kitchen and motioned to Travis to join her.

"I want to show you something outside."

Paula took Travis' hand and led him across the meadow behind his house to the brambles at the edge of the forest.

"There's a pathway, a glade. We call it the stagecoach road. It leads to our property. A nice walk. About five minutes. Maybe ten."

"Good to know."

"When will I see you again?"

"We can exchange numbers." Travis took out his cell phone.

When they'd finished creating contacts, Paula hugged Travis and felt a tingling of desire as she leaned in to kiss him. She wanted it to continue, to taste him for as long as possible, but forced herself to pull away. She took a tentative step onto the stagecoach road, then a few more, and turned her head.

"Hope you're a slow learner."

TWENTY-SEVEN

TRAVIS WATCHED PAULA DISAPPEAR into the woods. He knew indulging in physical pleasure and instigating a connection were risky distractions. What was he doing? Sorinah had stressed restraint. Sexual involvement with a mortal was taboo, and yet he felt unable to resist the temptation. He'd never had such a convenient arrangement.

He wasn't sure which was stronger: his spell or the effect Paula unexpectedly had on him. He felt an emotional excitement he knew existed. He'd finally sampled what others shared but he had always ignored. A strict focus on advancing himself to one day avenge his parents hadn't allowed him romantic intrusions of any sort. Living as a ward with his mentor had been enough, until now, out on his own, an ocean away from home. It was time to explore.

"I'm sure you can sense my confusion," Travis transferred. He lounged on the grass and looked toward the woods. "It's something irresistible."

Our lives have a mission, and emotions dilute the focus, Sorinah answered. *You already have plenty to do. How did this even happen?*

"A strand of hair, an eyelash, and finger grease from paper muffin cups."

You couldn't let it go? What do you hope to gain from her? It seems superfluous.

"I'm not sure. I did it out of habit, a reflex after years of controlling humans. But now I can see that it's something more. An experiment for myself."

We keep our distance from mortals. Do you like her?

"Yes. She is smart and attractive. I am lonely and open to explore. It's unexpectedly diverting to be seen as an object of desire and to be a source of physical pleasure. It's a novelty. I can see why it's popular and drives a lot of human behavior. You know I've never indulged. You've never allowed it. We've never delved into superficial matters like sex. I don't know what to expect."

You mustn't become weak with human entanglements. Keep focused upon mastery of the conjurings. The goal is to empower yourself sufficiently to stand against the coven.

"But that's always been the response. The solitary focus on advancement. This is different. Let me experience something new. Something emotional, not rational. I'm lonely here."

My parents travelled frequently and left me behind. I learned as a child to push loneliness aside as an emotional weakness. Sorinah paused. *Perhaps I was wrong to expect you to do the same.*

"I'm a witch, not a robot."

Knowledge and reason are forces of nature, incompatible with the frivolous lure of erotic pleasure. On these grounds, we've skirted sexual discussions. Any blame for your inexperience falls my way. Perhaps I've failed you.

"No. I owe you everything." Travis paused to consider. "But subjective sides of nature should no longer be ignored. This is a time to grow. I want to explore multiple fronts while I'm here."

Your development as a witch was my only goal because your bloodline demanded elite preparation. Sexual arousal was something superfluous, a nuisance to be tamed and controlled, something to delay until you someday rejoin witches in Bucharest to generate an heir. Until then, there is no rational reason to indulge in sex. The incantations of your parents must persist. Nothing can nurture heirs like the coven of your birth. It was taken from you.

"Return and revenge is years away and may never happen. I need something now."

I suppose indulgence is inevitable. You're in America, after all. Our lives can span centuries. When does one stage cross to the next? It's easy for me to compartmentalize. I believe feelings interfere with advancement over the course of a lifetime.

"There are repercussions from isolation. Perhaps more than you know. You are too far gone."

You may be correct. I see erotic encounters only in terms of control and release. The power that flows from a mortal lover who fails to resist erotic temptation comes with a pleasant rush. Exactly as power flows from slaves who fight to free themselves or think they've escaped only to find themselves immersed ever-deeper in a trap.

"I don't want that. You are an island. I want to be liked."

Continue as you must. But the sooner you complete the conjurings—correctly, carefully, next time—the sooner we confront the coven. The rest is a distraction. Goodbye for now, my Travis.

Travis sprawled on the lawn and worried that he'd annoyed Sorinah. Perhaps he was weak and unworthy of the station his parents had hoped for, inferior to the hardliners, a diluted, deluded offshoot. Even his first trial had gone bad.

He thought about Paula. Did he even need a spell? He'd bewitched her only to ensure she'd like him. But now emotional results would be tainted. It would be better to release her. Did he dare? Risking rejection was new and unwelcome and time was limited. What if she had no interest in him beyond being neighborly?

He realized his desire and loneliness signaled the arrival of a larger issue: proof the mentor/ward dynamic of his existence needed to evolve. He needed broader experiences. It was an important consideration he'd ignored. He could never go back to live in the solitude of the Bratislava mansion. Sorinah would never need anyone else.

Paula had opened his eyes. Already it was late.

TWENTY-EIGHT

SOPHIA AND RACHEL SAT at a table on the outdoor terrace of their favorite bistro in the center of town after a long and difficult day. The funeral for Mia had started at 11 a.m. and was followed by the burial. The overflow crowd in the church spoke to the town's shock. They'd helped Sophia's parents with a reception at their house for the afternoon.

"You can tell it's darker earlier," Rachel said. "Look at the sky."

"I know. So depressing," Sophia said. "A normal August's bittersweet. This one's unbearable."

Sophia fiddled with the tie of her ponytail holder while she sipped iced tea. Rachel stared up at the colors of sunset and tilted her head back, monitoring daylight's tenuous hold on the day. They both wore black mini dresses and heels that begged to be removed as soon as they sat.

"I feel numb," Rachel said. "I don't know what to do next."

"There's nothing to do except survive. We can't just fall apart."

"I want to."

"Not realistic."

"Mia wouldn't kill herself. We know it. Something's not right."

Sophia flicked her wavy, auburn hair over her shoulder. "Could her father have done it? I think he's a douche."

"Wondering the same thing. He could have snuck in and then covered his tracks by breaking down the door. Twisted, but possible."

"More likely someone got up and down the tree, and the police are morons."

"Her brother told me she'd been Skyping." Rachel nibbled at a cracker. "Her computer was lying on the bed. It was Emma from Austin. She told police she couldn't see anything. Just heard a strange voice in the room with Mia."

"I've got to track down that Emma. She knows more than anyone."

"Definitely," Rachel said and sat up in her chair. "Any idea what you want?"

"Let's just do Cobb salads," Sophia said and motioned to the waiter. "Maybe start with the flatbreads?" Rachel nodded, and they ordered.

"We need to stay grounded," Sophia said. "It's better than freaking out."

"Mia wouldn't want us to fall apart."

Sophia nervously flicked at the charm on her bracelet. "Don't forget your ring."

"I'll talk to MK next week," Rachel said.

Throughout dinner, they forced the conversation toward their final preparations for college. Both families would help them move. Some suitcases were already packed. They agreed their mental health required a focus on September.

They sat for a while when the dishes were cleared, serene in the cool night air and relieved the day was over. The comfort and peace of the moment was fleeting, and they knew it. They grabbed their heels by the straps and meandered barefoot to the parking lot, hugged, got in their cars, and drove their separate ways.

Sophia's route home took her away from the town center toward rolling foothills that grew little by little as they merged with a mountain range in the distance. The neighborhoods became more rural than suburban as she continued with single homes situated on acres of land instead of multiple homes on small, adjoining yards within developments.

She turned left at the single blinking yellow light she was so familiar with onto the narrow road that led to her parents' house. The headlights carved a path through the darkness, illuminating a mist that had risen after sunset as the temperature dropped to chill the humid air. Sophia strained to see as a fog drifted in and out of view.

A flicker in the distance on the edge of the headlight beams caught her eye, but it disappeared as soon as she fixed on it. A moment later, she saw it again though the shadows. A seagull? She shook her head and in an instant thought she caught a glimpse of a figure. A waving arm? Something floated above the road's shoulder. Sophia could make out flashes of white fabric when the light hit just right.

She strained to look more closely, and it became clear that someone was standing on the pavement. A woman waved frantically and motioned to Sophia to take a sharp turn that was coming up on the left. Sophia knew the dirt road. It led to a public reservoir that required a pass to enter. The park was closed after dark.

She put on her signal and pumped the brake to barely make the left turn, waving to the woman and scanning the scene to look for an accident or some kind of trouble. She drove a few yards and rolled down the window, slowing the car and looking in the rear-view monitor for the figure as the car came to a stop. Sophia leaned out the window and craned her neck, but the woman had disappeared.

Hands steady on the wheel, Sophia faced forward and gasped when she noticed a white gown drifting in and out of the mist at the outer reaches of the headlight beams.

How did she get in front of me?

Sophia strained to focus on the figure and realized the white gown was torn and dirtied and draped the undulating frame of what looked like a distraught, old woman.

Is she a vagrant living in the woods?

The wraith's hair was disheveled, and she seemed to float toward the car, arms wafting like jellyfish tendrils, pointing at the road as it sloped steeply downhill deeply into the woods and toward the reservoir. With a ghostly translucence, the wraith drifted out of range of the headlights and was swallowed by the mist.

Sophia drove ahead, slowly at first but accelerating in an attempt to catch up to the mysterious figure.

How does she go so fast?

At last the gown again came into view, and Sophia sped up. The wraith turned toward the car, motioned into the trees, and drifted from the beams into the darkness of the woods on the side of the road.

Was someone hurt in the forest?

Sophia continued cautiously and pulled over where the wraith had disappeared from view. She reached into the glove compartment and fumbled around for a flashlight.

First time I ever needed this. Surprised it even works.

Sophia stepped out of the car barefoot, walked toward the shoulder, and searched for the woman. Moonlight struggled through ominous clouds, crickets sounded like locomotives.

"Hello? Are you OK?" Sophia asked in a loud whisper as she took steps off the road and approached the edge of the forest. She pointed the flashlight into the void.

"You're scaring me."

A branch snapped in the woods. Sophia swung toward the sound and gasped as the wraith emerged from the mist. In the flashlight beam, the woman's skeletal features appeared translucent and untethered by gravity. She recoiled from the light, frantic, eyes darting and burning through hollow sockets and a fringe of straggly hair. An off-kilter jaw flapped as though trying to form words.

"What's wrong?" Sophia whispered. "What's happening? I'm going for help."

"Don't leave me!" a despairing voice, scratchy yet feminine, pleaded and made Sophia break out in goose bumps. "I beg you. With all my heart. Give me what's mine."

"What?" Sophia's pulse raced and she froze.

"The bracelet! I beg you. With all my heart." The wraith reached out with billowing arms that moved with an ethereal smoothness.

Sophia recognized the words from the charm. She

screamed and scrambled back to the shoulder, dropping the flashlight but not stopping.

The sound of footsteps trudging on gravel made clear she wasn't alone on the road. Sophia shot a look into the darkness behind her and bolted for the car.

"Keep away from her!" the wraith raged out.

Sophia made it to the headlight beams and tugged at her bracelet. It chilled her that the woman knew of the engraving on the charm. Sophia didn't understand how or why, but she wanted the bracelet off her wrist.

"Take it!" Sophia shouted as she fumbled with the clasp.

The wraith drifted into view on the side of the road, and Sophia threw the bracelet toward her. Rippling, elongated fingers intercepted it. The wraith evaporated with the passing mist.

With a jolt, Sophia spied a man staring and brooding from just beyond the headlights. As he marched forward, trampling the gravel, Sophia noticed he wore what looked like a military uniform, pants tucked into tall black boots.

"Thank God," Sophia said. "Police. Help! There's someone in the woods." She waved toward the trees. "Behind you!"

When the man didn't turn, didn't answer, and charged toward her with a scowl, Sophia ran. She was nearly to the car when he grabbed for her ponytail. She managed to elude him without slowing and without looking back.

Sophia was about to pull on the door handle when the assailant seized her wrist and spun her around. She shrieked and tried to break free. Without a word, he dragged her away from the car and back into the woods, pulling savagely, making her stumble in the undergrowth.

Sophia struggled to stand and fought to escape as the man plunged deeper into the dark. A blow to the head sent Sophia into a dream state until she emerged all at once, horrifically aware of a searing pain to her chest. She opened her eyes to find a pointed fence post pressed against her flesh, poised above her heart, and held firmly in place by thick hands wrapped over hers.

"With all *your* heart," Sophia heard the man whisper until there was nothing.

TWENTY-NINE

TRAVIS KNEW HE'D BEEN TRACKED. He held the shovel as a weapon as he crept past Sophia's car in the moonlight. He'd watched the man emerge from the shadows through the eyes of the wraith. He was sure it was Radu, the hardliners' leader, the one who'd whipped him with a belt the night of the pyre. The enforcer looked the same, and Travis remembered the boots.

Sophia's flashlight was still on. Travis retrieved it and scoured the woods on both sides of the road. A grotesque calling card reflected light. Radu hadn't bothered to hide Sophia's body or the whitewashed fence post in her chest.

Travis didn't know if Radu were watching and remained on alert to defend himself. He worked quickly, infuriated by the intrusion, terrified by its significance. He removed the stake and shoveled up bloodied earth as he dug a shallow grave on the forest floor that he disguised with stones, leaves, pine needles, and scattered branches.

A voice came down from above. "Nicely hidden, for now, orphan."

Travis shot the flashlight beam toward the voice. Radu stood on a tree branch, stable and steady on a slender limb.

"I could kill you now, though it would be far too easy," Radu said. "You took the bait like a stray kitten."

Travis hurtled a nerve bolt and knocked Radu from his perch. The burly man disappeared before hitting the ground.

"I'll bide my time and watch your world collapse," Radu's voice echoed through the forest, "bit by bit, until you surrender. It is your time of reckoning. Do not resist. You've been lucky. But no one runs forever."

Travis vanished and took Sophia's car. He guided it to her driveway, left it, and spirited home. He realized he was shaking when he reached the attic.

"The coven's found me," Travis transferred to Sorinah as he gripped the arms of his chair.

You must take immediate steps, Sorinah answered, alert and ready because she'd already perceived Travis' danger. *Tell me everything.*

"Radu is here, in Sussex. He killed Sophia, the second subject. She was free and would have returned home unharmed. Her death complicates matters. The town will grow suspicious. He knows it. He's sabotaging me."

Where is the body?

"In the woods beyond an isolated road. There were no witnesses. Sophia escaped the wraith only to be impaled by Radu. He planned the whole thing. He left her body as evidence to ensnare me. I buried her and guided the car back to her house. No one is yet aware she's missing."

How did he find you?

"The coven tracks the wraiths. I was a fool to forget. Now I must stop."

No! That's what they want. You need to get as strong as possible. Radu sees you as an inferior. It's an advantage.

"He quietly watched as I buried Sophia. He could have killed me already."

He's gauging what he's up against.

"He taunted me from a perch. I shot him down, and he disappeared. He swore he would make me surrender."

Protect your house and property. Now. Repel him.

"It wasn't supposed to go this way. They brought the fight to me. We were going to confront the hardliners together, in Bucharest. I need you here with me."

I will come as quickly as possible.

"Thank you."

Do not underestimate your strength. You are proof of the potency of your parents' methods.

"Do I dare conjure another?"

You must. You need the power to fight him. You need fuel for your weapons. He cannot stop a conjuring once you've initiated the cycle. He can only interfere with the aftermath.

"Or attack me."

You are powerful enough to defend yourself. Nerve bolts. I will be there soon.

Travis opened his parents' ancestral volume. There were ways to secure his turf. Travis seethed that the coven had seized the upper hand and had turned his American excursion from laboratory to crucible.

THIRTY

RACHEL TEXTED SOPHIA as she finished a cup of coffee Sunday morning, *I had horrible dreams. Someone's after us. Mia tried to warn me. Did you sleep?*

When she didn't get an answer an hour later, Rachel texted again, *Let me know. I'm needy. I gotta get out of the house.*

It was unlike Sophia to delay answering texts and frankly unacceptable. Rachel took a shower and felt the day called for comfort: jean shorts, a peach camisole top and mocha Birkenstocks. She poked at her phone as she drifted to the kitchen to eat a soft-boiled egg with avocado toast, and then called Sophia. It went directly to voicemail.

By 10:30 a.m., Rachel decided to drive to Sophia's house to get an explanation.

She should be texting by now; we weren't out late. She knows I'm a mess.

Rachel checked her phone multiple times in the car en route across town.

She pulled into the driveway and parked behind Sophia's parents' car, the one Sophia had driven the night before.

Rachel went to the side entrance and knocked. Sophia's mother answered the door.

"Morning, Rachel. You guys go out for breakfast?"

"No. We met last night for dinner."

"Sophia's not with you?"

Rachel shook her head and stepped into the kitchen. "She didn't answer my texts this morning. I came over to offer my iPhone charger. It's the only excuse I'll accept."

"She might be finishing up a run," Sophia's mother said. "She was already out and about when we got up."

"She's not in her room?"

"No. The door's open. The bed's made."

"Did you check the car?"

"Haven't used it yet today."

Sophia's mother and Rachel hustled out to the driveway.

"Didn't hear her arrive last night. We were already asleep. You guys were late."

"We finished dinner at 8:30 p.m."

"She still wasn't home at 11 p.m. Where did you guys go after dinner?"

"Nowhere."

Sophia's mother opened the door on the driver's side of the car. The keys were in the ignition. Sophia's cell phone sat on the passenger seat, her heels lay in the footwell.

"That's odd."

"What?" Rachel asked.

"She left her cell phone in the car."

"Something's wrong," Rachel said. "She would never do that."

They both searched the car but found nothing suspicious.

"Sophia?" Sophia's mother called out, in no particular direction, but toward the bushes on the side of the garage.

"Were you out drinking?" she demanded.

"No. Nothing. I swear. You're sure she's not inside? Maybe with earphones on the couch downstairs?"

They ran into the house and began to search, calling Sophia's name. The couch in the family room downstairs was undisturbed. They went upstairs and searched the bedrooms, including closets and under the beds.

They returned to the driveway and checked around the yard. In less than an hour's time, they decided to call the police. They might be overreacting, they admitted, but they were jittery following Mia's funeral.

Rachel was questioned and recounted the events of the previous evening with as much specificity as possible. She recalled Sophia's little black dress at dinner, and with the police they searched her bedroom for evidence she'd changed clothes to sleep. There was no trace of the dress in the hamper or closet, and her pajamas remained stuffed in a drawer.

By early afternoon, Sophia's mother was nearly unhinged and inconsolable, screaming her daughter's name and searching even illogical and impossible hideouts of their house and yard, including kitchen cabinets, under the front porch, and inside trash bins in the garage.

Rachel held out hope there might be an explanation and that Sophia would suddenly appear as if nothing had happened. But the abandoned cell phone signaled something darker. It was simply not possible that Sophia would leave it on the car seat unless she were drunk or otherwise impaired when parking the car. Where could she go barefoot? Had she been abducted in the driveway?

The police searched for drops of blood, ripped clothing, and fingerprints inside and outside the car. They inspected the property and neighboring yards but found no clues. The flashlight was missing from the glove compartment, but Sophia's mother couldn't recall the last time she'd seen it. It might have been months.

Within a few hours the police declared Sophia missing because she was linked to Mia, and the abandoned cell phone was impossible to ignore. Had she been unhappy at home? Would she have reason to hide or run away? Why was a duffle bag packed and hidden in her closet? A boyfriend? What about her father? Was he still out on business? Rachel was grilled about the possibility of a suicide pact.

Rachel tried to console Sophia's mother until late afternoon when Rachel realized it was pointless, and she would have to return home. She gripped the steering wheel with sweaty palms and trembled as she drove. She was barely able to focus as she fought off a stupor.

What is happening?

The world had taken a nightmarish twist with her best friends stricken out of nowhere. She doubted Sophia would reappear. Whatever force had destroyed Mia had somehow struck again, and it was foolish to hold out hope for Sophia to miraculously return. A week ago she might have believed it but not now, not after Mia.

Rachel pulled into the driveway of her parents' house, turned off the car, and sat for a while, unable to move. Then a terrifying thought overcame her: *What if whoever got Sophia also comes looking for me?*

She had to get inside. Nothing was safe. She slammed the car door and bolted for the house.

In the kitchen, she tried to hold it together but started crying and shaking as soon as she told her parents that Sophia was missing. They'd had dinner the night before, and now her friend was gone. They'd driven home separately, and Sophia didn't seem to have spent the night in her bedroom. She'd disappeared or run away.

Rachel's parents tried to remain calm and asked her for more information, but Rachel blurted out that she couldn't talk and had to lie down. She thought she heard them ask if she wanted something to eat, but through a fog she found herself on the way up the stairs.

She lay on her bed for a while and then thought of James. He needed to know what was happening. She'd completely forgotten about texting him while trying to help Sophia's mother. She called his cell, and it went into voicemail. She immediately called again, and this time he picked up. The distress signal still worked.

"Sophia's gone," Rachel said. "Missing. Disappeared."

"Wait. Slow down. What? How's that possible?"

"No one knows. I spent the day with her mother. We looked everywhere. I saw her last night. We had dinner. We each drove home, but in the morning she was gone."

"Maybe she had to run away, like me."

"To where? The car's still there."

"I wouldn't panic yet. I'm sure she'll turn up."

"Can you come back?"

"What good will that do?" James asked. "I'm having a decent visit with my dad."

"I'm freaking out."

"I'll be home on the weekend."

"I could be dead by then. What if I'm next?"

"Don't be so dramatic."

"My best friends. My core. I'm all that's left."

"She'll turn up. You'll see."

"I know there's something wrong. The keys were there. She left her cell phone on the car seat. She'd never do that."

"Maybe she didn't want to be tracked. Stay calm."

"I'll try, but I'm terrified."

"What if Sophia couldn't handle that Mia killed herself? Maybe the funeral freaked her out. Maybe she literally needs to disappear for a while. Wouldn't be the craziest thing I've ever heard."

"She would have told me something at dinner."

"Are you sure? Everyone has secrets."

"I can't think straight. I haven't eaten. I need to rest."

"Take care of yourself. Call me whenever you want until I get home."

Rachel hung up and closed her eyes. A moment later the phone vibrated, and she grabbed it and scanned it to find a marketing email from Amazon. She closed her eyes again and took a deep breath. She thought about eating something but gagged. She realized she was still trembling.

It seemed clear something awful, something inexplicable, had stricken Sophia just like Mia, and she was never coming back. Rachel feared her own fate might already be locked, a ticking time bomb. Her mind drifted to a scene in the movie *Halloween* that had always chilled her. The heroine explains to her teacher that some writers sometimes defined fate as an astrological element, like fire or water, something that could not be altered. Fate was fixed and there was no escaping it. Even now, something evil watched her and crept closer exactly as it had already ravaged her two best friends.

The idea of packing and moving to start college now seemed pointless. It was a lie that promised a future when, in fact, it was already spent. What did anything matter? Mia and Sophia were gone, and she was next. It was only a matter of time. She shuddered and pulled the comforter over her head, curled into a ball, closed her eyes, and gripped her phone.

THIRTY-ONE

THE BEST PART OF EACH DAY for Paula was suddenly any time that included Travis. James was in Massachusetts with Aaron. Katherine's last days of summer found her at the lake or the backyard parties of friends. Paula was free to have dinner with the neighbor or to head to his house for a bottle of wine after eating with Katherine.

The new routine exposed to Paula how lonely she'd become. It had also rekindled her sexual nature, something she'd packed away as expired after the divorce. Evenings with Travis were like entering a time machine. It was undeniable; she felt alive again.

They both admitted they shared a strong physical attraction. If they lacked chemistry, they'd both concluded there would be no motivation to continue. Fireworks were completely normal and necessary at the beginning, or relationships were fated to fail; she knew, and Travis had agreed.

Still, her own behavior surprised her. She'd never been particularly sexually adventurous or aggressive, but she had uncovered a wild side. Perhaps Aaron had been sexually selfish, and now she was finally learning what she'd been missing with Travis' generosity. She was fortunate to receive the gift of recovering lost time.

Travis seemed unaware of his attractiveness. It was uncanny and exciting. Paula sometimes felt as if he were under her complete control with an innate knowledge of exactly where, when, and how to move to bring her pleasure. She felt lust for the first time. Just eyeing his physique was enough. She was under his sexual spell. She knew it and liked it.

"Almost ready?" Katherine asked as she watched her mother from the entry to the kitchen. "You're legit staring into space. Earth calling Mom. Come in, please."

Paula gasped and realized she'd been lost in a daydream. She regained focus on the table she'd been setting. "Yes. Perfect timing."

"Maybe you should invite him over here for dinner," Katherine said.

"You wouldn't mind?"

"No. It's obvious you like each other. You're there every night."

"I've never slept over."

"It's been less than a week. Not saying much."

"Should I skip tonight? Slow things down?"

"You should do what feels right. I think you've been lonely."

"It's fun for me like I haven't had in years."

They sat down to eat and talked about what Katherine might need for the upcoming school year and inevitably about Sophia, who was still missing after five days. Though

Katherine was two years younger, she'd known Sophia through her connection to Rachel. Sophia's disappearance so soon after Mia's suicide had crept into conversations across town and put everyone on edge. Search parties had turned up nothing. No one had come forward with any leads. Parents sat their children down, probed them with questions, and imposed curfews. Anything even slightly strange was to be shared immediately.

"Kidnappings and suicides happen elsewhere," Paula said. "Not here."

"They do now," Katherine said.

"You need to be careful. You and your friends. Keep your eyes open."

"Everyone's jumpy, wondering who's next, who's unstable."

"Don't jump to conclusions."

"It's obvious things aren't so perfect. Like *Twin Peaks*. Someone else is gonna snap."

"Are you doing OK? Want to talk?"

"I'm more worried about you. You're acting strange. Don't get hurt again."

When they finished dinner, Katherine cleaned up so Paula could get going. She went to her room and buzzed between the closet and the mirror. She settled on patchwork Bermuda shorts and a fitted, button-back tee. Without much thought, she threw a change of panties and her phone charger into a handbag just in case. Why did it sometimes seem she couldn't think straight? Cupid's arrow had struck her brain.

She returned to the kitchen and found Katherine at the sink. Paula hugged her around the waist from behind before getting the car keys.

"I'm driving, so I don't have to walk in the dark," Paula said. "Be back later. Love you."

Paula took the main road and parked in the driveway behind Travis' pickup truck. The evening air felt warm and drenched with the sweetness of honeysuckle. She walked to the back door entrance off the kitchen and knocked. Travis appeared in the doorway and smiled broadly. He pulled a multi-colored bunch of long-stem roses from behind his back. Paula took them and followed him into the kitchen.

"You can use this until you're ready to go," Travis said and pointed to a vase on the counter already filled with water.

They plunged the roses bound with paper and rubber bands into the vase and went to the living room. He opened a bottle of wine. They settled on the couch with a comfortable distance between them.

"Tell me about your day," Travis said.

"Nothing special. I'm happy tomorrow's Friday."

"Me too. Lots going on."

"With your business? What's happening?"

"Struggling to figure things out. Second thoughts. Regrets. Unforeseen complications."

"Everything OK?"

"I need to solve a major problem before I can return home."

"Do you want to talk about it?"

Travis pushed against the back of the couch and stretched his arms across the cushion. The cling of a black t-shirt accentuated his physique. "My past is coming back to haunt me."

"Did you have a difficult time?" Paula asked and swiveled to focus on the contours of his face as she took a sip of wine. High cheekbones with his dark features and square jaw made him appear beautiful in the flaming light of sunset glazing the picture window. "Tell me more."

"It was bad when I was young. Sorinah raised me after my parents died."

"How did they die?"

"In a fire."

"My God."

"I owe Sorinah everything. She's coming to help me. She's still a mentor."

"She knows your business?"

"Better than I do. I'm playing catch-up."

It was suddenly clear to Paula why she'd rushed things over the past several days; the unpredictability of Travis' sojourn in Sussex had liberated her. The urgency she felt to act and to be free from inhibition made sense. From nowhere he'd appeared, and to oblivion he could just as easily return. She felt a twinge of empowerment, of purposefulness, that surged with her compulsion to seize the moment without concern for consequences.

She reached along the back of the couch to gently stroke Travis' soft black hair. He leaned toward her hand and closed his eyes.

"I'd like to meet her, of course," Paula said. "When she arrives."

"I expect her tomorrow night. I'll feel better when she gets here."

"What's happened?"

"A fierce competitor. It will literally kill my business if he gains a foothold."

"I hope you figure things out." She shifted closer and rested her head on his upper arm.

"I thought there would be more time."

"Do you think you're ready?" She slipped her hand under his t-shirt and rested it on his stomach.

Travis put his hand over hers. "I'll find out soon. If I disappear, you'll know the answer. It means things went bad." He leaned to kiss her. "Should we fight temptation?"

"No," Paula said and went higher. "I don't want to fight. And I don't want you to disappear." Travis lay still while Paula's hand came to rest on his chest.

"I would hate to disappear."

Travis swiveled to a reclining position with hands behind his head, propped up against the arm rest of the couch. He shifted his legs from the ottoman and pushed one along the back edge of the sofa cushion. Paula nested in the gulf between his thighs and playfully examined the lumpy terrain of his shorts. She climbed aboard to press down on his swelling as she lay flat on top of him, lifted his t-shirt, and rested the side of her face on his chest.

"Try to resist," Paula said with a flirtatious smile and slid up to kiss him.

Paula felt the urgency and the purposefulness of the moment spur her to take control. A stroke of incredible luck had brought Travis to the neighboring house. And the whole situation was incredibly, irresistibly tenuous.

She wriggled against the gentle force of his thighs closing more tightly around her waist. A trail with the tip of her tongue from his nipple stopped where his t-shirt bunched up under his armpits, so she pulled it over his head.

"I'm helpless against you," Travis said. He locked his fingers behind his head, eyes closed, muscles taut.

She swiveled to kiss a bicep.

"I'll go slow." Paula's hand invaded his waistband. "Try to resist."

She captured him with probing fingers, and Travis released a low moan. She applied more pressure as he tensed and pushed against her grip with nudges of his hips.

Paula felt a tremor and marveled at the neighbor who'd magically appeared in the Malloy house and awakened her.

"Now, it's my turn," Travis said as he wriggled to a sitting position and undid the buttons on the back of Paula's shirt. "I worry this may be our only night together."

"Why?"

"With Sorinah arriving and trouble in town from Bucharest, nothing's certain. I may have to return much sooner than expected." Travis managed to stand while holding Paula's hands. "Let's go to my room."

"Maybe it's better I leave."

"I want you so much. You don't know how alone I've been." He stepped toward the hallway and extended his arms. "You have free will. We'll only do what you want to."

Paula studied Travis as she stood from the couch. She too knew loneliness. They were both intrigued. She wanted to be bad. It seemed like a last chance. No one this sexy lived in Sussex. For once, she would break some rules. She sauntered to him and then sprang. Travis pulled her close and kissed her as she swayed against his core. He shook free of his shorts as he unfastened hers. They kissed passionately between pauses to gulp breaths and strip, piece by piece. Travis rubbed against Paula while standing. They took synchronized steps to the wall behind the table and she wriggled low to clutch his muscled buttocks.

"Please stay," Travis whispered. "It's important."

"Why?"

"I want to protect you. It's late. Leaving now might be dangerous."

She nodded and bit his lower lip, holding it carefully between her teeth as he pulled back against the pinch. He scooped her up effortlessly and carried her to his bedroom. They kissed deeply on top of the quilt and explored each other's bodies, glistening in the humid night air.

"My property's secure," Travis said with a grin and raised eyebrows. "For now, my bed's the safest place."

THIRTY-TWO

KATHERINE POKED AROUND THE KITCHEN at 9 a.m. and was surprised there was no coffee brewing. It was usual for her mother to be up first and to have a carafe ready as part of her routine before work. Katherine walked to the window to check for a car in the driveway, and it wasn't there.

Perfect, Mom. Katherine went to the counter to make the coffee herself.

At bedtime the night before, Katherine had known that her mother still wasn't home but saw no point in waiting up. Lecturing her mother in a role reversal was the last thing she'd wanted to launch into before trying to sleep.

Katherine finished her breakfast and checked the time. Paula still wasn't home and hadn't bothered to call. Was she already at work?

Katherine texted her mother: *Seriously? You never came home. Is everything OK?*

An hour later when Paula still hadn't responded, Katherine called Paula's office. Her direct line rang four times and went to voicemail, so Katherine dialed the general number. She identified herself as Paula's daughter and was told it was the last summer Friday and only a skeleton crew was working; her mother was off.

Katherine apologized, hung up the phone, and began to worry. Why hadn't her mother told her she had the day free? She dialed Paula's cell phone and grew increasingly frustrated when it bounced to voicemail. Katherine left a message to call her ASAP.

Katherine showered and changed into a white cropped *Star Wars* tee with frayed black cut-offs. She decided to take matters into her own hands and head directly to Travis' house to get some answers. She slipped on black suede Puma sneakers and made her way to the stagecoach road. As she sped through the woods, she checked her phone almost by the minute.

When she reached Travis' property, Katherine headed toward the farmhouse. From a distance, she spied her mother's car in the driveway. There was a truck parked behind it, and a man worked nearby. She assumed it was Travis, but as she got closer, she saw it wasn't because his hair was blond. She watched as the man unloaded a piece of equipment from a trailer hitched behind the truck and wheeled it toward the shed.

Katherine reached the driveway, peeked into her mother's car, and decided to watch the worker. The machine he'd unloaded looked like an oversize vacuum with a long, strong hose. He opened the lid of the canister and lifted out a plastic bag, which he twisted to secure. He carried the bag to the shed and went inside.

Katherine drew closer and spied several other identical bags lined up on a platform. The worker placed the new bag next to the others, checked his phone, wrote something with a pen, and labeled the bag.

The man noticed Katherine as she stood behind him in the doorway.

"Looking for something?" he asked.

She scrutinized him for a moment. He wore a dark blue polo shirt with a Town of Sussex logo that looked like a uniform.

"Sorry," Katherine said. "At first I thought you were Travis."

"He's inside."

"I'm looking for my mom. Sorry to bother you."

"They're in the kitchen." The worker smiled, pointed, and closed the door to the shed.

Katherine started down the driveway and heard her mother's laughter. Annoyed yet relieved, she charged toward the sound and strained to listen. The door to the kitchen was open, and Katherine peered through the screen to try to catch a glimpse. Though Travis was seated at the kitchen table alone, without a shirt, she decided to knock.

"Come in," Travis said with his back toward the door.

Katherine tentatively turned the knob and stepped into the kitchen. It was warm, with no air conditioning, only a breeze through the screen door.

"Hi, Travis. Sorry to intrude. It's me, Katherine. Is my mom here?"

As she approached the table, she realized with alarm that Travis wore only a black speedo. His arms were secured behind his back, wrists bound by a black leather bootlace that wove between the chair supports.

"Sorry. I thought you were Dylan," Travis said as he swiveled to face her.

"Sorry. Should I go?" Katherine asked.

Paula appeared in the kitchen, wearing one of Travis' dress shirts, unbuttoned and not able to conceal that she wore nothing else.

"Be right back," Paula announced, and raced away.

"I'm afraid you've caught us in a prank," Travis said.

"I think I'll wait outside," Katherine said.

"It's OK. She'll be right out."

Paula reentered the kitchen with shirt adjusted, jeans on, and a large towel that she draped over Travis' shoulders. She nonchalantly untied the cord.

"Seriously?" Katherine asked. "Why didn't you call?"

Paula looked at her phone on the counter. "I'm sorry," she said as she walked to Katherine and put her arm around her. "My battery died, and his charger's a Samsung."

"You couldn't call from his phone?"

"I lost track of time," Paula said. "Spontaneous. Realized it was a Summer Friday. Didn't think you'd mind. You knew where I was."

"I called you at work. Why didn't you tell me?"

"I completely forgot. I swear. I didn't remember until an hour ago. I took it as a sign that I needed a break."

"Do you want some breakfast?" Travis asked. He stood wrapped in the towel and headed toward the hallway.

"Thanks. I'm OK," Katherine said. "I'll leave you two alone. Awkward." She wanted to be anywhere except Travis' kitchen. She took tentative steps backward and looked at her mother. "Do you plan to come home?"

"Yes, before noon," Paula said. "So sorry about this. It was a silly game. We might go to the beach. Don't tell James. It won't happen again."

"Sure, Mom," Katherine said as she opened the door and stepped outside, intending to call James the instant she was out of earshot.

She walked across the driveway and passed in front of the shed. Dylan, his truck, and the vacuum were gone.

Katherine crossed Travis' lawn. She looked behind her, and the house was far enough away. She dialed James.

"You're not gonna believe what's been going on," Katherine said.

"What now?" James asked.

Katherine heard a slurp that she assumed was coffee. "Mom's out of her mind."

"Yeah, now what?"

"Travis. The neighbor. She's been over there every day since you've been gone. Didn't even bother to come home last night. Didn't call or anything. I went over to check and just caught Travis tied to a chair in the kitchen in a speedo. Legit."

"Jesus."

"Arms behind his back, tied by a shoelace. Like bondage. Mom comes out nude with one of his shirts wrapped around, all like, 'Oh, I'm sorry.'"

"Crazy. Shouldn't she be at work?"

"Another Summer Friday. They barely work."

"What about him? Doesn't he work?"

"He was getting some kind of delivery from the Town of Sussex. I read it on the worker's uniform."

"So?"

"Looks like a bag of homegrown."

"How would you know?"

"Just a guess. That's how my friend's older brother sells it."

"So Mom's dating a drug kingpin?"

"I don't know. The Sussex guy worked near the kitchen door. He loaded a bag from a big-ass vacuum into the shed. And it didn't bother Travis at all. The worker could've easily caught them too. He probably heard what was going on inside through the screen door."

"Did Mom tie Travis?"

"Yes. Who else? He couldn't do it himself." Katherine continued to walk toward the stagecoach road. "She's become a nympho."

"Is Travis nice to her?"

"Seems like it. But she's obsessed with him. She goes there every day. And spending the night without a care or a call takes the cake. She blew me off. She's legit out of control. You should get back here and see for yourself. I can't handle her."

"Rachel's a mess too. She's completely freaked about Mia and Sophia."

"I don't blame her. Just come home. Things are going wacko."

"I'll come tomorrow, a day early."

"How's Dad?"

"Seems good. Not exactly the picture of stability, either. But at least he's starting to admit what he did to us."

"I guess that's something."

"Said he regrets it. Wants to make it up to us."

"I can't even. He's sorry, and now Mom turns psycho."

"Should I tell Dad?"

"Why not? Stir the pot. And please tell Rachel thanks for the earrings."

They said their goodbyes, and Katherine put away her phone. She continued toward home and tried to make sense of what she'd seen in the kitchen. She was stunned, perhaps more so now that she had gotten away.

How could her mother have gone so crazy so quickly? She was equally at fault because regardless of who'd brainstormed the fantasy, she'd thought it was a fine idea. Was Travis kinky? It was TMI. And why had he even allowed her to enter? Couldn't he have shouted, "Just a minute," as a signal to Paula? Was he an exhibitionist? Paula could have covered him and then pretended they were getting dressed or some other attempt at a lie. But they were both blasé about the intrusion as if they'd been caught making French toast. The whole scenario was a joke.

Katherine navigated the stagecoach road, flipping through her phone while avoiding roots, weeds, and branches. About halfway she heard a sharp cracking sound, like two rocks slamming together somewhere behind her. She paused a moment but saw nothing and so resumed her walk and her analysis of her mother.

It especially bothered her that Paula hadn't tried to call even with the excuse of a dead phone battery, which sounded lame. Who just lets their phone die? Her mother knew breakfast together most mornings was the norm and skipping one was certainly reason enough to call from Travis' phone to leave a message. Why hadn't she considered that?

Again, Katherine heard a sharp crack in the woods, and she froze to look. She thought she saw someone in the trees at the far end of the bend behind her. Was she being followed? Or was it a trick of the sun rays breaching the leaves overhead? She strained to listen and could make out what sounded like footsteps breaking branches and crunching dried leaves.

"Mom?" she called out. "Is that you?"

There was no answer after a moment's pause, so she pressed on when the forest again fell silent. She was nervous now and fought to focus on anything to take her mind from the footsteps. Her mother would have lots of explaining to do when she got home from fantasy island, Katherine decided as she began to sharpen a mental list of questions.

A man appeared, seemingly from nowhere, not far in front of her. He was dressed as some sort of policeman although more like a storm trooper than a cop. As he drew closer, he looked muscled, macho, and mean—not her favorite combination.

"Are you looking for something?" Katherine called out.

He didn't answer and marched toward her in tall black boots. A whooshing sound followed a large log that sailed from somewhere in the forest and crashed into his gut. The man doubled over and groaned. He stood livid, eyes canvassing the area. From within the trees, a barrage of stones whizzed at him and struck. A spear-like fencepost drew blood. He shouted something foreign, jumped for cover, and vanished into the woods.

Katherine gasped, and her heart pounded. What if she had been just steps ahead in the road? Who was that thug, and where did he go? She tried to make sense of what was happening. Hardwoods towered and swayed over the pathway. Perhaps other limbs were ready to fall, so she edged forward, she knew she couldn't freeze.

Katherine noticed the wind pick up. Shadows created a mosaic on the overgrown pathway that made it woozy and volatile. A strange groan, pained yet threatening, rose from behind her, becoming audible over the wind. Was the man critically injured?

Katherine stopped and stared as a second figure emerged from the trees. The groans came from a frail woman with a straggle of wispy hair and a dirtied, tattered gown. She seemed to advance along the pathway without moving her legs.

"Hello?" Katherine called out. "Can I help you?"

Katherine's heart raced as the wraith drifted toward her with a tortured expression.

What's wrong with her?

A moan escaped cracked lips and sent chills through Katherine as the wraith seemed to be crying. She drew closer with skeletal features in a pained, desperate visage that tried to form words. She broke into berserk grasps at the sides of her head, as if fighting a swarm of bees. Katherine screamed and fled toward home.

For how long she ran, Katherine didn't know as the stagecoach road became a blur. She listened intently, and shot a look behind her. The woman was gone, so Katherine ducked behind a tree trunk to catch her breath and hide. She got low to the ground and searched for any sign of the thug or the wraith. Quiet sobs rose from behind her and quickly became hysterical. Katherine screamed and scrambled onto the pathway. She bolted and looked backward and saw the wraith emerge from the brush, drifting toward her, arms lengthy and billowing, fingers clutching at her hair.

"The earrings," the wraith managed to say, plenty loud to hear. "Save yourself."

Katherine picked up her pace as the apparition gained ground.

"Get away from me!"

Katherine ran a dozen steps and shot a sideways look and realized the wraith somehow had kept up with her. The white gown seemed to soar on the periphery of her vision as Katherine continued to run but couldn't escape talon-like nails that grasped at her hair.

Katherine ducked into a ball and rolled, trying to dodge. She looked up with horror to discover the wraith was floating, rising above her in a prone position, arms extended, hair and tattered gown rippling in an ill wind.

"The earrings," the wraith implored.

Katherine squirmed and dodged the woman's measured lunges at her ears as she loomed overhead.

"Give them to me. Save yourself."

Katherine scrambled away from the flying horror as best she could, using both arms and legs in a frantic, backward crab-walk.

The wraith sobbed and seemed perplexed by the girl's terror as she descended upon her. "The earrings. Stop. Please listen to me!"

Katherine collapsed in a mud puddle. "OK. Take them!" She grabbed her earrings and hurled them at the wraith, who snapped them up with an effortless sweep of one hand.

Then all was silent. The wind, the cries, and the wraith were gone.

Katherine jumped up and ran. She trembled violently but didn't stop. She shot a look over her shoulder and quickened her pace. All that mattered was getting out of the forest and finding her way home. Adrenaline coursed through her and surged when she at last recognized the thinning of trees that marked their property line.

As she ran across the lawn to the house, Katherine convulsively looked back toward the forest, eyes frantic. What was she running from? She couldn't remember, but forced herself forward, reaching the driveway and gasping for air as she climbed the back steps. She went numb and could think of only one thing to do.

Katherine opened the door to the kitchen closet and slammed it behind her as she jumped inside. In the darkness, she huddled in a far corner. She tried to quiet her breaths. She burrowed under coats and boots, as low as she could go, to make herself completely disappear.

THIRTY-THREE

RACHEL KNEW SHE NEEDED to rouse herself into some sort of action. She'd remained in her room for most of the week, checking her phone for possible updates, but knowing in her core that Sophia wasn't going to reappear. The police had peppered her with questions for hours Monday. For at least the hundredth time, it seemed, Rachel had recounted details of their last dinner together, but without any grand revelations. She'd confessed she knew that Sophia had sometimes fought with her parents. She knew about the packed duffle bag, but arguments wouldn't be enough to make Sophia flee, especially since she was moving to NYU in a week.

Despondent as bleak days advanced, she'd hidden herself away, turning down work and finding herself ambivalent about college plans. She would descend to the kitchen for meals only when hunger pangs became impossible to ignore. Mostly, she spent long hours sequestered in her bedroom with the door closed.

By the end of the week, she grew restless and concluded that self-inflicted isolation wasn't solving anything. She called MK to schedule a shift at Old Gold on Saturday. In a near frenzy she resumed packing and pile-making for the move to college. Rachel vowed to proceed as if nothing had changed, in honor of Mia and Sophia, whom she knew would have wanted it. Action felt better than paralysis. She reinitiated Sophia's plan to track down Mia's friend, Emma from Austin. It now seemed she'd wasted valuable time by hibernating.

Rachel scoured Facebook and found groups for incoming college freshmen. She searched the Mount Holyoke listing and with a bit of digging uncovered several Emmas, one of whom included being gay as part of her profile. Rachel messaged Emma and identified herself as a close friend of Mia's. She soon heard from Emma. They chatted and agreed to talk.

Emma called Rachel and told her about the video chats. They'd made Emma feel like a mentor to Mia, who was still using her gay training wheels.

"I'm glad she found you," Rachel said, lying back on her bed. "Tell me about that final night. Only if you can."

"We were Skyping. Everything was normal, talking about outfits and what to pack." Emma paused. "She complained about a noise at the window, a scratching sound. She walked away but then came back and said it was a tree. We talked some more. Then she heard it again. She went to the window. She never came back."

"And then what?"

"She said there was someone outside, someone coming for her. And whoever it was got in because I heard a strange voice—a woman, but spooky, like from a movie."

"Did you see anything?"

"No. Only a pillow. Then the bed shook. The computer flipped up at the ceiling."

"Was Mia playing with you?"

"No way. Someone got in. Someone scary."

"My God. I knew it wasn't suicide."

"The woman wanted something, a locket."

"Mia had just gotten one. Vintage, from the store I work at."

"Mia asked who she was. And the girl said her name. Carol Stilton. I remember because I jotted it down. I'm glad I did, or I would've forgotten."

"Then she's the killer. Simple. A robbery. Did you tell the police?"

"Yes, but let me finish. Things got really confusing. Mia screamed when the laptop tipped up. I couldn't see anything. There were whispers, and crying and gasping. It was hard to hear what was going on. Her father was shouting and pounding on the door at the same time. He broke into the room and found Mia. I never saw what happened, but I heard him freak out. He came to the screen and demanded answers. I told him someone else was there. He looked around but didn't find anyone. They accused me of having something to do with it: the police, the media, and Mia's father. Some sort of lesbian auto-erotic mumbo jumbo that I lured her into. She was in her underwear because we were figuring out outfits."

Emma started to cry.

"They never found anyone or any clues. I'll never understand. I'll never forget. It all happened so fast. One minute everything's fine. The next, she's gone. I'm not crazy."

"I believe you," Rachel said. "Maybe her father had something to do with it."

"He was pounding on the door to get in."

"What if he was already on the inside? You couldn't see."

"What about the voice? Carol Stilton?"

"Could he have faked it?"

"Mia would have said something if her dad were in the room. There's something more. Carol Stilton was the one sobbing. That makes no sense. Maybe Mia faked it? I'm so confused. Maybe I got it all wrong." Emma went silent.

Rachel waited a moment. "You didn't. The whole thing is very strange. That's why they won't close the case."

"They can't because of me. The voice I heard. I told them about her cries, and they laughed about the wailing thief."

"Thank God you were chatting. You are important."

"And then there's the locket."

Rachel's heart pounded. "What about it?"

"Mia showed me on the screen. A girl's photo in black and white."

"That's the one. On a long chain."

"The police said there wasn't any locket anywhere. They think I'm making that up too. Making up everything, even the voice. They think the sobs were Mia's, who was actually mentally ill and about to kill herself. I'm not sure where they found the chain. They won't give me details."

"The locket wasn't that expensive. Why would that Carol want it, of all things? Random. What about Mia's wallet?"

Rachel paused to take a sip of water. "Something else scares me. We had a mutual friend, Sophia. The three of us were always together. Everyone knew it."

"Mia talked about both of you."

"Now Sophia's missing. It happened on Sunday. We had dinner Saturday night. I was the last one to see her. She was perfectly fine with no secret plan to leave. Nothing. She would have told me if something were wrong. But in the morning she was gone."

"What do you mean, gone?"

"Car was parked in the driveway, but she was nowhere to be found. Disappeared. Her phone was on the front seat. I know she'd never leave it. Police came and searched the house and searched the neighborhood. The whole thing. Her parents freaking out. Everyone's questioning me like I know something and I'm covering for her."

"That's what happened to me. I'm a suspect. I'm the one who's crazy. The police have finally left me alone for a while."

"Sophia's face is plastered around town on 'missing' signs. It's freaky, and the whole town's on edge, especially after Mia. People don't just vanish or hang themselves in their bedrooms, not in this small town. They were both starting college next week."

Rachel held back tears as she continued, "I'm freaking out. I know it's selfish. But what if some psycho didn't like us, the three of us, and held a grudge? Everyone knew us. Maybe we did something or hurt someone's feelings. And now it's time for revenge, one by one, hunting us, and I'm next. It's fate."

"Shh, shh," Emma soothed as Rachel's sobs grew louder. "No one's coming for you. The robbery is random. They'll find something. And Sophia still might turn up."

"I really hope so," Rachel said, gathering some composure. "Fate changes, right?"

THIRTY-FOUR

PAULA PULLED INTO THE driveway and parked the car off-kilter near the back door.

On the short drive from Travis' house, she'd grown increasingly nervous and guilty that she'd spent so much time with him. What had she been thinking? It was after noon, and she'd squandered the whole morning. Hadn't she promised Katherine she'd be home sooner? And why exactly had she decided to stay over? To savor a final night? The excuse felt selfish. But the sex was hot and she'd do it again if offered the chance. He'd gently massaged semen on her stomach to her breasts as she climaxed. It was oddly arousing and intimate. He'd whispered in Romanian and said it would protect her. What did *that* mean? Something was definitely lost in translation.

On some level she admitted she'd deliberately hidden from Katherine that she would be free on Friday. But why hadn't she texted her daughter when it was clear she wasn't coming home? That it hadn't occurred to her was frightening. Even more so was that she had packed her charger and didn't bother to pull it out. She hadn't cared. She'd wanted to act out. The urgency and purposefulness of any time she could get with Travis had taken over.

And how much had Katherine witnessed in the kitchen? They'd talked about a trip to the beach, but he questioned his skimpy speedo in the States. Paula remembered tying Travis' wrists as a lark. He'd joked only a physical restraint could keep him from her. She could recall kissing a trail from his lips to his chest. Arm muscles fought the bootlace, bulging, trembling slightly. His arousal was clear as he'd struggled to catch her as she scampered away wearing his shirt and he was helpless to follow. Was that when Katherine appeared?

She smelled sweet and spicy musk on her skin as the sun hit. An explicit mental image of his body, solid and smooth over hers, powerful yet gentle, made it clear the risks had been worth it. But now it was time to face the consequences.

Paula shook her head to focus on damage control as she entered the kitchen. She unwrapped the roses Travis had given her and filled a vase. The house was silent, and Paula fussed with the flowers before putting them on the table.

"Katherine?" Paula called out as she peeked through the window on the refrigerator door and realized she was famished. "I'm home, honey. Sorry about this morning." She gathered a few things for a sandwich, brought them to the counter, and opened the bread box.

"Katherine? You hungry?"

When there was still no answer, Paula abandoned the Hellman's to check Katherine's bedroom. Was she resting or listening to music? Paula searched upstairs and down, but the house was empty.

She returned to the kitchen and plugged in her cell

phone. *Duh, Paula. What were you waiting for?* After a few minutes, she accessed the messages Katherine had sent her earlier in the day, both text and voice, but there was nothing from the afternoon. It was reckless to leave her phone uncharged and ignored. She felt a fresh wave of guilt. She was as irresponsible as Aaron.

Paula sent a text message:

Hey. I'm home. Where you at? So sorry about last night. And this morning. Call me. xoxo

Paula went back to building a sandwich and sat at the table. When she finished eating, and there was still no response, Paula dialed Katherine's number. It rang, and, oddly, Paula thought she could detect a buzzing somewhere in the house. She concentrated and hustled to the living room. Another buzz, but barely audible. When it stopped, she shot back to the kitchen and punched her screen again.

After a few rings, she eyed the kitchen closet. It seemed to be coming from inside. She opened the door, and the buzz grew stronger, muffled but audible. She turned on the light and stood silently to look and listen. The phone was definitely close. Paula's gaze fixed on an igloo in the far corner. She pushed aside coats and boots and found Katherine curled into a ball. Her eyes were open, her face expressionless. The back of her white t-shirt was smeared with mud.

"Honey, what's going on?" Paula asked as she kneeled down next to her. She placed her hand on Katherine's face and felt her forehead. "Let's get you out of here."

Paula put her arms around Katherine and lifted her to a standing position. Paula detected an odor and realized

Katherine had soiled herself. Paula gently maneuvered her toward the kitchen table, grabbed a dish towel, and settled her in a chair. Katherine sat upright and supported herself unassisted. But the vacant stare on her face rattled Paula.

"Honey, what's wrong?" she asked as she hugged her daughter. "I'm so sorry about this morning and last night. I know I should have called. There's no excuse."

Paula sat and held both of Katherine's hands.

"Are you angry?"

Paula looked into Katherine's eyes. "Why won't you talk? Please tell me, honey. I didn't mean to hurt you. I promise. It will never happen again."

Paula studied her face. Katherine's lips puckered, then moved slightly, as though forming words. But there was no sound. Paula leaned toward her.

"Take your time. Talk to me, honey."

Travis intervened: *Tell her. It's for the best. There's danger near. He knows your house.*

Katherine's breathing quickened through her mouth. It seemed as if she might hyperventilate. She shook her head as if to say "no" as a young child. "My God," she whispered.

"What's happening, Katherine?"

Katherine remained in a stupor without focus, eyes fixed, but finally spoke: "On the stagecoach road. Something happened. Something bad."

"What?" Paula cried out and gripped her hands.

Katherine's words came slowly and quietly. "Someone chased me. A horrible, flying thing like a witch, something ghostly, someone haunted. It was real like a nightmare, but I couldn't wake up."

Katherine took shallow, rapid breaths through her mouth and spoke haltingly.

"A skeletal, scary face, with burning eyes. I tried to get away, but she kept coming. She was desperate. I've never seen such pain, like an abused animal. We were both terrified. She soared over me with fingers like claws grabbing at my hair. I thought she wanted to kill me. She wore a ragged dress that flapped in the wind as she flew. Somehow I got away. But she's still out there. She must be. We have to hide. We have to get out of here! She knows where we live. She's terrified of something. She's in misery, a desperate witch in the woods."

That's enough. Thank you, Katherine. You'll be done soon, Travis transferred.

Katherine shuddered, exhaled sharply, and then seemed to hold her breath. Her face again became expressionless. She stopped talking and visibly withdrew.

Paula tried to engage her but soon gave up and called 911.

A squad car and an ambulance arrived quickly. Paula recounted what she'd witnessed, and the paramedics examined her daughter.

Katherine refused or was unable to speak, though she responded to appeals to walk and obeyed when coaxed to the bathroom with her mother to wash up and change her clothes. The police searched the grounds outside, and Paula directed them to the stagecoach road. Paramedics continued to observe Katherine.

"We've got to take her in," one EMT announced as Paula reentered the kitchen. "She's in some sort of shock, incommunicative and catatonic."

"Of course," Paula said. "I'll ride with her."

"Has she had any history of mental illness?"

"None whatsoever."

"Violence or abuse in the household?"

"Of course not."

"Any recent changes?"

Paula paused to consider. Should she mention her daughter had caught her just hours ago in a naughty game with the neighbor?

"Divorce."

"She will need a physical and psychological evaluation."

Paula went upstairs and quickly pulled together some clothes and toiletries. She realized she was shaking. Was there a crazy woman in the woods? How could Katherine have come up with such a story?

Thoughts of Travis popped into her head. She had to warn him. Someone bad might be lurking.

She rushed to the kitchen and watched as the paramedics wheeled Katherine to the ambulance on a gurney. Paula grabbed her cell phone and the charger. She called Travis.

"Something's happened to Katherine," Paula said. "I found her at home, hysterical."

"Is she OK?"

"She says she was chased in the woods between our houses on the stagecoach road. The police are searching as we speak. There might be danger."

"What did she tell you?"

"She was out of her mind. A witch attacked her, flying above her. She barely got away. She's in shock, insane, dazed. They're taking her to the hospital now."

"You've got to get out of the house. Go with her now. It will be much safer in a public space. Stay there until Katherine's better."

"I've packed supplies. We're ready to leave. Be careful. Call me if you see anything."

Paula shut off the phone and bolted from the kitchen to join Katherine in the back of the ambulance. Her daughter stared at the ceiling, lost in a trance.

THIRTY-FIVE

TRAVIS FELT HIS GRIP on control disintegrating and anxiously awaited Sorinah's arrival. It was hard to gauge next steps. Katherine and Paula were at the hospital for now. Radu was nearby. Events could spin out of control very quickly, he was learning firsthand, just as his parents had so long ago in Bucharest.

Travis studied the scene outside his dormer widow. He spied two policemen near the entrance to the stagecoach road. He watched as they strolled about and probed the undergrowth. An officer surveyed his property with binoculars, so Travis stepped out of sight. He went downstairs for a last-minute check of the guest bedroom and readied a tray with a pitcher of ice water, fruit, and cheese in the kitchen until the doorbell rang.

Sorinah stood on the doorstep. A cascade of burnt caramel hair spilled over a floral chiffon blouse. She pushed back a pair of black Prada sunglasses with delicate fingers, nails lacquered in obsidian. "Sorry, I'm a bit later than expected."

They embraced, and Travis grabbed her suitcase. "I'm so

happy to see you. Thank you." He led her to the sofa in the living room and hustled back with the tray from the kitchen.

"We're within a zone of control?" Sorinah asked.

"Yes. Radu's barred from the property. All witches. Except you."

"After all this time, they tracked you down. I thought by now they'd have given up. But they've brought the battle to us."

"I'm worried. But perhaps it's for the best. They've saved us a trip."

Sorinah and Travis both grew silent as they settled into their seats.

"Do you feel ready? What has happened since the conjuring?" Sorinah asked.

"The girl is resting in the hospital until things calm down. Her mother's with her. I suspect Radu knows where they live."

"I'm not surprised your lust got them into trouble. It seems you used her daughter as a decoy. And now there are messy consequences."

"Katherine's chase was a necessary test."

"A risky one." Sorinah poured water from the pitcher.

"I had to test my ability to fight. How do I stack up against an elder? We need to know. It's the whole point of the conjurings. I was certain the wraith would lure Radu. I ambushed him and forced his retreat, bloodied him with a picket fencepost for my own gratification. I sent him a message. It was a gamble I had to win."

"You saved her from Radu only to face the wraith?"

"Yes, that came next. But she freed herself and released

the wraith. Her distress generated potent fuel, crucial to the fight against Radu, in accordance with my parents' spell. No one died this time. That's the way it's supposed to work. At least, in theory. But I see pitfalls."

"Elaborate." Sorinah put her sunglasses on the table and pulled her hair back.

"My parents envisioned an elevated approach."

"Empowerment without kills."

"Exactly. The ancestral spell perfectly erases the torment of the subject." Travis locked eyes with Sorinah. "But the torment of the wraiths themselves is vexing. I have no power over their agony. It's unnerving. Something dark. I cannot ignore it and presume elevation."

"It will be your focus for future advancement of the work."

"I cannot justify the mistakes and residual pain. I have no solution for Mia's family. Radu killed Sophia, but I caused her predicament. Even my parents admitted that the forced amnesia left confusion and a troubling void after the subjects broke free." Travis stood, went to the picture window, exhaled a long, slow breath, and then returned to his seat.

"Where is Katherine now?"

"She's resting quietly, not wanting to speak. The fugue will pass when we're ready to confront Radu. It buys time so we can plan."

"Does it look suspicious?" Sorinah put a slice of gouda on a rice cracker.

"Her silence appears rooted in catatonia or some other psychological disorder they can use to rationalize her case."

"The diagnosis will need to be based on something."

"I'll leave that to the imagination of doctors. They're good at postulating."

Sorinah again reached for the tray, and Travis pushed it closer.

"And what is left to gain from involving the girl's mother?"

Travis paused and his eyes shifted. "Remember? We discussed emotion."

"I tried to warn you. It isn't real. You're foolishly indulging yourself." She pursed her lips and shook her head.

"Let me try. We lived with a singular focus. I became your passion project. But what of my existence?"

"An intentional lapse on my part." Sorinah exhaled and folded her arms.

"You never allowed me to explore emotion. Now it's a problem."

"A game for fools not worthy of your station."

"I remove the spell when we're together. I want to gauge how she feels. Last night she wanted me without it. I don't need it, except to clear her memory when I'm gone."

"That sounds like weakness."

"To be desired is weakness?"

"For a witch? By a mortal? Yes."

"We've lived alone in that mansion for so long. I want to experience more. Am I nothing without a spell?"

"What's the value of trying?"

"To learn about connection. Something you can't teach."

"I suppose there could be value, if only to better understand your own folly."

Travis paused and studied her face. "Are you angry?"

Sorinah's cold beauty broke into a smile. "No, my Travis.

Stumbles are unavoidable, but carelessness is intolerable because it undermines your achievement. The stakes are high, and Radu is dangerous. Emotional involvement is risky because it changes behavior in observable ways and arouses suspicion. And the knowledge gained from it? Is it worth the risk?"

"After so much time alone? I thought so."

"Katherine witnessed your ludicrous display, and her escape from the woods was never guaranteed."

"I needed a crack at Radu to intimidate him."

"Fortunately, it worked. How would Katherine's death have been explained?"

"The body would be hidden like Sophia's somewhere in the woods."

"That's not good enough. She was on the way home, and you live nearby. Too many disappearances for one small town. They would find the corpse this time. Don't underestimate the resolve of a town under siege." Sorinah took a deep drink of water from her glass.

"I'm losing control. Things happen so quickly."

"Such is blindness created by lust. It is dangerous. I regret I failed to teach you about its downward lure. Perhaps I could have guided you better. One day you will sire an heir, but with a witch in the coven of your birth. Until then, sex is not something I condone for any purpose other than a quick shot of fuel or as a stepping stone to an achievable goal. When you wallow in physical pleasure, you needlessly lower your mental state from the higher plane."

"And what of being desired?" Travis raised his eyebrows and stared at his mentor.

"This is also a danger. You will find a suitable partner. But with a mortal it is folly. Elements of hiding and control would always create distance. Age and time would separate you further and tear you apart. Emotion would make you weak."

Travis shook his head. "I was lonely before Paula. It went away."

"Only Radu matters now. We need a plan. I'd better unpack."

Sorinah stood and folded her sunglasses. Travis grabbed her suitcase.

"I'll show you the house," he said. "Welcome to Sussex."

THIRTY-SIX

JAMES SPIED THE VASE OF ROSES on the table as he entered the kitchen. He was hungry after the three-hour drive from Massachusetts and happy to find lunch supplies out on the table. He touched the package of honeyed ham, and it seemed cold enough, so he made a sandwich.

His mother had texted she would be home from the hospital any minute, so James ate as he waited. Why did things have to erupt during the millisecond he'd set aside to spend with his father? Everything seemed to have unraveled in a week: Mia dead, Sophia gone, Rachel frantic, Katherine hospitalized, and his mother lost in a mid-life crisis.

Nonetheless, he considered the visit a success, a first since the divorce. Katherine's phone call had prompted him to tantalize his father with updates on the new neighbor. *They have wine every night.* As James could have guessed, Aaron launched into a jealous rant, though he clearly had no claim. *Damn. I even left out the part about the chair in the kitchen. He'd go berserk.*

James heard Paula's car pull into the driveway. He cleared the table and rinsed plates in the sink.

"How was your trip?" Paula asked as she entered, and they hugged.

"Better than expected. I'll tell you later," James said. "What's going on with Katherine?"

"No one knows. She's gone silent, in some sort of shock." She pointed behind James. "I found her burrowed under a pile of coats in the closet."

"Crazy. What did she say?"

"At first, not a word. Imagine my reaction. Finding her in there and just silence. But then her face changed, and she blurted out a horrific story about being chased in the woods behind the house by a flying witch or something. Can you believe it? On the stagecoach road! Then she went silent again and hasn't spoken since. They're monitoring her at the hospital."

"What do they think happened?"

"Some kind of trauma. She's withdrawn within herself."

"Did something bad happen? Like a crime? She called me from Travis' backyard. She was on her way home. She was fine. She said you were the one acting strange."

"I saw him a few times while you were away. It was unexpected."

"Maybe that's what bothered Katherine."

"It's possible. It may have set her off. I told the doctor. He said the first sign of romance after a divorce could trigger a reaction. She might've been more upset than we'd realized. It was something hidden. She wasn't even aware of it herself until I upset the balance."

"Did she lie about getting chased?"

"No idea. Police checked the woods but didn't find any clues."

"Doesn't really prove anything. *Something* must've happened."

"I know. But her story's so extreme. And her silence is frustrating. Scary, even."

"Was she hurt?"

"Scratches from falling. Nothing serious."

"What's been going on between you and Travis?"

"I sometimes went over after dinner. On Thursday I spent the night for the first time. I should have known better. I should have called Katherine. I admit it. But I wanted time to myself. He might be leaving soon and it clouded my judgment like a teenager."

"We're the teenagers. You should have at least sent a text. Katherine said she caught you in the kitchen the next morning. Sounds a bit crazy."

"She told you?"

"No wonder she's traumatized." James shook his head and raised his eyebrows.

"I know. I kept that part from the doctors. It was only a game. It won't happen again." Paula paused and gazed at the flowers. "This was a wake-up call. Katherine's really upset. Now she's my main focus. Anyway, Travis' partner is arriving and it looks like our time's up."

Paula opened the refrigerator and put away the condiments.

"I'm grabbing a few things upstairs and going back to the hospital," Paula said. "They don't know when she'll be released."

"Have they ever seen this before?"

"Not exactly. They can't explain why she won't talk."

"Is she just stubborn, or pretending she stroked out?" James asked. "I've seen her fake it."

"It's not a stroke. She's aware of everything. They tested. She doesn't even try to speak."

"Is it PTSD? Like from what chased her? Or shock?"

"I don't know. But if they don't have anything to offer, I want her home. Maybe then she'll snap out of it. Maybe she needs time. I think she's punishing me. The silent treatment."

"I need to see for myself."

"Come to the hospital for visiting hours. I'll text you all the info so you have it."

"Perfect. I'm gonna check outside. I'll see you at the hospital later."

He hugged his mother goodbye, went out the kitchen door, and made his way toward the woods to spy around.

As he walked the stagecoach road, James kicked aside brush and fallen branches, looking for a clue—a ripped article of clothing, a spiral notebook, anything—that might show Katherine had passed through or had tripped, but he found nothing to support her story.

After meandering for about twenty minutes, weaving zigzag and pushing fronds and bushes aside with this foot, James reached Travis' property line. He crept into the clearing and surveyed the meadow between the woods and the farmhouse.

He spied a large pick-up truck parked near the storage shed. He looked more closely and saw a man moving some equipment down a trailer ramp. James slinked toward the house. He made his way to a large maple several yards behind the shed with a good view of the driveway.

James watched as the man wheeled what looked like an industrial vacuum or water pump toward the shed. The worker pushed aside the hose, swung open the lid on top of the canister, and lifted out a black plastic bag. He pulled the drawstrings to seal it and carried it into the shed.

A delivery of trash?

James wanted a closer look and crouched low to scurry to the front of the man's truck. He inched along the far side and ducked behind the back tires to get a view inside the shed. James noted a collection of bags arranged on a wooden platform. The worker placed the new one behind the others. James watched as he went to a shelf, checked his phone, and filled out a label, which he affixed to the bag.

What's he up to?

The man surveyed his work then walked outside. He closed the doors and returned to his equipment. James noticed a logo for the Town of Sussex on the worker's shirt and remembered Katherine had mentioned it. The man wheeled the vacuum toward the trailer. James dropped to the ground and wriggled under the truck with his stomach flat on gravel as he got between the tires and watched.

The man finagled the vacuum up the trailer ramp. He secured it, jumped down, and slammed the guard gate shut.

James decided to trail him. It would be the fastest way to gather evidence. Something seemed suspicious, and his mother needed to know. A quick answer would go a long way. And he might get caught in the driveway, or run over, if he didn't make a move.

The man started toward the driver's cab in front, and James froze in place. He waited for the man to pass, and then shimmied to the back of the trailer. When he heard the driver's side door open, James crept over the back of the trailer as quickly as he could and immediately lay down flat. The vacuum obscured a clear view from the rear window of the cab, and James got low enough to avoid being spotted in a mirror.

His heart pounded, and he breathed deeply when at last the engine ignited. He tucked himself into the space between the vacuum and the back gate. The truck lurched into reverse, backed onto the grass to turn around, and then started down the driveway.

The driver turned left onto a dirt road and continued to the intersection with the main highway, leading to the center of town. James locked his fingers and placed his hands behind his head to cushion it from bouncing against the metal floor.

James watched the sky above and noted signs, traffic lights, and landmarks as they floated past. For now, he knew where they were. He invented a lie he would tell if he were discovered. *Sorry, man. I just hopped in when the truck slowed at the train tracks to hitch a ride. The bus never came.*

From his prone position, James recognized the tops of federal-style red brick buildings as they passed through the town center and watched as the view changed to pines and telephone poles. A few minutes later, the truck slowed and pulled to the left side of the road, and James saw a black wrought iron fence. The driver turned onto the narrow dirt road of an old cemetery. James had driven past the place countless times but never given it a second thought. It was simply a town landmark filled with time-worn gravestones.

The truck crawled along as it hugged the outer fence of the cemetery, and James realized it was time to ditch. Keeping as low as possible, he jumped from the back of the trailer and rolled when he hit the ground toward the brush on the side of the road. Laying motionless in tall grass, he listened as the truck lurched forward. James didn't get up until it turned a corner and came to a stop on the other side. He crouched down, found a spot to spy from behind a bush, and watched as the man drove a tree planter from where it was parked in front of the truck and up an embankment toward the graves.

The Sussex man parked the rig, read the inscription on a headstone, and then studied others nearby.

Is he paying respects?

The worker knelt in front of one, pulled out his cell phone, and photographed it. He positioned the tree planter adjacent to the grave, took the controls, and raised the arm of the drill with the tip pointed downward. The man left the auger menacingly poised while he unloaded the vacuum and wheeled it graveside.

That's not right. There's nothing to plant, nothing to vacuum.

James moved closer to the work area, remaining low and concealed beneath a shrub. The man jogged to the truck and returned with tools. He plunged a spade into the grass just to the side of the plot. He carved a circle, outlining the edges a few times until it was cleanly cut. With a thrust of a pitchfork, he dislodged a thick chunk of sod, and hoisted it behind his equipment.

Is he testing the soil?

James watched as the worker mounted the back of the

tree planter, started the engine, and took the controls. The auger rose higher with jerking movements until the man was able to stabilize its position precisely above the circle he'd carved. The drill bit began to rotate, and he penetrated the ground at an angle. Dirt spilled out around the auger that fit precisely within the shape of the sod patch, like a spear piercing through its target yet remaining within the bull's eye.

Why would a tree be planted there? Why is he boring at an angle instead of straight down? Isn't he getting way too close inside the grave?

The scene looked criminal and sinister. There was nothing to plant.

Dirt continued to spill out of the hole as the drill drove deeper and deeper. Resistance sometimes rocked the equipment and held the auger at bay, but the man powered through it with both hands on the levers, forcing the drill further, thrusting his body in sync with the swaying motion until the blockage cleared.

James examined the angle of the auger and calculated the six-foot depth of a grave.

Is he actually drilling into a coffin?

James' heart began to race. He watched as once again the auger stalled against something hard inside the earth.

He's hit the casket.

The man coaxed the drill bit backward, waited a moment, and then reapplied pressure. James heard a sickening *thump* and watched as the equipment rocked but then rested.

He's into the casket.

James knew he needed pictures. He steadied his phone

camera and captured what he saw, including the man's face. He looked perfectly normal. Handsome, even.

The worker withdrew the auger from the earth and backed the tree planter away from the hole. James held his breath as he watched him wheel the vacuum into position, and then, incredibly, unhook the thick hose from the canister and feed it into the freshly bored hole, using both hands to guide it. Nearly the entire length of hose disappeared into the ground. James took more photos as the man stood over the grave with the hose trailing behind him into the canister.

A moment later he switched on the vacuum. A sound like the machine-gun fire of gravel bits immediately crackled as refuse entered the plastic hose.

What exactly is coming out? Dirt? Bones?

James watched and listened as the rattle within the tube slowed but resumed when the man jumped down to coax and twist it. What sounded like something clunky entered the tube and jammed. The worker wriggled the tube with both hands to dislodge it, and the blockage scraped along the ribbing of the hose as it traveled up to the surface.

The man rushed back to the canister and shook it, listened for additional noise, and then switched the power off when it stayed quiet. He unfastened two clips, swung the lid backward, and poked around inside with a stick before lifting out a shred of fabric on the tip.

James gasped.

Someone wore that. They were buried in it. Something favorite.

James considered what he'd witnessed, and it seemed clear the Sussex man had devised a way to suck out caskets.

He was a grave robber, and no doubt Travis kept the stuff. The bags from the vacuum were stored in his shed. Drugs would have been better.

James started trembling and tried to take a shot of the open canister, but he was unable to frame it.

Wearing work gloves, the Sussex man cajoled something out, and held it up. James gasped at what seemed to be a skull remnant with no lower jaw.

In a panic, James rolled to his stomach and pulled himself with his elbows while shimmying with his legs to steal away from his hiding spot beneath the brush. He scrambled toward an oak and peered back toward the man, but the gravesite was hidden behind a knoll. James bolted toward the main entrance.

At the cemetery gates, James paused to catch his breath. The sights and sounds of traffic on the main road created a veneer of normalcy that suggested he'd escaped the horror at the gravesite. He darted across and started down the sidewalk toward town. He shot a glance behind him, but nothing stirred amid the gravestones except leaves.

The eye sockets of the skull fragment burned in his memory. Was he losing his grip on reality? His breathing slowed as he continued to walk; his panic calmed by the displays of ordinary life that surrounded him as he approached the center of town. Cars and pedestrians buzzed about their business at the dry cleaner, Chinese takeout, florist, and bridal shop. He looked over his shoulder every few steps to make sure he wasn't being stalked.

James realized he needed a destination. His mind settled on Old Gold to find Rachel. He had to tell her what he'd witnessed. He hoped she would be working and grabbed for his phone to check. Empty pockets as he patted them down confirmed the flash of dread he felt. He must have dropped it. He remembered scrambling from under the brush. There was no way he would go back now to get it. The cemetery was too scary and dangerous. First he had to find Rachel.

He grew more determined to see her with every step as he drew closer to the store, desperate even. She had to be there. He felt a sudden surge of loss that she would leave any day to start college. She'd been right all along. He should have been more concerned about planning his future. The idea of a gap year seemed like a colossal waste and wasn't a plan at all. How would it look in a few months? Did he seriously expect to blame it on his parents' divorce and say that he'd needed time to himself? And what exactly did he have to show, academically or otherwise, to look like a good candidate for a job or college?

A free-floating nervousness about his future morphed into dread as his mind shot back to the cemetery. He had to dump it all out on Rachel: about the gravesite, about his fear of the future, and about his failure. He found himself trembling.

Please be there.

James turned onto Bank Street, raced to the entrance to Old Gold, and peeked in the window. A wave of relief surged over him when he saw Rachel behind the cash register. She noticed his face peering in, raised her eyebrows, and waved as he entered.

"Seems like you've been gone forever," Rachel said. She stepped forward, and they hugged. "So much shit."

"Even more than you know," James said. "Can you talk?"

"It's not that busy, and MK will take over soon."

"You'll never believe what I just saw. You gotta help me."

"What?" Rachel pulled a stool close to the counter and motioned for James to sit. "Tell me everything."

"I'll backtrack. I got home around lunchtime. Already things are bizarro. My sister's in the hospital. I gotta go see her tonight."

"What happened?"

"She had some kind of mental breakdown. She's silent, except for a rant to my mother. She said she was chased by a witch through the woods. Insane."

"Sounds about right," Rachel said as she fixed on James' blanched face with rapt attention, "the way things've turned out. Go on."

"Katherine called me before she flipped out. She'd gone to find my mom at a neighbor's house and caught her in a sexy game in the kitchen with Travis."

The temperature in the store felt oppressive and James realized his gray t-shirt was soaked and clung to his chest. He pulled at the fabric, but it snapped back.

"Who's Travis?"

"The new neighbor. The guy my mom's seeing. Anyway. I went to spy around the woods after lunch. That's where Katherine said she got chased. There's a trail that cuts through to his house. I watched a guy who works for Sussex unloading a huge vacuum and moving a trash bag into Travis' shed. There's a bunch of them lined up inside. I thought it was suspicious, homegrown or something. So I followed him."

"How?"

"Jumped in the back of his trailer and hid behind the vacuum." James rotated on his stool nervously. "He drove to the old cemetery downtown, the one near the tracks. Then I spied on him."

"The cemetery?"

"Wait. It gets better. He fires up a tree planter."

Rachel raised her eyebrows and fanned herself with the top of a shoe box.

"A large drill mounted to the front of a tractor. You can dig like six feet deep and two feet wide."

"And? He works for Sussex. He plants trees."

"He drilled into a grave."

"To dig a hole for a tree?"

"No. He literally drilled into the side of the grave—bored straight into a casket underground."

"That's not even funny. Are you joking?"

"I've got photos to prove it."

"Show me."

"I freaked out and dropped my phone when I ran. We have to go back when MK comes and you get off work." James ran a hand through his spiky blond hair, but the wax barely budged.

"Maybe it just looked like it."

"He fed the vacuum hose into the hole and sucked things out of the casket."

"Are you serious? You're scaring me."

"He opened the canister. Dug around and pulled out a piece of fabric. It creeped me out. Dug around again and held up a part of a skull. I panicked and got the hell out. That's when I lost my phone."

Rachel stared at James for a moment without speaking. She pulled at a thick chestnut tendril that hung loose from her messy bun. "You're really freaking me out."

"I'm sorry. I know it sounds crazy."

"It does. What could he want? I would think you were completely nuts, except for all the strange shit that's happened. We've got to find your phone. And I want to see the grave. You have to prove it. Can you go back? What if he's still around?"

"Hopefully he'll be gone when your shift ends. We can pretend we're paying respects."

"I've never seen anyone there. It's basically deserted."

"Let's get our story straight. We're tracing our great-grandmother."

"That's rock solid," Rachel said with a face.

"I'm sure no one will ask. I've got to get my phone. You've gotta see the pix and the hole in the ground."

James sat quietly as two customers walked in. Rachel left her perch by the register to greet them. After a few minutes of steering them to their sizes, she came back to the counter.

"I don't understand the connection to Travis," James said. "Why would he have these bags or want them in his shed?"

"Do you know him?" Rachel asked.

"We visited him once. My mom, me, and Katherine. He seemed nice. I want to see if the bags in his shed are filled with stuff from the graves. Maybe they're something else entirely. The Sussex man's digging might be random. I'm gonna check out the shed myself tomorrow."

"It's too dangerous. What if you get caught?"

"My mom's involved with this guy. If there's shit in his shed, I want to know."

"Just go to the police."

"Not until I get my camera and find proof. Otherwise, I'll sound like an idiot. Think about it."

"I wouldn't have believed it. But now I'm open to anything."

James waited as Rachel checked in with a pair trying on dresses and returned to the counter to ring up a sale. She shifted focus to James after they left.

"What happened with Mia was impossible and doesn't add up," Rachel said. "Her friend Emma was Skyping with her the night it happened. Emma heard someone else in the room. There was crying and whispers, and she thinks Mia's killer came in through the window. A scary woman who stole her locket. And I believe her. We spoke last week."

"And what about Sophia?" James asked. "Still missing?"

"Yes. Again, something's off. I saw her the night before. We had dinner. And the next morning she was gone. It's impossible she ran away or somehow just disappeared. She would have said something. You know how close we are. Someone killed her and hid the body, or she was kidnapped. I just know it. There's no other explanation. Someone's after us."

Tears began, and she held her face in her hands as she leaned forward on the counter.

"We were so excited. The three of us starting fresh on three separate paths. We would plunge into a whole new universe at exactly the same instant and share it all: the nervousness, the excitement, and the fun of being on our own for the first time."

James stood and put his arm around her.

"We worked hard for it, James. You know it. We got the grades, prepped for the exams, and had recommendations that weren't made up. I'm not bragging. Really. The point is, all that effort was for nothing. We played by the rules, and it blew up in our faces. Mia's dead. Sophia's missing. But I know she's dead or maybe chained in a basement. And I'm next. It's fate. At least, it looks that way."

Rachel stood and pulled out her phone. James leaned over to see the screen.

"This is the last photo we ever took together. Right here in the store on top of the jewelry case. I owe it to them to continue, to keep this memory alive, and to honor them by refusing to just collapse, which is what I want to do."

She led him from the register to the front of the store.

"We all chose something," Rachel continued. "A token to remember."

She unlocked the back of the jewelry case and took the bloodstone ring from the top shelf.

"This is the one I picked. Mia got a locket necklace. Sophia chose a charm bracelet. We took the selfie and posted it. We never thought it would be an epitaph."

"Why didn't you keep the ring?"

"MK wanted me to hold off before I got it at discount. She gave me the costume earrings instead. But since it's still here, I'm gonna take it. I'm lucky no one nabbed it. I'll pay full price. Fuck the discount. It's worth it."

Rachel placed the ring on her finger, and James opened his palm and cradled her hand.

"It beautiful," James said. "You definitely need to take it."

He put his arm around her and wiped tears from her cheeks. Rachel smiled, and they went back to the register.

"I'll pay MK when she gets here," Rachel said. "And then we can go."

They both settled onto stools by the counter. A few new customers entered, and Rachel rang up their purchases. When the store quieted, Rachel folded, organized, and re-hung clothing she found in the changing room as she told James more about her chat with Emma, of the search parties, and about the posters around town for Sophia.

MK arrived at exactly 4 p.m. and breezily greeted Rachel and James. She pushed aviator sunglasses to rest above her stick straight blonde bob, and wore a dark wash denim miniskirt with a camisole top and vintage Dr. Scholl's. Rachel finished unpacking a box with curated accessories from a trade show that she'd abandoned when James had arrived. She prepared to end her shift, but first led MK to the jewelry case and showed her the selfie. Rachel explained the significance of the bloodstone ring.

"You need to have it, obviously at no charge. The whole thing makes me nervous and depressed." MK struggled to compose herself and dabbed at her eyes. "I'm thankful you guys found things you liked. I'm so sorry. Please cherish the memory. Everyone's so worried about you. If you ever need to talk, I'm here. Don't do anything, you know, crazy."

"I won't. I'm just numb. It helps to work. I want to pay for the ring."

"I'll get new rings. I have a new supplier. We'll make a fresh push for fall. The jewelry's doing well. This one's yours." MK clasped Rachel's hand.

Rachel nodded and smiled. "Do you want the earrings back?"

"No. You can keep them. You're going through so much; it's the least I can do."

"Thanks for understanding. It means a lot." She handed over her time sheet and they hugged. "If you're all set, we'll head out."

"Of course. I'll take it from here. See you tomorrow afternoon? You sure you're OK?"

Rachel nodded; James said goodbye, and they headed outside to Rachel's car.

James grew anxious as they approached the cemetery in silence. Rachel parked conspicuously in front of the wrought-iron gates as if they were legitimate visitors. James led Rachel along the dirt roadway on the perimeter until he spotted the tree planter parked against the gate in the back. There was no sign of the man's pick-up or the vacuum.

"He must be gone," James whispered, unsure why. He took Rachel's hand and walked toward the bushes that he'd used as cover. He found his spying spot and got down on all fours to search for his phone. He probed the undergrowth and pushed aside the grassy camouflage. Inching toward the dirt roadway, he found his phone about ten feet away.

James grabbed it and tapped the screen. "Check this out."

He opened the photo library and scrolled through it, tilting it toward Rachel.

"See? There's the man. He's using the tree planter to drill a hole." James stopped on another. "Here's the vacuum hose he stuffs in the hole."

"Where did this happen?" Rachel asked.

"Right there," James said as he pointed. "At that grave with the cracked cross."

James led Rachel up the slope. With the equipment gone, he was unsure he'd targeted the correct plot. He scoured the grave until he discovered loose dirt in the grass and knelt down.

"Look here," James said and traced his finger along the rough edge of sod.

He dug his fingertips into the thin gap in the grass and carefully pried up one corner. He got a grip with both hands and pulled the sod patch away. He swiped at the dirt below, clearing the surface layer to reveal a circular hole filled with earth that was more loosely packed than the solid ground surrounding the edges.

"The hole is here," James said. "It's just hidden."

He scratched at more earth from inside the hole to prove his point.

"My God," Rachel said. "Let me see the photos again."

James handed her the cell phone then knelt back down to push the earth back into place. He stamped on the ground to pack it in firmly and then replaced the sod.

"What should we do?" Rachel asked. "I think we should go straight to the police."

"Not until we have more evidence."

"We've got the photos."

"There's no proof he took anything."

"They can dig up the grave to check. We can find more holes in the grass."

"They're almost impossible to find. And it's getting dark. There's no time. They'll never believe us without more proof.

I don't want to sound crazy. I need to check the bags in Travis' shed to see for myself and to get pix. I can find that skull. That's proof. We aren't ready."

"It's so creepy," Rachel said. "I'm really scared. Can we get out of here?"

James nodded and stuck his phone in his pocket. "I've got to visit my sister."

They silently rushed along the dirt road to the cemetery gates and the safety of Rachel's car. They jumped in and sped toward James' house.

"Tomorrow morning park in our driveway before work," James said. "We'll take the trail to Travis' house and scope things out. I know good places to spy from. We'll sneak into the shed, get some photos, and go straight to the police before your shift."

"What if there's nothing?"

"Then Travis is clear, and we'll nab the Sussex guy."

"What if we get caught in the shed?"

"We'll make up a lie."

"For breaking in?"

"I'll say my mother dropped something. We went to find it, and the door was open."

"Yes. We'll say we heard a sound. A scream inside."

THIRTY-SEVEN

KATHERINE LANGUISHED IN A HOSPITAL BED set at an incline in the far corner of a sterile room. A single window on the fourth floor faced a brick wall from a building that appeared close enough to touch. Overhead fluorescents cancelled out whatever natural light filtered in as the sun dipped low, barely clearing the slate black rooftops.

She watched as three people entered and greeted her mother, who had been reading in a chair near the foot of her bed. Katherine recognized the first two visitors as doctors who in the afternoon had annoyingly probed her with fingers and questions; for how long she couldn't say. Her brother followed and kissed his mother's cheek.

On some level Katherine knew she should want to reach out to greet him, but she felt completely content to vegetate and observe them as they all observed her. There was nothing to say. Something urged her to freeze, to play the Helen Keller game that was actually quite amusing and made the time pass. She lay expressionless as they arranged chairs around the bed and closer to her pillow. She breathed and blinked, and that was all.

James stood and took her hand. Katherine heard him explain, seemingly to her, that he would have arrived sooner, but he'd lost his cell phone and didn't know where to go. However, he'd miraculously recovered it from where he'd dropped it in the grass, and it was a long, strange story that he'd explain some other time.

Katherine felt him return her hand to a resting position on top of the crisp bed sheet. She wasn't sure if she were frowning or had any air about her at all. It simply didn't matter. There was no reason to interact. She liked the isolation, the cozy cocoon. If she didn't need to eat, she surely wouldn't. It was too much of a bother and an interruption of her pleasant state of suspension. Yes, that described it perfectly. She understood implicitly she was simply suspended until further notice. Everyone could just wait a bit and kindly calm down.

But at times hunger and thirst came forward. The doctors, nurses, and her mother were thrilled when she made any effort to consume water, applesauce, oatmeal, or anything they could levy as bait. Why they were so excited, she couldn't guess. A feeding tube would be much easier to tolerate than the baby talk they used to push food on her as if she were some sort of captive pet, a stray they'd uncovered on a closet floor and were obsessed to nurse back to civility.

Katherine's focus meandered back to James. She watched him talk to Paula but didn't care to listen. It was so easy to block out whatever around her she chose to ignore. She let her mind wander and recalled the hurt and anger of the morning. Her mother spoke of lunch meat, skirting entirely the topic of man meat, in a speedo bound to a kitchen chair.

Speak of that, Mother, and perhaps I'll engage. Until then, taste the silent treatment.

She didn't know why she'd settled on this particular style of punishment, and didn't care, but it seemed best just to float, just for now.

Katherine had no impulse to laugh or smile and coolly ignored the attempt of one of the doctors to offer an anecdote he apparently thought was hilarious. James chuckled and smiled warmly at her. Were they trying to make her laugh? On some level, buried deep and far away, she knew she should want to smile back. It seemed proper to acknowledge her brother and to return the simple gesture. But at the same time, she felt blissfully cocooned in a silken sachet.

Katherine!

Her pulse raced with the shout of her name inside her head.

Snap out of it. Now! Tell them about the witch in the woods. She tried to kill you!

The storm trooper's stern command intruded into her reverie with a stabbing pain in her right temple. Katherine gasped, and the doctors jumped to attention. She watched them stare but didn't mind because now something was very wrong.

She pushed the voice away and focused on the light fixture. The pain subsided, and she became aware of the doctors, her mother, and her brother asking her what was happening in unison. They clamored like they really cared for her. They gathered closer and stood above her on both sides of the bed.

Tell them. Now! You cannot resist. Or I'll pop a blood vessel in your brain.

Katherine winced from a searing jolt behind her right eye. A whimper escaped her lips. She couldn't suppress it, and a second cry escaped. She shook her head and looked toward the window. The storm trooper made clear he was all that mattered. He was in control.

A shroud of mist darkened the natural light and swirled around an otherworldly glow outside the window. Katherine felt an overwhelming sense of dread and knew with complete certainty that the man who had appeared and then disappeared from the woods had uncovered her hiding spot in the safety of her hospital bed.

The otherworldly light confirmed he was just outside.

Tell them! Or I will torture you when everyone leaves. Visiting hours are almost up.

Katherine heard taps on the window pane. She craned her neck to look as the sound grew louder and resonated after each intermittent thump of knuckles on glass. She heard a snigger.

Why won't anyone help me? Please go to the window! Can't you hear him? I beg you!

She watched as outstretched hands on thick forearms materialized in the window. Palms pressed against the panes, pushing, threatening to shatter glass.

Katherine fought to close off her mind, to return to the cocoon, but instead screeched and signaled toward the window. She gasped for breath and rocked her head on the pillow to try to escape the man's hold and wake from this diabolical stupor.

Katherine knew people were touching her, rubbing her arms, and trying to soothe her.

Gate the windows. Do something! Draw the blinds. James?

Katherine stared wide-eyed at the window. The storm trooper's face materialized with the same look of disdain she remembered from the woods. Katherine screamed.

The man sneered and pointed at her.

The visitors turned their heads helplessly between the window and Katherine, unsure of what was happening, blind to any threat except her explosion.

Katherine captured their full attention when she shrieked:

"There's a witch in the woods! She tried to get me. Travis sent her. We have to kill him! He's the one tormenting us. Stop him!"

Katherine threw her head back against the pillow and repeated the diatribe, loudly at first, and then as murmurs between frantic gasps for air.

"What's wrong with her?" Paula shouted at the doctor next to her and grasped Katherine's hand.

The girl kicked under the covers and forced herself to a sitting position to look beyond the visitors who had closed in around her and blocked a clear view of the window.

"She's biting herself!" Paula shouted. "Her lip!"

Katherine stopped whispering and strained to see the window. Only the ghostly glow remained, rippling in the mist, little more than a fading reflection. But Katherine knew that he knew exactly where she was. There was no escaping him.

Nicely done. But not effective. They think you're crazy. I'll try your mother, too.

Katherine freed her arms and covered her ears with her hands. She shook her head furiously, burrowing into the pillow as she tried to silence the storm trooper's voice.

"The bad man's coming for us!" Katherine shrieked with eyes closed tight.

Everyone in the room stared and stepped away from the bed. Katherine continued to rock her head, ears covered, tangles of hair covering her face smeared with tears and blood from her lip.

"You've got to do something!" Paula cried.

"An IV drip with a sedative!" one doctor yelled. "STAT."

"What's wrong with her?" Paula demanded.

"Hysteria," the doctor said. "She's clearly a danger to herself and others."

One doctor ran from the room, and the other attempted to wipe Katherine's face with a towel. She arched her back and seemed oblivious to the doctor's touch.

Hospital staff entered the room with rolling equipment and monitors. A nurse coaxed Katherine's hands away from her ears and calmed her as she affixed arm restraints to bars on the sides of the bed. She prepared an IV. If Katherine understood what was happening, she didn't acknowledge it. She hazarded glances at the window while the nurse affixed the needle.

"She's quieting," the doctor said. "The sedative kicks in quickly."

Katherine settled back, expressionless and exhausted. She closed her eyes.

The doctor handed a control to Paula. "Press this button for help. You can stay two more hours."

When Katherine's breathing slowed and vitals on the monitor stabilized, the staff left the room.

Paula and James sat in two chairs near Katherine's pillow. "I came as fast as I could," James said.

"I'm glad you're here," Paula said. "We should talk outside so she can rest."

James gave his sister's hand a squeeze and went to the waiting lounge. Paula leaned in to kiss her daughter's cheek and followed her son outside.

"What the hell happened in there?" James asked as Paula settled next to him on a sofa in a corner. It was after hours, and the check-in desk was abandoned. "Did you hear what she said? It doesn't even make sense."

"That's the worst she's been."

"It's like she's possessed."

"I thought she was improving. I thought this might be over."

"I'm going to call Dad."

"Don't get him involved."

"He has to know about Katherine. He has the right."

"He's not staying with us."

"He can stay in a hotel."

"Don't mention my personal life."

"He already knows about it. I told him after Katherine told me. Don't worry, nothing about the kitchen."

"Do what you want," Paula said. "I can't stop you anyway." She lay back on the sofa. "I need a minute before I go back in. I'm still shaking."

"I'm gonna step outside."

Paula nodded and watched James until he disappeared behind the elevator doors. She closed her eyes and tried to make sense of what she'd witnessed. It seemed clear now that her affair with Travis had traumatized Katherine. Her daughter blamed him and wanted to kill him. The witch she'd invented as a metaphor. To help her daughter, she would have to tell the doctors about the incident in the kitchen. Embarrassment was the price of recklessness.

Paula realized she was starving and walked to the vending machine. A *ding* from the elevator caught her attention, and she watched as an imposing man with fitted khakis tucked into black boots entered the lounge with a tray from the cafeteria. He made his way toward her.

"Do you happen to know the way to room 402?" the man asked.

"Yes. It's just around the corner," Paula answered and pointed toward the hallway. "That's my daughter's room. Who are you?"

"I'm Radu. One of Katherine's teachers from Chemistry lab. I heard she was ill."

"Word travels fast."

"Smart phones. I got worried. Strange things around town."

"Now's not the best time to visit. She just fell asleep."

"How's she doing?"

"Not great at the moment. I hope tomorrow's better."

"I understand. I came earlier, but no one was around." Radu motioned with the tray. "I brought up snacks. A few things in case anyone's hungry."

"Very kind of you. I'm actually starved. But I don't want to impose." Paula stepped back from the vending machine. "Please, let me pay."

"It's totally fine. Help yourself." Radu crossed the room and placed the tray on a side table. "There's a burger, fries, and a salad if that's your thing. Extra napkins. Utensils."

Paula followed him. "Are you sure you don't mind?"

Radu smiled and nodded.

"I really appreciate it," Paula said as she sat next to the table and reached for the burger. She unwrapped it and opened a ketchup packet.

"My pleasure."

"It's been a long day. Didn't plan for dinner." Paula struggled to open the salad container and then speared a cucumber with her fork. "Not sure I remember you from last year's open house. I thought Katherine had Mrs. Murphy for chemistry. I'm Paula, by the way."

"Nice to meet you. I supervise experiments and bonded with Katherine over some misfires with her lab partner."

"You have an accent. Eastern European?"

"Yes. How did you guess?"

"Met someone recently from Bucharest." She paused. "Went my whole life not meeting anyone from the former Eastern bloc. Now, you're everywhere. Funny how that works."

"Things happen in sequence. Usually for a reason. Like chemistry."

"Or everything's random. We just hope there's meaning." Paula paused to squeeze dressing from a packet.

"I'll keep quiet so you can eat in peace," Radu said, and settled into his seat on the opposite side of the table.

"It's OK. Again, I really appreciate it." They chatted between bites until Paula had finished half the burger and most of the salad. "Your outfit. Is it a uniform?"

"Security. Something extra for over the summer. Does it look bad?"

"No. It's dapper and official. Thanks for making time to see Katherine. I'll tell her you stopped by," Paula said. She wiped her lips and fingers with napkins. "That was perfect. Thank you so much. I'll return the tray later. It's the least I can do."

"No, I'll do it. I insist. You've got to get back to your daughter. I hope she feels better."

Paula smiled and again offered payment, which Radu dismissed with the palm of his hand and motioned toward room 402.

When Paula turned the corner, Radu took the tray, called the elevator, and disappeared behind the doors. He coaxed everything he would need into a Zip-lock bag and left the tray on the floor. With a *ding*, the doors opened in the lobby, and Radu faded into the night.

THIRTY-EIGHT

JAMES FOUND A BENCH outside and called Aaron.

"How was your trip back?"

"A lot's happened."

"Everything OK?"

"Not really. I'm in the hospital. Katherine's here. She's had some kind of trauma."

"Is she hurt? What's going on?"

"She said she was chased by a witch in the woods. She refused to talk, so they brought her to the hospital for tests. Nothing's broken or anything. It's psychological."

"A witch? That doesn't sound like Katherine. She's rational."

"I know. But something's very wrong. She just freaked out in her hospital bed."

"Doing what?"

"Screaming about the witch. She's traumatized, like something bad happened to her. She announced to everyone we need to kill Travis, the neighbor. She caught Mom messing around with him in his kitchen. Maybe it messed her up. Maybe she wasn't ready to see Mom with someone new."

"What's with this Travis?"

"He lives in the Malloy's house across the woods from us. Mom went over there every night last week. But that's nothing."

"What else?"

"I witnessed something really strange."

"What?"

"I checked out the woods where Katherine told Mom she was chased. I didn't find anything. But I snuck into Travis' yard and spied on a delivery guy. He dropped off a trash bag that he pulled from a big vacuum. He works for the Town of Sussex."

"How do you know?"

"I saw the logo on his shirt. Anyway, it seemed suspicious. I got closer and peeked in the shed where the guy put the bag. There's a bunch of them lined up."

"So what? It's not your business."

"I know. But why would a town worker bring him bags of trash? From a vacuum? I thought it might be marijuana. I trailed him to find out more since Mom's involved."

"That was dangerous and stupid."

"I don't care. There's been strange stuff happening. I jumped in his trailer and hid behind the vacuum. He drove to the old cemetery downtown past the train tracks. Then I followed him on foot. This is where it gets freaky."

"What? Tell me already."

"He's got a tree planter parked by the back fence. I watched him take it and use it to drill into a grave. I watched him from under a bush. Then he took that vacuum, fed the hose into the hole, and sucked stuff out."

"Are you crazy? What's wrong with you?"

"I have photos to prove it. I'll send them right now. I think he drills straight into the casket. Then he vacuums it out and carts it away inside the trash bag."

"Sounds impossible. There's something you're missing."

"He neatly covers his tracks with a patch of sod. I swear. Wait 'til you see the photos."

"So, what do you want me to do about it?"

"I need you to come here. Tomorrow. Drop everything."

The phone went silent for a moment. "OK. And then what?"

"First, look at the photos. There are good ones of the guy's face. Maybe you can spy around that cemetery. You know the one. It's after you pass the train tracks downtown. Look for the blue uniform shirt, or at least find the tree planter. You can see what I'm talking about."

"I'll pick you up before lunch. You can show me."

"I'll take you after lunch. First, I gotta check out Travis' shed. That's the real proof: the bags, what's inside."

"Breaking and entering."

"Grave robbing's worse."

"Should I stop by the house first? Go to the hospital?"

"Mom said you couldn't stay with us. Just get a room. Then let's meet for lunch. We can compare notes and visit Katherine in the afternoon."

"It all sounds nuts. There's gotta be an explanation."

"I saw part of a skull. The guy held it up."

"Go to the police in the morning."

"We need more proof. We need the bags. I'm still not sure how Travis is involved or if they're the same bags. I need to find out for Mom's sake."

Neither spoke for a moment.

"I'll get a room and check out the cemetery. Don't bother with the shed."

"I've already made a plan with Rachel. We'll make it quick then meet up with you."

"Have you told any of this to your mother?"

"Not yet. She might ask Travis about the shed and tip him off. If he hides the bags, we've got nothing."

"Send me the photos. Don't do anything stupid. See you tomorrow. Tell Katherine to hang in there."

They said their goodbyes. James scrolled though his photos and selected a few with the worker's face, the drill, and the vacuum.

Somehow now the photos didn't look so bad. Wasn't the man simply doing grounds work? It was difficult to assign sinister intent. James suddenly questioned everything. No one would believe it. And had he been certain about the skull? Maybe his mind had played a trick.

He stared at the screen, numb, and lumbered back to the lobby to call the elevator. The doors opened and James spied a plastic tray on the floor with nothing but an empty salad container. He was grateful for the sloppy reminder; he'd forgotten about dinner. He scanned the directory panel for the cafeteria, and tapped the button for the 7th floor.

James grabbed the tray to return it. *People are pigs.*

PART FOUR
ELEVATION

THIRTY-NINE

RACHEL SIDESTEPPED THE PILE OF boxes, bags, books, and a huge wheeled suitcase she'd deposited in the downstairs family room close to the garage. All that remained to pack were toiletries and summer-weight clothes still in play before moving to campus on Thursday. She checked her phone reflexively every time it buzzed or chimed, hoping to find a message from Sophia. How long would she cling to false hope? Months? A year? She needed a new routine, and fast, before something tiny might be enough to push her over the edge.

She believed James' macabre story and agreed they had to investigate the shed. Sure, the photos were odd. But maybe there was a legitimate explanation. An infestation or drainage problem? Rachel told herself these things, but on a darker level, she hoped they would find something awful like bones.

She believed Emma. A crazy woman had entered Mia's room, robbed her, killed her, and then escaped down the tree outside her second-floor window.

And Sophia's disappearance could be described as

301

supernatural, in the sense that it would be completely unnatural for Sophia to run away on her own without a word to her best friend.

Sussex weather in late August could swelter or chill on the same day. Rachel checked the temperature and changed from sweats to Adidas gym shorts with a slim fit Lacoste. If they were playing detective, she wanted to be comfortable and presentable for work in the afternoon.

Rachel said goodbye to her parents in the kitchen and told them she would be home after work. But first she had breakfast plans with James. No, they weren't getting back together.

She drove her mother's Nissan Sentra to James' house and parked on the far side of the driveway near the grass so her car wouldn't be in the way.

James came out to greet her as soon as she stopped.

"Right on time," he said. "It's already hot. Want any iced coffee?"

Rachel stepped out of the car and closed the door. "I'm good. Got up early to do more packing. Nervous energy." She paused to check out his jean cut-offs and tight navy polo, his blond spikes waxed in place. "You look nice."

"You too. Need to look respectable if we go to the police."

"Where's your dad?"

"He just arrived, finding a place to spend the night."

"He's not coming here first?"

"That would be hard for my mom. I'll meet him for lunch."

"Did you tell him your story?"

"Yes. He's going to the cemetery to check it out. Hopefully he'll back me up. We'll both go to the police later with photos from the shed."

"Did you visit Katherine?"

"Yes. It was freaky." They walked from Rachel's car and past the garden. "She's bad. For a long time, she didn't even speak and didn't even acknowledge I was there. Then she burst out about the witch and threatened Travis."

"A threat?"

"She said Travis sent the witch, and we had to kill him. She's definitely upset about Mom and lashing out."

The witch reference spooked Rachel. What Emma had described in the room with Mia also sounded like a witch. They walked silently until they started down the stagecoach road.

"I've already searched the trail," James said. "It's where Katherine told Mom she got chased."

"Scary it's so close to home," Rachel said as they went deeper into the woods. "Strange she used the word 'witch.' Any idea why? It bothers me."

"It gets attention. My mom said she blurted it out when she broke her silence. Katherine was hiding in the kitchen closet. That's where my mom found her. Maybe she's punishing my mom by being dramatic and saying crazy things. She doesn't want my mom sleeping with Travis. And now she wants him dead. That's my guess."

"Too many strange things. We need answers."

They reached the meadow on Travis' property. James tapped Rachel's shoulder. "That's the shed. It used to be a chicken barn," he whispered and pointed.

The pair took steps forward and sidestepped mud slicks as they silently advanced and ducked behind brambles and clumps of cattails.

"We'll sprint to those pines, then to the oak." James leaned in close. "He can spot us if he looks out the back windows, so crouch low and keep hidden."

"I'm really nervous," Rachel said as she bent down and trailed him. The thick grass was soaked with morning dew. "We need an excuse in case he catches us."

"We came to look for something my mom dropped."

"By sneaking around?"

"We just can't get caught. Maybe he isn't home."

"What about the Sussex guy?"

"Truck's not in the driveway. He's not here."

"What if he shows up?"

"We'll hear him coming," James whispered as he took her hand. "We'll work fast. Break into the shed and check out the bags. We'll know very quickly if there's nothing. If it's illegal, we take pictures and get the hell out."

Rachel nodded, bent down low, and ran after James toward the second tree. They huddled together and caught their breath.

"From here it's a straight shot to the door," James whispered.

James dashed toward the shed. Rachel waited a moment to survey the scene. It seemed clear, so she sprinted. She kept watch as James fiddled with the latch.

"It's not even locked."

Chipped red paint exposed the weathered planks of the door, and it squeaked open on tarnished hinges. Daylight sliced a pathway on the hay-strewn dusty floor as they stepped inside.

Nine black bags were lined up in two rows on a raised

wooden platform. James went to the first one on the end and read the label: *DEIRDRE ROBINSON 1928.*

His hand trembled as he unfastened the tie and pulled the plastic open wide. James gasped and stepped away from the bag.

"You gotta see this."

Rachel came up next to him and peered inside. "My God."

A silver watch and a broken pair of wire spectacles rested on a folded swath of cream-colored fabric. A pile of dirt and debris filled the rest of the bag.

"Let's get out of here," Rachel said, taking quick breaths. "You were right. These are things from a grave. I feel dizzy."

"We need photos." James took out his camera to snap the name tag, the relics on top, and the bags lined up in rows. "I'm digging for more."

James gingerly pushed aside the fabric. He probed the top layer of dirt with his fingers and hit something. He burrowed deeper, grabbed hold, and extracted a broken rib that curved grotesquely lengthwise into the bag.

"Holy shit!" Rachel whispered and stepped away.

James rested the bone on top and photographed it. He held his finger to his lips.

"Please, let's go." Rachel's wild eyes scanned the bags.

"OK. I'm tying it back up. We've got proof." He plunged the bone back into the dirt, closed the bag, and refastened the tie.

Rachel choked and covered her mouth with her hand. James pivoted in surprise. With eyes wide she pointed to a bag in the front row.

"What?" James asked.

"That bag. The label." Rachel's forearm trembled as she pointed.

James reached for it and read aloud, "*Carol Stilton, 1949.*" He studied Rachel's stricken face. "What about it? Tell me."

Rachel's breaths were rapid and shallow. "That name. I know it. She was the one in the room with Mia. The night she died. Emma heard her say the name. She wrote it down. She told me the name."

James photographed the name on the label.

"Open it," Rachel said. "I need to see inside."

"We should get the hell out of here."

"She was in the room with Mia. We've got to look inside."

James untied the bag and gingerly pulled the plastic wide.

In exactly the same arrangement, a swatch of tattered fabric lay on top of refuse from the grave. Metal barrettes and an oval-shaped pendant sat on top.

Rachel didn't blink or hesitate. Still trembling, she reached inside and took out the pendant. Her lips parted as she opened and closed the cover over and over.

"This locket. What's it doing here? It's Mia's. I swear it. She bought it at Old Gold. It's in the photo we posted. This girl inside. I remember her exactly, in black and white. The sad smile. This isn't possible. It's the same locket." Rachel's eyes filled with tears.

James put his arm around her. "Put it back. Let's get out of here."

"The chain is gone. The pendant hung on a thick chain. But it's not here." Rachel paused and pushed away. "And do you know why? It's what Mia used to hang herself on the doorknob. No. No. No." She shook her head. "Carol Stilton used the chain to strangle Mia. Carol Stilton did it. I know it. This filth is from her grave. She somehow came back to kill Mia."

She tossed the locket into the bag and struggled to maintain balance.

"The jewelry. It's tainted. It has to be. It's a curse. There's no other way it could wind up here. MK's new supplier must be Travis. He's the witch. Katherine was right. I want this filth off me." Rachel pulled at the bloodstone ring. "It won't come off. God! I can't twist it."

"Your finger's swollen from the humidity. We'll use soap at home."

James held Rachel and tried to help her dislodge the ring. They didn't notice as the light dimmed and a figure loomed in the doorway.

"What are you doing?" Travis asked in a calm, quiet voice.

Rachel screamed and turned toward the door. James jumped backward.

"What are *you* doing with these bags?" James demanded.

"You're trespassing. Breaking and entering."

"The door wasn't locked."

"That doesn't give you the right to enter."

"I had suspicions. Just cause."

Rachel backed away from the door and inched toward James.

Travis folded his arms in front of his broad chest.

"What suspicions, James?" Travis asked. "I suppose it's perfectly normal to be protective of your mother."

"You're in a lot of trouble," James said. "I have photos."

"Of what, exactly?"

"Drilling in the cemetery. And now these bags. Absolute proof."

"Dylan and I were aware of your spying around. Sorry you got scared and ran. Perhaps your time would have been better spent helping your sister in the hospital. You could have protected her against an unwelcome visitor."

"What?"

"You could have guarded her room."

"You knew I was in the cemetery?"

"And I watched you under the truck. This is none of your concern."

"You're breaking the law."

"Only to solve a bigger problem. Matters of life and death."

"You're grave robbers."

"To what end?" Travis asked. "You need to calm down."

"To sell stuff." James inched toward Travis, fists clenched.

Travis took a step into the shed and blocked the door. "Don't do this."

James lunged at Travis and swung at his face. Travis effortlessly dodged the blow and countered with a punch of his own. James staggered and took several steps backward, scrambling to regain his balance, stabilizing himself against the back wall.

Travis marched toward him as Rachel bolted out the door, shouting, "I'll get help!"

"Run!" James yelled as he jumped on Travis and locked an arm around his neck, swiveling behind him. Travis rotated and took forceful steps backward, pressing James against a support beam. He slammed them both backward until James' grip went soft.

Travis pivoted behind James and locked an elbow around his neck. Travis grabbed his other arm for leverage and forced James' head forward. James struggled but could only groan against the sleeper hold. He went limp, fell to the floor, and didn't get up.

Travis knelt next to him. He ran one hand slowly through James' hair. He massaged his scalp firmly, gathered a few strands, and clenched them in his fist.

"I regret it's come to this," Travis said as he stood and stepped away. "I don't expect you to understand. I'm not sure what's next myself."

He closed the door, latched it, and left James with the bags in the musty gloom.

Travis took a few steps beyond the shed, scanned the meadow, and watched Rachel disappear into the forest.

"Every drop of fear," he whispered. "You won't remember. It won't be wasted."

FORTY

AARON DROVE PAST THE CEMETERY near the railroad tracks several times before pulling up directly in front of the gates. He knew it had to be the one; no others were near the center of town. Aaron parked and stepped out of the car.

He was tired from the three-hour drive and wandered through the entrance gate to look for a spot to relieve himself. It was his first time back to Sussex since he had packed up and left Paula, his first time facing humiliation in the town he grew up in. He'd lost custody of his kids. He resented that he had to hide behind a tree in the corner of a cemetery to pee. He was banned from the house he had lived in for years, paying down half the mortgage.

He still hadn't checked into a hotel because he wasn't sure he would stay the night. He had to see how the day played out and if there were any point spending hours of time with Katherine in the hospital. It seemed doubtful, considering what James had relayed about her psychological state. He also dreaded running into Paula. James would have to text him about her whereabouts.

Aaron didn't admit it to his son, and he had tried to play

it cool when they'd tossed a football in the backyard, but the idea that Paula had moved on bothered him to his core. He knew he had no right to feelings of jealousy, but he couldn't help himself. He'd yet to connect with anyone beyond hookups. Maybe Paula really was his superior. The proof was accumulating.

Zip up your pants, and step away from the tree.

He had to do better. Returning to town with no pot to piss in wasn't good enough. Was he more than the irredeemable ex-husband? He would have to prove himself better than a cliché.

He'd already bonded with James during the past week. They'd talked in a deeper way than ever before. Aaron had finally admitted that his incessant focus on athletics may have hurt his son's chances to do much of anything else. But the past didn't have to dictate the future. Now was the time to figure out options.

Perhaps Katherine was a lost cause. She'd always taken her mother's side, anyway. But he could show empathy if she would open to him, at least, one more time. He was learning in therapy what it meant to share and consider the point of view of others. He'd been narcissistic. Who knew? Apparently everyone but him, especially Paula. He would take the high road if they crossed paths. He would force himself to stop imagining her in bed with the neighbor. Of course, it all depended on his ability to step up, a difficult task for someone not wired to put others before himself. The narcissist thing: he couldn't escape it.

Aaron tugged at the drawstring of his black track pants and walked the dirt road along the fence. What he expected to find, he had no clue. James had sent photos of the Sussex man drilling a hole. It looked strange only because it was jarringly close to the gravestones. He hoped to find the tree planter to corroborate James' story. He would then meet his son for lunch and continue to the hospital.

Aaron became aware of the sound of a motor running on the other side of the cemetery. It wasn't loud and almost blended into the background like a lawnmower, but it was something to focus on.

He quickened his pace and spotted a pickup truck with a trailer parked next to the fence around the far corner. It had to be the one James had snuck a ride in.

The wind shifted, and the motor was louder now. Aaron could make out its source: a tree planter boring into the earth with a man at the controls. Aaron matched the worker's traits with the photos James had sent: blue shirt, blond hair, muscles. It had to be the same guy.

Aaron crept toward the Sussex man. Maybe there was a legitimate explanation, and he wanted to get answers that would sober his son's vivid imagination. Aaron hid behind a tree with a good view of the gravesite.

Exactly as James had described, the auger was mounted over a grave, the large vacuum parked at the ready just behind. The man drilled from a side angle against the slope of a hill.

Aaron was fascinated. Was this really happening? The auger bored unmistakably into a grave amid the headstones. He could hardly wait to see if the vacuum would be used. He *hoped* it would be used; for the Sussex man to plant a sapling at this point would be a letdown.

Aaron's blood started to pump. He wanted to catch the man red-handed, to watch him squirm, to overcome him, to capture him, and to turn him in, just like an action hero.

The drill met resistance and rocked the tree planter. The driver manipulated the auger up and down until grating gave way to churn, and pumped his fist.

I'm going to kick your ass.

As Aaron watched his quarry, he realized his heart was racing. He felt aroused and primed with adrenaline, ready to strike.

Busting someone is the best. Screw coaching. I want to be a detective.

The Sussex man withdrew the drill and backed the planter away from the grave. He dismounted and pulled the vacuum toward the hole, unwinding the large hose from the canister.

James was right. He's really doing it. He is so burned.

The man bent and fed the tube into the hole. When it would extend no further, he stood and switched on the vacuum. The sound of debris coursing through the tube and intermittently firing into the canister overcame the whir of the motor.

Aaron decided the perfect moment had arrived to confront his prey. He strode behind the Sussex man, who'd bent to coax the hose with both hands.

"The hell's going on here?" Aaron asked, muscled forearms folded across his chest.

"Who wants to know?" the Sussex man asked with a start as he leaped from the ground and faced Aaron.

"I'm in mourning."

"I work here. The name's Dylan." He extended his hand, but Aaron ignored it.

"Hell of a job you're doing. Care to explain?"

"Extermination. Pest infestations in old graves. Moles."

"That's a crock. I've been watching."

"Watching what?"

"The drill. The vacuum. Everything. We're going to the police."

Dylan switched off the vacuum. "Good luck with that," he said and stared at Aaron defiantly. "Be on your way before you get hurt." He held himself solidly and took a belligerent step toward Aaron.

"Dying for an excuse," Aaron said as he raised his fists. "I'm gonna kick your ass, leave your carcass by the drill, call the police, and watch you cuffed."

The two men faced each other and locked into stances of defense, circling slowly, sniffing out each other's level of skill, weaving and shifting in search of an opening.

Aaron swung first, but Dylan anticipated it, blocked, and countered with a powerful stomach jab that forced Aaron to recoil and groan louder than he could muffle.

"You'll die for that," Aaron said and shook off any sign of damage. He feigned a lunge at Dylan, who leapt left to avoid it, and caught the grave robber with a blow to the side of his face. Dylan grunted, stumbled back, and spit out blood.

"Give it up while you still can," Aaron said.

Dylan scoffed and motioned Aaron forward with a slow, taunting wave of the fingers of his right hand.

The men circled. Dylan surged forward with multiple punches that Aaron blocked without much trouble until an uppercut grazed his chin. Livid, Aaron lunged and managed to wrap an elbow around Dylan's neck, swiveling quickly behind the younger man and buckling his knees, forcing Dylan to the ground.

Aaron twisted his body behind Dylan and attempted a rear naked choke, but Dylan powered out and countered with repeated blows with his elbows to Aaron's ribs until Aaron was forced to release his hold completely and struggled to his feet.

The men faced off again, breathing heavily, furious and primed to kill.

Dylan launched an assault of body blows with strikes of both fists, landing some of the punches, surging forward. He forced Aaron into a defensive stance that opened him to an unguarded, powerful blow to the side of the head.

Aaron reeled and figured his only chance to win would be on the ground. Aaron tackled Dylan with all his strength, managing to topple him and to pin him face down. Aaron forced his right elbow under Dylan's neck and pulled his head backward by the hair. Dylan groaned and flailed his arms. He reached rearward and grabbed at Aaron's shirt as he tried to escape.

"I'll snap your fucking neck!" Aaron said with spittle in Dylan's ear.

He began to twist Dylan's head to the side, using his body weight to add pressure. Aaron covered Dylan's mouth and nose with his right hand, blocking air, squeezing his jaw while trying to break his will. Aaron planted his thighs tight against Dylan's torso to keep him pinned.

"Submit, you son of a bitch."

With a surge and despite the vice on his neck, Dylan snapped his legs up under his stomach and rocked his powerful lower body to buck Aaron off his back.

I must not fail Travis.

A reptilian survival instinct overcame Dylan. He twisted himself in midair and scrambled on top of Aaron. Dylan gulped in air and unleashed a barrage of punches on Aaron's face. When Aaron pulled his arms up to shield himself, Dylan attacked his ribs. Aaron screamed with rage as it became clear he could not defend himself.

Dylan stopped his attack, rose up, and slowly stood over his opponent. He backed away to savor his foe's collapse.

Aaron found his footing, shook his head to rally, and lunged at Dylan, who saw him coming and pushed him aside. Dylan followed with an elbow to his back, and his opponent staggered, unable to contain a groan.

"It's over," Dylan said as he hammered the base of Aaron's neck with his fist.

Aaron collapsed on the ground.

Dylan stood over his rival and prodded him with his foot. "Stay down."

Excellent work. Your defeat would have also been mine. You are most worthy. Recover yourself. You are done with the cemetery. Pack up and bring him to me.

Travis' communication elated Dylan. Whatever pain he felt lessened. He found himself smiling and sat a few feet from Aaron to catch his breath. He rubbed his throbbing neck and massaged his jaw until the soreness from Aaron's grip grew tolerable.

Dylan studied his vanquished foe: solid and muscular, an

athlete, a worthy opponent. What happened was real, not a regulated Golden Gloves bout, but a primal fight to survive. Dylan felt an urge to stand, place one foot on the defeated man's chest, or maybe his neck given the residual pain of his own, and to roar like Tarzan. For the first time, he understood that animalistic impulse.

He opted instead to remain seated.

Why had the intruder tried to kill him? He was only doing his job for Travis.

Dylan returned to the vacuum and retracted the hose. He wrapped it around the canister and checked inside. Like many of the bags he'd collected, he could discern nothing within but decrepit earth and fragments of debris. It didn't look like much.

Dylan shoveled dirt back into the hole, raked the grass, and replaced the patch of sod. He parked the tree planter next to the fence and wheeled the vacuum to the trailer.

He didn't want to carry the muscled bulk of his opponent farther than necessary, so he backed the truck up along the fence and got it closer to the body.

He lifted the man carefully, hooking his arms beneath his armpits as if applying a headlock, and pulled him toward the truck backwards with both his legs dragging along the grass. The man's head fell forward and bobbed. Dylan hoisted him onto the trailer and positioned his body beside the vacuum. His opponent lay helplessly on his back.

"For the record, I kicked your ass," Dylan said as he closed door. "I'm worthy."

He climbed into his truck and headed for Travis' house to deliver the seemingly useless canister and his captive.

I'm worthy.

FORTY-ONE

JAMES SOARED WITH SEAGULLS and marveled at the mountain tops, verdant pastures, and a sliver of lake that shimmered to eternity. The gulls counted him as one of their own as he sailed in formation, his trajectory steered by featherless beats of outstretched arms.

He felt an exhilarating rush with each pass through the clouds that broke into open sky over sun-flecked water. He swooped low, craned his neck, and spotted the gulls soaring higher, ever smaller. He raced to catch them, his flight now lumbering. They abruptly changed course and began to pull up and away. Then the gulls disappeared.

James recognized he was falling hopelessly behind, and he struggled all at once to defy gravity. First he was above the clouds, then he was trapped below them within swirls of vapor and thick, soaking droplets of mist. He watched with dread as the countryside drew closer.

Sometimes the dangerous drag would ebb, and James could get high enough to view the seagulls. It seemed he might even catch them. But with a menacing rumble somewhere below, the drag would resume. The gulls didn't wait. James strained to remain aloft, aware he could crash out of the sky. His arms ached from flapping furiously against what he knew, as dreams make such things innately clear, was something evil far below. He had to escape, or it would kill him.

As he further descended, landmarks and buildings he recognized from Sussex came into view: the shopping plazas, the fairgrounds, and a new office building in the historic center. His spirits lifted, and flying was effortless again. It seemed the force that had singled him out had forgotten about him. He waved at fairgoers in the upper carriages of the Ferris wheel that soared thrillingly high. They waved back as he glided just overhead. His fingertips grazed the outstretched hand of a fan who recognized him from the football field.

He soared over the central downtown crossroads and over the small train depot nearby. An enthralling sense of wonder began to morph into foreboding as he spied the stone crosses and monuments of an old cemetery just beyond the train tracks visible through breaks in the trees.

Again the drag found him. His most frantic attempts to stay aloft held him just above the pricks of upper branches. He scoured the landscape for the source of the downward pull. His eyes were drawn to a cluster of tightly packed marble markers. A fresh, open hole on top of a grave was pulling him down. Dirt spilled into the grass around it, like an anthill. The high pitch of a motor from deep within overpowered all other sound.

He knew he would crash and flailed his limbs in midair. He found himself rapidly shrinking in size and realized with alarm he would soon be small enough to be sucked into the hole. No other debris entered: no leaves and no birds. It was clear whatever was inside wanted only him. Trapped within the suction, he entered the opening in the earth. He was tiny, no larger than a bumblebee, flying through the pitch-black expanse of a dirt tunnel.

Terror swept over him as he descended deeper and deeper into the hole, pulled by a force in the dark. He was not in control of his propulsion, and the unsettling sensation made him wave and kick reflexively. A crash would be torture, an endless tumble along the edges of the tunnel perhaps all the way to hell.

As time passed, he realized he wasn't flying at all, but simply floating. He stopped fighting the downward spiral. He drifted and didn't collide with the dirt walls for what felt like hours, but perhaps was only seconds.

At last there was a focal point in the endless void: a soft, warm, red glow in the distance. If it were light from the embers of hell, he welcomed the beacon as a resolution.

He'd approached heaven with the seagulls and hoped to get in, but the gatekeepers rejected him, closed the doors, and watched unperturbed as the suction swept him toward a fate they knew couldn't be good, but rules were rules, and he didn't pass muster.

Now, it didn't seem so bad. As he drew closer the glow flickered, subdued and inviting.

He watched with wonder as he floated through the threshold of light into a wide, open space of red satin. He gently landed on cushioned, pillowed fabric. He rolled with joy several times, luxuriating on the smooth, silken softness and savoring stability after the tumultuous journey through decrepit earth. At last, he closed his eyes.

When he awoke, to his delight, Rachel had joined him, along with Mia and Sophia. They lay together side-by-side, laughing and chattering and then settling on their backs to stare upward at a movie that began to play on the large, flat surface directly above them.

Scenes from a football game starring James on the field with Triple Trouble cheering from the stands looped a few times before cutting to a formal dance in the school gymnasium, decorated to look fancier than it was or ever could be, with James sneaking kisses with Rachel as Mia and Sophia stood nearby, swaying their bodies with the band.

The movie faded as it had started. Rachel, Mia, and Sophia stood, joined hands, and smiled down on James, who luxuriated on his back. He found himself at the center of a circle they'd formed. He watched them dance around him, arms held high, lowered for an instant, then raised again with faces beaming.

Again a movie started high above them; this time it was a scene from *The Wizard of Oz*. The room reverberated with melancholy, almost desperate shouts of *Bye! Good bye!* from the Munchkins as they chased the large, floating, fading bubble that would slowly deliver Glinda the Good Witch to a faraway place.

Rachel, Mia, and Sophia broke the circle, still holding hands, and moved away from James in single file with slow, backward steps. They turned and chanted *Bye! Good bye!* along with the Munchkins. Rachel waved with her right hand. She was first in line, leading Mia and Sophia toward the entrance to the tunnel.

James pleaded with them to stay.

I'm coming! Let me go with you. Wait! Please wait.

He stood and shouted as loudly as he could. But they didn't stop and soon disappeared within the darkness. James panicked and ran toward the hole, but to his horror realized he was growing in size and could no longer fit into the tunnel that had transported him inside.

The desperate shouts of the Munchkins morphed into the shrill, evil laughter of a witch, and a terrifying chill overcame him.

He watched helplessly as he continued to grow until his head touched the padded ceiling of the room. James threw himself onto his back. He soon filled the confines of the space, his face just inches from the satin ceiling.

He screamed and pounded with both hands on the sides and top of his keep. He knew he was trapped in a casket, buried alive. Whatever warm light had previously illuminated the space faded to black, though the laughter from the witch continued from a distance somewhere deep within the tunnel on the way back up to the cemetery.

James felt around for the hole in the side of casket and managed to force his hand into the opening. He clawed his fingers into the packed earth.

He screamed for help and realized the air was thin and depleted.

His fingers probed and felt the tunnel walls turn to mud. A rapid stream of cold water surged through the hole into the casket, soaking him as he convulsed in the dark.

"My God!" James cried out as he shook his head and abruptly sat up.

Travis sat next to him on some hay strewn about the wooden floor toward the back of the shed. "You've had quite a dream."

"What's happening?" James asked as he drew in rapid, shallow breaths. "Where am I?"

"You're OK. Everything's fine. Just relax. Here's some water." Travis handed him a chilled bottle of Poland Spring, and watched as James's eyes shifted warily from the window to the door to the collection of bags on the platform.

"It was horrible." James took a few gulps from the water bottle. "The worst nightmare in my life. I was there. I'm shaking. It seemed so real."

"Dreams *are* real until you awake," Travis said. "But it's over now."

James became aware of a large patch of wetness clearly visible in the front of his shorts.

"I'm sorry." James covered his eyes and exhaled deeply.

"Don't worry. Your mother's on her way with a change of clothes."

"I still don't know what's happening. My mind's blank. Except for the dream." James took another sip.

"You're in the storage barn behind my house."

"But why?"

"You don't remember?"

"No. Nothing."

"You offered to help me with these bags of debris, to load them into my truck and take them to the landfill. I think they can be composted. A few are heavy."

"Why was I asleep?"

"I came back from the truck, and you'd passed out. I think you fainted. It's hot. You slept soundly, deeply immersed in a dream. Your arms twitched, and you struggled to speak. I didn't want to wake you until the nightmare ended. You know the superstition."

James reached behind his head and felt a lump. "Never fainted before."

They sat quietly and listened to the crunch of gravel on the driveway as a car pulled close.

"Your mom's here. I called her." Travis got up and waved outside. "She wants to check you out and see if you also need a trip to the hospital."

Travis went back to James, and Paula entered with the strap of a duffle bag slung over her shoulder, eyes wide and focused on her son.

"How's your head?" she asked. "Let me see the bump."

James swiveled and bent his head down, and his mother probed gently.

"The swelling's not bad," she said. "How do you feel? Do you think it's a concussion? Like from football?"

"I feel OK," James said. "Just confused. And embarrassed." He looked down.

"I brought a change of clothes," Paula said.

"Loss of bladder control could be the sign of a concussion," Travis said.

"It was from the dream," James said. "A horrible nightmare. Water flowing in dreams always made me wet the bed when I was little."

"Let's get you inside and changed," Travis said. "Then we

can see how you're doing. Any pain, headache, or dizziness, and we'll decide what's next."

Travis led the way out, and they followed. They entered his house though the kitchen door, and Travis showed James to the bathroom.

"Take a shower. Everything you need's on the counter," Travis said. "Just leave your old stuff on the floor. Come out when you're ready."

James took the fresh clothes, entered the bathroom, and closed the door. He undressed and fiddled with the shower controls before stepping into the spray. He shook his head to try to clear it. He had no recollection of helping Travis, none at all. Only fragments from the dream remained and invaded his thoughts as he attempted to sort out what had happened. He soon gave up digging for more and surrendered to the allure of the water. He probed the lump on the back of his head. It was sore but not remarkable. He got dressed, and left his soiled clothes in a clump to disguise their wetness.

When he finished in the bathroom, James found Travis and Paula in the living room.

"Any better?" his mother asked.

"Still disoriented," James said. "But not bad."

Travis stood and motioned to the sofa. "Relax and catch up. Are you hungry?"

"Maybe a little."

"Head for the kitchen," Travis said. "Your mom knows where things are. It'll give me a few minutes to put things in order."

"Take your time," Paula said. "I'll get James something."

They went to the kitchen, and Travis left the room.

"How's Katherine doing?" James asked. He sat in a chair at the kitchen table.

"No change. But at least she's quiet," Paula said. "None of that screaming like last night."

"Are you going back?"

"Depends on what happens with you. I left the hospital when Travis called. Swung home to grab your change of clothes."

"Sorry for the extra work. How did he know I needed them?"

"He must have noticed your shorts. Sorry you got hurt. Are you still confused?"

"I have no clear memory of this morning." James paused a moment. "I was with Rachel, but I think she went to work. And Dad's in town."

"For what?"

"To visit Katherine. He's finding a place to stay the night."

"That's awkward. I'm not ready to see him."

Paula poked through Travis' refrigerator and put supplies on the table. She pulled three plates from the cupboard, and found the silverware. A loaf of fresh country bread sat ready on a cutting board on the counter. She made sandwiches and placed them in the middle of the table. James devoured one half with a relish that surprised him because he hadn't felt hungry or hadn't been aware. He reached for another and forced himself to slow down.

When they finished, Paula gathered the plates and cleaned up at the sink. Travis came down the attic stairs and appeared in the kitchen. He gripped a small bottle.

"How are you feeling, James?" Travis asked.

"Better. I needed to eat."

"Let me check you out."

James swiveled his chair away from the table. Travis murmured quietly to himself, as if in a moment's prayer, as he stepped in close. He tilted James' head gently forward to examine the lump and massaged the back of his neck with one hand.

"That feels good." James exhaled deeply. "So much better."

Travis placed his fist below James' chin and raised it. They locked eyes for an instant.

"Is everything OK?" Paula asked.

"Yes. But I need to protect him."

"From what? You told me the same thing the other night." Paula joined James at the table.

"There's trouble nearby. A dangerous countryman."

"Maybe we should call the police."

"Sorinah is handling it."

"I forgot she's here. I would like to meet her."

"You will soon."

Travis placed a hand on each of their shoulders. He shifted his gaze to the son.

James reached up to grip Travis' forearm. He wanted the neighbor to like him. "Can I help with something?"

"Something small." Travis smiled and gave him a squeeze. "Take out your phone."

James reached into his pocket and held it out.

"Delete photos from the cemetery and today in the shed," Travis said. "Also from the chat with your dad."

James silently attended to his task.

"What photos?" Paula asked.

"It's not that important," Travis said.

Paula pursed her lips but kept silent.

"Do you believe in witches?" Travis asked her.

"That's a strange question."

"What about magic? Supernatural things."

"Don't try to scare me."

"That is not my intention."

"Witches are evil."

Paula's eyes widened, and she stared at Travis. He sensed her alarm, and took her hand. She squeezed it and exhaled deeply.

"Many people define evil for their own convenience," Travis continued. "Everyday things can also be evil and never get a second thought."

"Like what?" James asked. He put his phone away.

"Eating animals can be seen as evil."

"We need to eat," James said.

"There are alternatives. But we declare our urges more important."

"You're getting philosophical," Paula said.

"Humans fighting wars for self-serving definitions of virtue is evil."

"What about the witches?" James asked.

"Untold millions die in human wars. But only scattered individuals fall to witches and always for a specific goal. It's always a matter of survival for the witch."

"What are you saying?" Paula asked. "Witches aren't real."

"Didn't one chase Katherine?" Travis asked.

"She was crazed," Paula said.

"Maybe not. I am open to the idea."

"Of a witch?" James asked.

"Seems possible," Travis said. "I have a vivid imagination."

"I had a witch in my dream."

"From *The Wizard of Oz*?"

"How did you know?"

"Just a guess."

FORTY-TWO

RACHEL SPRINTED FROM THE SHED and didn't pause to catch her breath until she made it to the stagecoach road. She shot a glance behind her. Was anyone coming? Maybe James had managed to escape. She bent over with both hands on her knees and sucked in air. Should she go back to help him? She rejected the thought. She had to run. There was nothing she could do against Travis. James would have to fend for himself. Rachel cut her rest short and bolted into the woods.

The tree cover was reassuring, and Rachel focused on getting back to James' house and the safety of her car. She considered 911. What would be the nature of her emergency? A fight in the neighbor's shed? But she couldn't provide many details and would have a hard time explaining what they had been doing there in the first place.

Trespassing?

Yes, ma'am, because we were suspicious about trash bags in the shed of my ex-boyfriend's mother's lover.

Suspicious about what?

That he's in cahoots with a grave robber. We've got photos from the cemetery. We found bones and old jewelry in the bags. We think he's a witch.

No, over the phone the story sounded crazy. She would have to report it in person formally at the police station ASAP. She would insist they send a squad car to Travis' shed. Rachel surged forward. Step by step: get to the house, drive to the station, send help to James.

But what if I'm too late? What if James is captured? What if the witch tries to kill him? What could possibly explain the pendant? Katherine said we had to kill Travis.

Change of plan. She had to act immediately.

She pulled out her cell phone. The farfetched story didn't matter. She would throw in domestic violence. Travis was beating up his girlfriend's son. She didn't know the exact street address, but could describe the location. *Across the woods from James' house. Very helpful.*

Rachel fumbled to unlock the phone. She thought she heard her name, a whisper somewhere in the distance yet loud enough to hear. It seemed close, but filtered through a great distance as if from another dimension of *Star Trek.*

The voice was unsettling, and she broke out in gooseflesh. Rachel turned toward the sound that lingered in the stillness of the trees just behind her. She saw nothing but instinctively fled as fast as she could.

Her heart pounded, and she gripped her phone tightly as she ran, pumping both arms. Again came the whisper, close yet faraway. She screamed as the crack of dried leaves and broken branches sounded from somewhere out of sight. Footsteps? Was someone following her? Rachel kept her focus on the trail and continued to run.

A woman's sobs rose above the footsteps, haunting and despondent. Then came a voice: *Please stop, Rachel. Let me catch you. I can't stand the pain. Please help me.*

The use of her name filled her with dread. She whimpered through rapid breaths and forced herself onward. From somewhere behind, again came the whispers. Rachel focused on getting out of the woods. She blocked out the sights and sounds around her except for the contours and obstacles of the stagecoach road.

Rachel saw the light of the meadow come into view through the thinning trees. She dashed for James' property line, unsure if whatever was following her were still in pursuit and too afraid to turn around.

She ran until she'd cleared the woods. She slowed to catch her breath and focused on her car parked near the house. She looked behind her but saw nothing and pressed on. Her breathing was forced and shallow. She felt a cramp in her gut.

As Rachel approached her car, she saw a flicker near the old maple that towered above the edge of the driveway. A flash of fabric caught her eye as the train of a dress seemed to float and then disappear behind the tree trunk. Was it James' mother?

"Is anyone there?" Rachel called out and then proceeded cautiously. "Paula?"

Aware of the wind swaying its branches, Rachel studied the tree, attuned to any movement. Slowly emerged a woman in a tattered evening gown, her hair a brittle, gray tangle that failed to conceal her pained grimace.

Rachel strained to study the stranger. She moved fluidly,

limbs wavering within torn bands of water-stained fabric, her skin a translucent, dried veneer concealing bone. The wraith floated across the grass toward Rachel with a gracefulness that belied her skeletal features. Frantic eyes darted and burned within vacant sockets framed by the silvery snarl of hair.

My God. It's the witch that chased Katherine. It isn't Travis. Maybe the bags are hers.

The clouds shifted and sunlight hit the wraith's face. Rachel listened with horror as the ghostly whisper, the one from the woods, wafted from the woman's lips, enunciating her name as if the two syllables were two separate words.

"*Ra-chel.*"

Rachel screamed and backtracked toward the forest. She trembled and held her arms out defensively as she withdrew from the apparition.

"Stay away from me!"

The wraith whimpered and repeated the whisper of her name. The sounds were eerily amplified as if reverberating in a deserted cavern. Haunting echoes of spasmodic sobs surrounded her. Rachel scanned for a place to run. She refused to reenter the woods. She knew she would never come out. She focused on her car. She slapped her pocket and felt the keys. She tripped on a tree root as she edged backward and dropped her phone. She left it because it was too scary to take her eyes off the pathetic horror suspended above the grass.

Rachel improvised a plan to lure the witch toward her, closer to the woods, far enough away from the driveway. She would sprint past the witch and make for the car. The wraith drifted slowly, and Rachel was sure she could outrun her.

"Rachel," the woman pleaded as she drew closer. Her jaw opened wide, and she clutched at her breast as if corroding from within.

"My God. What happened to you?" Rachel continued to walk backward slowly, allowing the witch to gain ground and draw dangerously close.

"I don't know where I am." The wraith shook her head, bewildered and stricken. "I was thrust to a circle of hell and delivered to the Devil."

"You're scaring me. How do you know my name?"

The woman found a voice between sobs. "The witch told me. He ousted me. He did this. The Devil's near. I beg you to listen. Only you can save us. Get me out of here!"

The wraith extended her palm, and Rachel screamed. She darted left, then turned to the driveway and dashed for her car.

"Stop! Please listen. We haven't much time. We can both be free. The ring."

Rachel ignored her, and reached the driver's side door. She glanced back at the wraith, who appeared crestfallen by her escape. Rachel put the key in the ignition, and revved the engine. She threw the car into reverse, turned, and sped out of the driveway.

In the mirror she spied the witch, who drifted in front of the maple as Rachel turned right on the main road and hit the accelerator. The police station was in the center of town not far from Old Gold. She could be there in no time.

About a half-mile down the road, fabric from the water-stained evening gown flapped in the wind and obscured the passenger window behind her. Rachel gasped and tightly gripped the steering wheel. She slammed the brake, and then sped violently forward. She glanced back, and the window was clear.

Rachel started shaking and her gaze zoomed between windows and mirrors for any sign of the woman. She hunched over the wheel and accelerated. There were no cars in the intersection, so she flew through a red light without stopping or slowing.

Quiet sobs rose from behind her. Rachel gasped and reeled sideways. The wraith was in the car. A stench filled the air.

"Leave me alone!" Rachel shouted. "What do you want?"

The woman materialized on the passenger seat next to her, the gown expanding and consuming the armrest and footwell.

"The ring. It's mine," the wraith whispered and swiveled toward her.

"What? My God. Tell me what to do!" Rachel begged and stomped on the gas pedal.

"Give it back. Now! You must." The wraith pointed with a quivering finger to Rachel's hand as she clenched the steering wheel. "Only you can save us. The Devil's near. I'm burning! Stop the cycle of the witch. The bloodstone. Please help me!"

With sickening clarity, Rachel realized the ring had somehow lured the wraith, and so had Sophia's charm bracelet and Mia's necklace. In a twisted way, everything suddenly made sense. They'd been players in some sort of nightmare beyond their control.

They truly were linked, marked by circumstance and random bad luck, their lives marred by antique baubles.

Carol Stilton's locket in the shed was proof. It had to be Travis. The jewelry was cursed. The wraiths conjured from the grave needed it back. There was no escaping fate.

Everything Rachel had known in her heart to be true from the beginning was correct. All of it. Mia hadn't killed herself. Sophia hadn't run away.

It was the work of a witch.

Rachel understood and grabbed at the ring. It was still tight, so she spat on her hand and twisted the ring in her saliva. It loosened and she forced the ring over her knuckle. The wraith looked desperate and extended a leathery palm as Rachel pried the ring off her fingertip and flicked it away. The bloodstone floated with supernatural precision into the wraith's grasp, and she clenched it tight. Rachel watched the woman's expression of gratitude become vacant as she dissipated into vapor.

A man came out of nowhere, and Rachel slammed on the brake. She swerved to avoid him and careened off the road. The car went into a skid and hurtled toward a stockade fence. Rachel screamed and hit the windshield when the car crashed through the seven-foot wooden planks. She collapsed on the seat as the car rolled to a stop on the lawn.

FORTY-THREE

DYLAN PULLED INTO TRAVIS' DRIVEWAY and parked near the shed behind the house. He walked to the trailer to unload the canister and check on his captive. Aaron remained out cold on his back. Dylan lowered the door, extended the ramp, and wheeled the vacuum down to the driveway.

Travis came outside to join him.

"The gladiator," Travis said. They embraced, and Travis gripped Dylan's hands. "I owe you everything. You should be proud."

"I had no choice," Dylan said. "Life or death."

"More than you know. You stopped a lethal complication. I am most grateful. Your freedom is the best reward. I want you to have it. This will be your last day of service."

Dylan looked confused and alarmed. "What do you mean?"

"Your work here is complete. I need nothing more from the cemetery. Your performance was perfect. I could never have done it without you."

Dylan pointed to the vacuum canister. "Do you still want me to unload it?"

"Yes, exactly as you've done with the others."

Travis mounted the back of the trailer and carefully pulled Aaron's grass-stained white polo shirt over his head. He folded it and wiped sweat, blood, and drool from the fallen man's face. He climbed down and went to Dylan.

"You'll find a bucket and sponge in the shed. Wash up. Then do the same for Aaron. Leave him by the side of the driveway."

"Do you know him?"

"I know about him."

"What if he tries to get away?"

"He won't. That's his wife's car," Travis said, pointing. "Ex-wife, I should say. You can handle him. You've already proven it."

"And then what?"

"When you're finished, return to the cemetery. Take the tree planter and vacuum to the storage garage at the town park. Consider them a donation. You can use them in your future work. Lastly, delete the photos you took of headstones over the past few weeks. It's time for you to pursue new subjects."

"That's it?"

"I would introduce you to Sorinah, my mentor, but she's away right now."

"You're the only one who pays me any mind. Now I need to leave?"

"Yes. You will be back on your own. You will never see me again. You will not remember. Neither will you care as soon as you drive away."

"That's cold. I don't want to go."

"It's for the best. Trouble's near. You will be much better off without me."

"But I have nothing else. No one."

"You will solve that. You need a companion, an authentic connection with emotion. I am learning about it too. I will leave you with that impulse. What you feel for me right now you will find with someone else, but for real and to keep."

Travis opened his arms. Dylan hesitated, but his devotion to the mysterious man overpowered his disappointment and confusion, and they embraced again. An instinct told him not to overthink what he couldn't fathom.

"I've got two guests waiting inside, and time is running short," Travis said as he pulled away. "Finish the tasks. Return to your life. You will find someone to share it with."

Dylan watched as Travis disappeared into the house through the door to the kitchen. He covered his eyes with one hand. Were there tears? Why did he feel so lost? Everything was so confusing. Dylan knew he never wanted to be without Travis. This couldn't be good.

He dutifully pushed the vacuum toward the shed. He pulled out the bag and processed it exactly as he'd done before with the others on the platform. Carefully following his enigmatic boss' final instructions, he collected the bucket and sponge and hauled them with the vacuum back to the trailer.

The cool water felt good from the spigot on the side of the house. He filled the bucket and washed his face. He removed his uniform and cleaned away smears of dirt from his chest and neck with the sponge. Still wet, he walked to Aaron, grabbed him by both ankles, and pulled him until his legs bent over the back of the trailer. Dylan reached for his wrists and pulled him to a sitting position. He hoisted Aaron and dragged him to the grass near the spigot.

"This'll be fun," Dylan said as he filled the bucket. He lifted it high and dumped it all at once on Aaron's face. The big man gasped and shook his head as he sprang up.

"What the hell?" Aaron shouted and wiped at his eyes with his hands.

Dylan refilled the bucket and dipped the sponge. He tossed the sponge to Aaron before depositing the fresh bucket next to him. "Clean yourself up."

Aaron wiped his face and upper body, rinsed blood and dirt into the bucket, and repeated. He recognized Paula's car in the driveway in front of him.

"Where'd you take me?"

"Travis' house," Dylan said. "Need more water?"

Aaron nodded. Dylan refilled the bucket and brought it over.

"Why are you helping me?" Aaron asked.

"No reason."

"I wanted to kill you. I remember. I am going to the police."

Dylan thought about a response, but found it difficult to recall how he even knew the big guy sitting on the grass. An instinct told him it didn't matter.

"I have to go now," Dylan said. "Do as you like."

A sense of loss and gloom overcame Dylan, a sadness with no source he could pinpoint. He figured it was because his time with Travis was about to end. Was he fired? He felt foggy.

Your own life is the focus.

Had someone just spoken to him?

Find someone to make you happy. To share your life. Simply. Together, not alone.

It was like from a dream, fading even as he tried to cling to the words.

You are most worthy.

What was that? He knew it from somewhere. He felt a tinge of pride, and knew to his bones he deserved it. He took steps on the driveway, and it felt OK to move on.

He remembered drilling in grass to plant a tree. But where?

The only drill work he could recall was at the Korean War memorial near the traffic lights in the center of town. His boss had approved the order for a new row of trees to shield benches from traffic.

Without a word to Aaron, Dylan put on his Sussex shirt. Why was it ripped? He climbed in his truck and pulled away from Travis' property with the vacuum on the trailer. He knew he needed to get to the cemetery, to load equipment, and to store it in the bunker at the town park. It was a donation from a man he used to help landscape. But he'd moved back to Europe. That much he knew. And even that was vanishing. What country? What was the guy's name? No clue. It was frustrating to dig. It simply didn't matter.

FORTY-FOUR

THE MAN IN BLACK BOOTS marched to Rachel's car and peered in the window.

"Keep away from her," Sorinah warned as she appeared from behind the broken planks of the stockade fence.

Radu reeled as she spoke and sprang up. "This isn't your fight. I'm here for Travis, authorized by the coven you deserted. I know who you are."

"The coven betrayed us." Sorinah stepped forward and glared at Radu. Lacy maroon sleeves from her shawl billowed in the breeze as she pointed. "Get away from the car."

She forced him to the fence with angry eyes. His thick arms stuck above his head as if under arrest; his legs stiffened, suspended above the grass.

"Let's talk this out. I have no quarrel with you." Radu took a few deep breaths. A smile slowly spread across his chiseled face. The tight knit fabric of pale gray trousers stretched against muscle as he managed to bend his knees to rest his boot soles against the planks. "I can ease your path to reintegration."

"We will take our rightful place with or without your

permission." Sorinah glared at Radu, clenched her fists, and increased pressure.

"Don't make this harder than it needs to be."

"You are misguided and aggressive."

"You are weak and deluded."

Sorinah flattened his legs. "You will recognize the inevitability of change. Let Travis show you. He can help the coven."

"Such gyrations to avoid kills. It's wrong to fight our nature."

"Kills leave corpses to investigate. Time moves on and rewards innovation. It's arrogant to speak one language and then expect others with greater skill to stifle themselves. We speak more than one. Leave us alone." Sorinah felt a wave of dizziness and could scarcely finish speaking. "Go back to Bucharest," she barely managed to whisper.

Radu fixed a laser focus on Sorinah's stricken face and folded his arms as he descended to the grass.

"I gave you a chance," he said as he strode to the car with an arrogant gait.

Sorinah stared at Radu as she found herself frozen in place. She tried to contact Travis but failed. Her eyes darted about, but her limbs were immobilized. She watched herself glide helplessly to Radu's side by Rachel's car.

"You are a greater prize than the girl," Radu said. "Perhaps she's dead already. It's time to show you what it takes to face an elder." He took Sorinah's hand. "Close your eyes."

Sorinah obeyed. She tried desperately to prod Travis. When she felt her legs on stable ground, she surveyed the scene. Radu had transported them to Travis' property, just beyond the woods. They stood in the meadow in front of the stagecoach road.

Radu pointed to Travis' farmhouse.

"He thinks I'm barred from entry. But as a vampire needs an invitation, one of my own is already inside, linked to Travis by his seed. An intimate. Prepare, orphans, to be schooled."

FORTY-FIVE

AARON WATCHED THE TRUCK pull away and got to his feet. His body ached all over. What the hell was going on? The Sussex guy he'd hoped to apprehend had driven off. They'd fought furiously, he remembered. Apparently, he'd lost. Was his car still at the cemetery? At least it was convenient he'd ended up hand-delivered at the neighbor's place. But why was he left unattended and shirtless? Surely lover-boy didn't expect him to lie down and play dead.

He remembered the cemetery photos James had sent him, the reason for all the trouble and something about trash bags hidden in the shed.

Aaron crept to the corner of Travis' house and perused the grounds. He spied a small barn about a hundred feet away. That had to be it. He darted across the driveway and made it to the door undetected. It was simple to open, not even locked. *What an idiot.*

Aaron stepped inside and saw ten bags lined up on a platform exactly as James had described. The evidence was here. Travis was definitely in cahoots with the Sussex guy doing something illegal. Aaron decided to leave the bonanza for the police. But first, he would make Travis sing, try to explain himself, and squirm. He would shame lover-boy in front of Paula.

Aaron cracked the door and peeked outside. Travis stood waiting. He burst in with one hand and seized Aaron's jaw. Aaron tried to break his grip, but the murmurs in a foreign tongue somehow soothed him. The pulsating pressure of fingers felt pleasurable.

"Can I help you with something?" Travis asked.

"James told me about the bags. He sent pix from the cemetery. The guy that lives here is a criminal. A grave robber. I caught his accomplice this morning. He transports stuff here."

"For what?"

Travis pulled the door open and stepped inside.

"I don't know. To sell shit? It's robbery. Illegal. Not to mention, immoral."

Travis rolled his eyes. "Take out your phone. Delete the pix. You won't be needing them. I'm Travis, by the way."

Aaron obeyed and returned the phone to his pocket. "I'm Aaron." He extended his hand.

"Nice to meet you." They shook, and Travis smiled. "I sense you need an intervention." He shifted behind Aaron and gripped his shoulders. He squeezed and worked toward Aaron's neck before digging in with fingers and thumb to begin a massage.

Aaron took deep breaths. "That's so much better. Rejuvenating. There was a fight."

"I know."

"What's your deal? A masseuse?"

"Not really. But I'm good at it. It's surprising. Most things I touch go dark."

"Dark?"

"It's not my fault. I blame my origin."

Aaron exhaled deeply. "I hear an accent. From where?"

"Bucharest. But the source of darkness goes deeper. It's inside me."

"Why are you telling me this?" Aaron asked, but he wasn't alarmed. Everything felt perfect.

"To help explain my predicament. Take it as a kind of confession. My needs have entangled you and your family. I feel I owe it to you. I didn't plan it this way."

"Are they OK?"

"At this moment? Absolutely. But I cannot ignore that my need to refuel triggers unintended consequences. That's what I've learned. That's my conundrum."

"Refuel?"

"Fear empowers me. But it comes from a very dark place, often with great pain."

"You're OK with that?"

"I can justify it in terms of my own survival. My time on earth ends without refueling. It is transactional, not personal, not a choice. No one usually dies from it."

Aaron took deep breaths and swayed in sync with the pulsations. "I don't understand."

"Do you eat meat?" Travis asked.

Aaron halfway turned his head and nodded.

"Why?" Travis asked.

"To live. Protein. Energy. It tastes good."

"All neat and clean and packaged in the grocery store."

"Yes."

"The tidiness belies the bloody process that gets it there."

"I suppose it does. Never really thought about it."

"A focus on the pain would ruin things. The fuel I need is not so different. It comes from human fear. I don't dwell on it because the frights are temporary. No one remembers."

"Maybe you should be a vegetarian." Aaron felt confused and euphoric.

"I've been thinking the same."

Travis stopped the massage and pulled a polo from his shoulder bag.

Yours got ruined. Take this one. We're about the same size.

How can I hear you? Aaron looked puzzled and pulled on the shirt.

Just part of the process. No time to explain.

Travis put a hand on Aaron's shoulder and ushered him toward the door.

Aaron stopped in the entryway and held deep breaths, in and out. Travis' grip felt reassuring and intoxicating, supercharged with endorphins. A step outside might break the connection. He wanted to linger, forever if possible. Paula had good judgment.

"We've got to move on," Travis said aloud after a minute. "There's danger about. James and Paula are inside. You'll be reunited later. You've got to stay hidden. No one knows you are here. Keep on alert. I don't know what to expect. You've already proven yourself a fighter. Now, you're revitalized."

Await my call. Be ready to protect your family.

Aaron nodded and stepped onto the lawn. He grabbed Travis' hand. *I'll be ready.*

FORTY-SIX

TRAVIS KNEW THE BATTLE WAS ON when Sorinah fell silent. He'd seen a vision of Radu pinned to a fence, but then it had disintegrated along with the last pulse from his mentor.

Sorinah had stolen away hours ago to witness Travis' handiwork and to shield Rachel from Radu's interference. The conjuring was risky. Insecurity had driven him to proceed no matter the outcome. Travis had no idea how he measured up against an elder. Now he was fully empowered, but Sorinah and Rachel's fates hung in the balance.

Travis scoured his parents' manuscripts and sharpened his arsenal. He'd underestimated the coven. He was now on the defensive, operating blindly and unsure of Radu's whereabouts. He hadn't even the seed of a plan. Only his property was secure.

"Why are you hiding?" voices called from the living room.

Travis realized he'd left Paula and James unattended while he'd immersed himself in his books. Should he send them home? He had no idea what to do. Radu knew where they lived. But there might be a window for their escape to the hospital while his foe struggled against Sorinah.

"Be right there," Travis called out as he descended the stairs and then found them in the living room. "Forgive me. Time got away."

Paula looked up and smiled. "James seems perfectly fine."

James sat next to her. "Just a small bump. I feel good."

"Excellent," Travis said. "You can both get to the hospital to see Katherine."

James stood from the couch. "I have plans with my dad."

"Think I'll stay the afternoon," Paula said. "You can meet your dad at the hospital."

Travis looked at her, surprised.

"I need a break," Paula continued. "Katherine's probably zoned out anyway."

"It's best you go with James. Make sure they're both doing OK."

"Only after a kiss goodbye," Paula said. She tapped James. "It's something you can tell your father about."

Paula stood and James eased away from the couch. She motioned to Travis, and he obligingly pecked her on the cheek. What was she doing in front of her son?

"That won't do." Paula grabbed Travis and pulled him close. He tried to withdraw, but with a sudden thrust, she pushed him to the couch and got on top of him. Paula arched her back and planted both hands on his pecs. Travis closed his eyes in embarrassment. James looked away.

Paula reached behind a sofa cushion and procured a dagger. Travis opened his eyes as she hoisted it and thrust it at his chest. He managed to block, and it lanced his upper arm. Travis yelled and rolled from the couch onto the floor.

Paula gripped the dagger and stalked him as he scrambled.

"You think you haven't caused pain? You think you're some kind of hero?" Paula smirked as she drew closer and raised her weapon.

Travis recognized the dagger from the cottage attack in Bucharest. Alexandra's black serpentine blade was unmistakable.

Paula slashed at his face.

Stop her, Travis transferred to James.

James leaped at his mother and pried the weapon from her hand. It crashed to the floor, and Travis snapped it up.

"How did you get this?" Travis demanded and jumped to his feet. Blood soaked the sleeve of his polo and dripped down his arm as he pointed the blade toward Paula and locked eyes with James.

Cotton and tape under the bathroom sink.

James nodded and ran out.

"You don't need me to tell you," Paula said. "Justice shall be served."

A deep unease gripped Travis as he realized Radu's control over Paula had superseded the protection of his property.

Travis kept both eyes on Paula and both hands on the dagger as James returned with supplies. He blotted the wound before wrapping it with cotton and tight tape.

This'll hold, James transferred. *It's not deep.*

"My son's not your slave!" Paula shouted. "You will die for this abomination."

"Let's see how much your new master cares for you," Travis answered.

In a move so quick it blurred, Travis restrained Paula from behind with his injured arm and put the blade at her throat with the other. "Transfer your peril to him now; I know you can do it. Tell him to release Sorinah."

Paula closed her eyes and trembled.

The room darkened as a murky haze gathered outside the picture window then turned to black as it swirled and passed through the glass. Radu rose up from vapor and faced Travis.

"You were barred from here," Travis stated in disbelief. He studied the enforcer's imposing build, and tightened his grip on Paula.

"How little you know, orphan."

"Where's Sorinah?"

"Bound to a tree, awaiting your surrender."

Travis readied the dagger. "Free her or Paula dies and it's on your hands."

Radu scoffed. "Why would I care? Her sacrifice only strengthens what I absorb from the spell. A soft heart will be your undoing. Your dalliances with humans make me sick."

Radu held an arm aloft, and James shuddered. Travis watched him twist and buckle under an invisible force that drew him toward the intruder.

I can't fight it! James transferred to Travis. *What's happening?*

James strained and flailed as he fought the pull toward Radu. He felt himself pivot, and an elbow locked in place around his neck.

"I'll kill him. I'll snap your slave's neck like a chicken bone."

Paula started sobbing. "Please, stop. Let us go."

"It's all up to Travis," Radu said. "He's the root of all the trouble. You should have listened to your daughter last night."

Travis released his hold on Paula and rested a hand on her shoulder.

"Leave them out of this," Travis said as he pointed the dagger at Radu. "They are innocent. This is between us."

"Spare me your nobility. You use mortals as pawns as it suits you." Radu shoved James to the floor, and he scrambled away. "We gain only headaches from two more deaths. Your punishment is all that matters. Your mission is finished. A death sentence awaits."

Travis fired the dagger across the room; it grazed Radu's neck before crashing into the window. The enforcer rocked and grimaced. Travis seized control of his mobility.

Radu seethed as he strained to clutch at the wound. "You may have drawn first blood, but you can't hold me for long."

"Take me to Sorinah," Travis demanded, and backed up his command with a nerve bolt that cascaded down Radu's spine.

Radu groaned. "You'll die for that, orphan." Muscles flexed and trembled within the tailored knit fabric of his uniform, testing the strength of the invisible constraints. The enforcer glared at Travis as he found himself hovering just inches above the floor.

Travis forced Radu through the kitchen toward the back door. The enforcer began to sweat from the strain of resistance but was unable to fight Travis' thrust out of the house. Paula and James followed silently behind, linked to opposite masters. From the lawn behind the shed, Travis canvassed the grounds for Sorinah or Aaron. The mental effort to dominate Radu kept Travis from using transference.

"Take me to Sorinah, or I'll find her myself. Your spell dies along with you."

Travis shot another bolt, and Radu winced as his black boots came to rest on grass.

"Use your legs. It's faster. If you want to live, march quickly."

Radu regained limited control and led the procession across the meadow toward the stagecoach road. As they reached brambles at the edge of the forest, Radu stopped.

"Look up. She's near. The treasure is yours to find, tethered in the pines."

"Don't play games with me," Travis sneered.

"I did my part. I can't make you see her."

Travis scowled at Radu and froze him to the spot. He then turned to James. "Guard your mother, and keep her away from him."

James nodded, grasped Paula's arm, and backed away from the stagecoach road.

"Don't touch me," she said, but didn't struggle. "I can walk on my own."

James swiveled behind her and placed both hands around her waist as he pushed. "It's for your own good. That man is evil."

"What about Travis?"

James herded her away from the woods. "He's different. You knew that before."

Travis treaded onto the stagecoach road and scoured the treetops. If he didn't find Sorinah soon, within minutes, he would kill Radu to break the spell. Empowerment through the wraiths had worked. He felt stronger than ever, fueled to fight even as the drain of restraining Radu consumed energy. He had the reserves necessary to launch nerve bolts or objects.

A shriek in the woods somewhere high above stopped him in his tracks. Stabs of sunlight pierced the foliage but wavered, and shadows played tricks. Travis watched the branches sway, and he detected a wail on the wind. He craned his neck. A woman's cries. His heart raced, and his eyes darted about. He heard a whisper in the distance and stole toward it deeper into the woods. He strained to listen again.

"Help me, Travis." The words came quietly, but unmistakably.

Travis crept forward.

"Sorinah? Where are you?"

He studied the branches swaying amid flecks of sunlight. A moan brought his focus higher. A spot of color. Sixty feet above. Something maroon contrasted green and brown. Wavy brunette streamers hung down, beckoning in the breeze.

"I see you!" Travis called out. "Hold on, Sorinah. I've got you!"

He sprinted to the spot below what looked like a bundle suspended from a lone, precarious branch over the stagecoach road.

A thick cascade of Sorinah's hair wafted below the bale, protruding from the bottom and lengthened by gravity. A rope constrained the cocoon and held her upside down. Her body seemed truncated, curled in a fetal position. The shawl was knotted at her ankles by a single cord that connected to the branch. The bundle swayed sickeningly, slowly.

Travis racked his brain to devise a rescue while restraining Radu.

With no time to spare, he decided to snap the branch and break her fall. He targeted the critical limb, and it began to creak and sway. A scream from within the bundle chilled him as the branch bowed, cracked, and then splintered as it snapped free. The bundle plummeted, and Travis seized control of its descent, cushioning its landing on the pathway.

The maroon bale lay motionless, and Travis rolled it over. He gasped when he saw Sorinah's hair crudely attached to the head of a scarecrow with duct tape and thread. It appeared she'd been scalped. He tore at the bundle.

A chuckle rose from behind, and Travis yelped.

"So easily distracted." Radu sneered and loomed over him. "Concentration of a mule. I knew you couldn't hold me."

Travis found himself suspended just above the ground, immobilized.

"You lied. Where is she?" Travis drifted higher, and his body tilted prone to the stagecoach road, face down, limbs outstretched and useless.

"You'll be reunited soon enough," Radu said as he strode along the pathway toward the farmhouse with Travis directly in front of him, "in hell."

Travis floated backward, nose-to-nose with Radu as they moved through the woods.

The procession continued with only the crunch of boots as Radu tramped and glowered at his foe. As they approached Travis' property, the enforcer halted.

"Remember this?"

He smiled and unfastened his belt. He pulled it free,

folded it once, and snapped the leather in Travis' face. The air brushed his nose, but only his eyes flinched.

"All this time, you thought you'd escaped the beating. I don't leave assignments unfinished."

Radu stepped aside and traced a line with his fingers down Travis' arm to his midsection. He shoved Travis' shirt to his neck and then pulled it over his head. He bunched it and tossed it to the weeds. Radu unfurled the belt and lashed out several times in succession. Travis winced and grunted with each crack.

"You were supposed to be taken alive. It's too late for that now. Blame my tumescence."

Radu flogged his prey, deliberately, pausing between strokes to relish the result from different angles.

"Bringing down arrogance bestows power. I'm feeding from you, aroused by your comeuppance. You squandered strength and beauty solely for revenge. I knew you'd grow formidable. I warned the council. You should have been satisfied with getting away."

Travis felt the burn following each sting while he probed to breach Radu's hold.

"You can't kill me without a trial," Travis wheezed. "There are limits."

"I'll deal with the fallout later. Elisabeta can be reasoned with. Her own political survival depends on it." Radu planted himself in front of Travis. They locked eyes.

"The traditionalists still control the council. Your techniques are dangerous and untested. Fear and amnesia invite as much suspicion as deaths. And your softness is an insult to the original disciples." Radu took a step back to study his captive and siphon fuel. With his fingertips he wiped sweat from Travis' brow to catalyze absorption. The gentleness belied his hate.

"You look like a bull on a spit with no rod and no pit. Time to add some flame."

Radu resumed the march with Travis splayed out in front of him, floating backward, until they emerged from the stagecoach road. The enforcer strode in front of his foe and left him suspended above the brambles. He motioned to Paula, who broke free of her son's grip and ran toward her master.

Tie your son.

Radu tossed Paula the belt. She grabbed it and turned toward James. He backed away, but she sprinted and unleashed a barrage of lashes. James tripped, and Paula leapt upon him, knocking him to the ground while struggling to bind his wrists.

Radu smirked and transported Travis to a marshy glade behind cattails at the edge of the forest. Travis saw a collection of stones arranged in a pattern. He recognized the pyrokinetic formation. His frustration and panic grew as attempts to free himself from Radu's hold proved useless. Transference was blocked. Sweat dripped into his eyes.

"I need to know if Sorinah's alive!" Travis shouted. "Grant me that."

"Oh, she's watching. Her response to your incineration will determine the length and degree of her punishment."

Travis stared at the rock formation, and an instant later an inferno ignited, blazing within the stones, smokeless, arising from mud. He felt himself propelled toward the flames.

Radu laughed and moved to the edge of the stones. "I want to see this up close. You've been living on borrowed time, all the while planning revenge. You should have perished along with your parents. At last justice is served."

Travis felt his legs rise and his arms come to his sides. His elevation dropped as he floated headfirst toward the flames. He struggled but was helpless to fight. His body leveled and his face veered away from the blaze and grazed Radu's boot. He elevated slowly until he was face-to-face with his captor, prone but eye-level. The enforcer stood resolute, primed by his dominance, hands on his hips. He beamed with a sneering look of triumph.

"You'll roast slowly, not all at once as tradition dictates. I know you like innovation."

"Please. I beg you. There must be another way." Travis' body was slick with sweat and it dripped from his chin and torso.

"There isn't. Banishment is serious. Your parents understood. You had no right to leave."

"Take me alive. I can help the coven. I can share advancements."

"I like the old ways."

Travis watched with horror as he shifted away from Radu and drifted over the blaze, facedown, headfirst. The tallest flames danced high enough to scorch him. He screamed in pain and rage. He saw the forest flash into view as he rotated on the other side of the inferno and then roasted on the return pass.

"You're still too high. We're just getting started."

Travis drifted by Radu and felt his elevation jerk

downward. He watched the mud turn to flame and back to mud as he passed over the blaze. He closed his eyes tightly as he felt himself twist, and then sear, and then cool again.

He opened his eyes and glimpsed Radu's ebullient swagger.

In that instant, Aaron tackled Radu.

Travis dropped to the ground. Aaron coiled around Radu and rolled. Travis immediately seized control of Radu to immobilize him. Aaron climbed off his suddenly calcified opponent.

Thank you. I'll handle him. Protect Paula and James. Get them into the house!

Aaron nodded and sprinted away.

Travis elevated Radu to an upright position, suspended just in front of him.

"I'll kill you now." Travis stared into Radu's eyes, livid. "Tell me where she is."

"Never, orphan."

"I'll drop you in your own fire." Travis sent Radu aloft, his boots tempting the flames.

Radu glared at Travis and managed to spit. The inferno immediately extinguished.

"Anything better?"

Travis sent a nerve bolt that visibly rocked Radu as he floated amid vapor rising from mud.

"Impressive," Radu said. "But not enough. It won't kill me. My power exceeds yours."

Travis said nothing and prepared to fire a second jolt.

"Only one thing will do," Radu said. "I'll even surrender."

Travis raised his eyebrows. "Speak."

"Fight me the old way. I like the old ways."

"I've already beaten you. You're done. Release Sorinah." Travis sent a nerve bolt and watched Radu spasm. "I'll kill you with the next." Travis felt a wave of dizziness as his weapon drained power.

"Try it. I find it invigorating."

Travis glared at Radu. He didn't like being goaded and fired another bolt to his spine with as much force as he could. It rocked Radu's body, and his foe could not contain a groan, but when the motion stilled, he smirked. Travis gulped deep lungfuls of air.

"You tried to kill me with magic and failed," Radu said. "I can block it. You have no answer for that. Face me. Make me surrender. Sorinah dies otherwise. You can't suspend me forever. Already your reserves are draining. I see the strain. Sweat betrays you. You cannot hide."

Travis studied his foe. Was it a trick? What else could he do? Did he dare cede his advantage? The time had arrived to risk everything. He had to see if his family's spell produced enough power to defeat an elder. He'd dreamed of revenge ever since the night of the pyre. It had motivated his advancement and driven him to conjure the wraiths. He had to take the chance to force his family's foe to surrender, the hardliner responsible for their banishment.

Travis lowered Radu into the steaming circle.

"How do I know you'll keep your word?" Travis asked. "It means nothing to me."

"You haven't much choice. Restrain me until your power drains, if you like. So much for the wraiths. It will prove your supposed superiority is nothing but a farce."

"One of us must surrender," Travis said.

Radu managed a nod, and Travis released him.

The enforcer shook out his limbs and took deep breaths. He paused before tramping toward Travis. "I've dreamed of this moment. Played it out in my mind, but this is better."

Travis put up his fists. The two men circled within the rocks.

Radu lunged at Travis, tackling him and forcing him to the ground on his back. He planted his legs on both sides of Travis' torso and pinned him while he locked both hands on his throat and squeezed. Travis thrashed from side to side and attempted to roll. But Radu held firm and continued the relentless pressure on his neck.

"Surrender, or I'll kill you now." Radu stared into Travis' face and tightened his grip.

Travis summoned reserves to send a bolt to Radu's spine and thrust his arms upward to grab his foe's neck with both hands. Blood sprang from Radu's nose, and he gasped with surprise as it dripped down but used his top position to his advantage. He pushed against Travis with all his strength and weight.

Travis held firm and applied more pressure to Radu's neck.

Both men's arms trembled and strained against vice-like clamps. Fingers dug in deeply to penetrate thick neck muscle to crush the other's airway.

The expression of confidence on Radu's face shifted to alarm as blood streamed from his nostrils and he found himself struggling to breathe. Radu released his grip and grabbed Travis' forearms. The enforcer wheezed and groaned as he tried to leverage his position on top to wrest Travis' hands from his neck.

Sweat drenched both men as they remained locked in combat. Radu's arms strained and trembled as he pulled, but he was unable to stop the counterattack that dug into the wound from the dagger on his neck. He raised his haunches higher to apply more outward pressure.

Radu slowly lost control of the position of dominance as the shift in body weight allowed Travis to force him sideways and to pounce on him. Travis planted his legs, arched his back, and squeezed relentlessly on Radu's throat, his grip unfazed by his opponent's desperate attempts to dislodge his arms.

As Travis felt Radu weaken, he shook one arm free and punched him in the face. Gulping for air, Radu attempted to block, but Travis landed another blow.

Travis sent another bolt. Radu clenched his eyes and bellowed.

Travis rolled and pinned Radu's arm behind his back as he forced him toward the stones. He pushed Radu's face toward the searing heat of rock.

Radu screamed and thrashed while Travis shoved his cheek against the surface. Radu bucked to escape the pain, but Travis shoved it again despite the smell of burning flesh.

"I surrender!" Radu shouted.

"Do you swear?"

"Yes. I swear."

Travis rolled away from the stones and jumped up while Radu moaned on his back, the left side of his face oozing below the eye.

"Where is Sorinah?" Travis shouted. "Release her!"

Radu closed his eyes. In the next instant, Travis felt Sorinah's presence.

I'm free. I can see you through the trees, Sorinah transferred to Travis. *I bore witness to his surrender.*

You're alive. I am so grateful. Are you hurt?

I can move. I can free myself. I'm coming now.

Travis surveyed the woods. He heard the snap of branches across the glade and watched as Sorinah emerged from a hiding spot. She stepped carefully with bare feet onto the wet ground of the marsh. She was nude and bruised, her scalp bloodied and pocked with clumps of hair. Travis rushed to her side and embraced her. Together they limped back to the clearing and confronted Radu.

"You bastard," Travis said. "You did this."

Radu frowned unapologetically and sat up.

An inferno within the stones suddenly burst to life, soaring, and they jumped away.

"What are you doing?" Travis demanded and glared at Radu.

Radu winced and shook his head. "It's not me. I swear it."

Travis was transfixed as a white hot ember rose above the flames, extended tendrils, and morphed into a glowing sphere that floated toward them.

Elisabeta emerged from the luminescence and loomed over Radu. A shimmering aura cloaked her translucent, billowing presence. Only the ethereal beauty of her face sharpened.

"What do you have to say for yourself?" Elisabeta asked.

"He drew first blood," Radu said. "I had to defend myself."

"Nonsense. Your conduct was a deliberate affront to my orders."

"I was authorized to use any tools at my disposal."

"Not against the mortals under his protection."

"It was a means to subdue him. He would never cooperate otherwise."

"You explained nothing and delivered only hostility. He was to be taken alive."

"Surely you understand. It was the fog of battle."

"You've always considered yourself above the law." Elisabeta glared, and Radu averted his gaze. "Your allies witnessed your surrender and are not impressed."

"The traditionalists would never betray me."

"You betrayed the coven with your hubris."

Radu struggled to his feet, stained with sweat and blood. "I did what I thought was right. Then and now. He will weaken us."

"You cannot act unilaterally."

"I understand the threats more than—"

"Silence."

Radu froze, and Elisabeta pointed at the enforcer.

"He has proven himself. You have been humbled in surrender and barred from the council."

Radu covered his eyes.

"The council, including hardliners, has ruled to reaccept Travis, as was the original intention."

Travis and Sorinah exchanged looks.

"It is the coven's desire to consider his methods." Elisabeta raised both arms, and Radu bowed. "You will contemplate your folly, for as long as it takes."

"Yes, Elisabeta."

"The coven will tend to your wounds before your isolation."

Erratic white tendrils flashed from her opened palms and encircled the enforcer. He stood stoically and closed his eyes. Radu levitated even as he shrunk to a glowing ember and hovered above the blaze. In a moment, he was gone.

Travis and Sorinah joined hands and turned to face Elisabeta.

"What now?" Travis asked.

Elisabeta came to rest just above the ground in front of them, still shimmering. She focused on Travis.

"You have the propensity to empathize. You've proved it here. There were others you could have killed, but you chose mercy and restraint, attributes hardliners like Radu cannot fathom. It is seen as weakness. You exacted no more cruelty than prescribed by our dictates. It tells us you are capable of pardoning your own for the death of your parents."

"Is it true? The coven always feared my revenge," Travis said. "The coven lied that I would be spared and sent the assassin to kill me and to steal from my parents."

"Alexandra acted of her own accord. It was never part of the plan for her to kill you or Lucian. She was blinded by her own greed: your parents' possessions, the silver, and whatever spells she could study. She would have faced the wrath of those in the coven who'd championed your survival. But you dispatched her. It was justified."

Travis focused on the weathered grace of Elisabeta's face as he spoke.

"You burned my parents. Why allow me to live?"

"The coven always knew of your potential. Your parents were gifted. Had you remained in Bucharest, in banishment, you would have perished alone in the woods. Had the coven received you immediately, you would have been blinded by hate and obsessed with revenge, an outcast. No one would trust you. So we arranged your keep at an outpost in Transylvania. Time was needed to intervene."

"Transylvania was a trap. Lucian told me."

"You would have found protection. Any plot would have been illegal and stopped. Time would have tempered the poisonous climate."

"Already so much time has passed."

"And no more should be wasted."

"Why accept me now?"

"The wraiths exposed your whereabouts. We watched. The elders are convinced of your talent and ability to innovate. They are more open to change. We are united in the offer of re-admittance, if only you can also forgive."

Travis looked into Elisabeta's eyes. *Can I trust you?*

Yes. You must. There is no other way.

Travis pondered her words and extended his hand, awash with relief and regret.

"What shall become of me?" Sorinah asked in a timorous whisper.

Elisabeta paused to consider the nude and vulnerable mentor who'd shielded Travis. "You deserted of your own accord."

"Because my parents were double-crossed."

"You've been alone for so long. Do you wish to return?"

"With Travis?" Sorinah asked. "Yes."

"Then you'd best approach us."

"How do we know it's not a trick?" Travis asked.

"The inferno," Elisabeta said as she pointed. "You have the power to extinguish it."

"Pyrokinesis is not a family weapon," Travis said. "The fire was Radu's."

"Access your core within. You will feel it, a connection from the coven. It is exactly as with the illumination from your parents. I watched as they enlightened you. The answers are there."

Travis closed his eyes. He felt a stirring within, the same as what Monica and Victor had transferred from the pyre. He sharpened his focus. The blaze withered, flickered, and died. Soon only vapor drifted above the marsh within the formation of stones.

Well done. We expect you soon. Elisabeta sailed away as a shimmering ember on the wind. *Welcome home.*

FORTY-SEVEN

"TELL ME AGAIN WHAT HAPPENED?"

Paula had no recollection of stabbing Travis or attacking her son. She sat on the couch and changed the cotton of his makeshift bandage. "It's not much more than a scratch. You must heal quickly." When she finished, he rolled down his sleeve.

"An intruder broke in." Travis put away the first aid supplies and retrieved the dagger from the floor. "He stalked me from back home, a troublemaker."

"Looks like something from a museum," Paula said, looking at it.

"He saw it as a trophy."

"What about the belt?" Aaron asked, and held it up. "She had James tied with it."

James raised his eyebrows and said nothing. He sat on a chair opposite his father.

"I don't remember doing it," Paula said. "It's as if I'd been drugged or was possessed."

"James said you've been acting strange all week," Aaron noted.

"What are you even doing here?" Paula asked her ex-husband.

"I'm hoping to visit Katherine. James told me about her psychosis or whatever. Maybe you should make an appointment with her doctor for yourself."

"What happened to your lip? Another bar fight?"

Travis raised the dagger. "Quiet, please."

He placed it on the table and transferred to the men, *Wait here. We need a moment alone.*

Travis extended a hand to Paula, and she stood from the couch. He led her to the kitchen and pulled a chair out from the table. Paula sat, and he leaned against the counter across from her.

"Thanks for dressing the cut," Travis said.

"It doesn't seem bad. Is the stalker gone? Are we safe?" Paula locked on his eyes. "I don't even know what happened today. It's scary. I want things to go back to normal."

"Yes, we're safe. The stalker surrendered." Travis folded his arms and exhaled. "The whole town can relax. My business here is ended. I will be returning to Bucharest."

"We knew you wouldn't be here for long, but I thought there would be more time." Paula paused and smiled. "So what now?"

"We need to say goodbye. You need to pick up Katherine. She needs you and her father. She's recovered from the stupor."

"How do you know?"

"The same way I know many things."

"Will I see you again?"

"Probably not. But you won't care. You will remember

only that my stint ended and I had to leave. Nothing to regret."

"I'll miss you."

"No, you won't. Not from the moment you pull away." Travis motioned to the backdoor. "It sounds harsh, but it's for the best. Let's go outside."

They walked silently to the driveway and leaned against the car.

"I need to feel again," Paula said. "Like before I met you. Right now, I'm numb. I think I'm going crazy. The whole afternoon's a blur. We found James in the shed, then nothing."

"I'm sorry I pulled you in and everyone else. Pain for some in town will linger forever. I've been deluded. I can no longer ignore it."

"Ignore what?"

"Pain and danger. Some is erased, but there's always more."

"I've been conflicted, irresponsible, and out of control. You brought it out in me. My worst behavior. But even now, something seems to soothe it all away. I recognize I should care. But I don't. A feeling tells me everything's quite fine although I know it's not. Katherine's in trouble because of me and my actions. That's all I know is true."

"It's not your fault," Travis said. "She'll be fine. You'll see tonight."

"I thought I loved you. Maybe I do. It happened so quickly. Though I always knew I couldn't have you, I still want you now despite all my confusion."

"I'll never know what's real." Travis hugged Paula. "Were you only under my spell?"

Paula smiled and touched Travis' cheek. "You were under mine. At least we had one full night together. Maybe it was enough. All that was meant to be."

"It helped me more than you know. Emotion is new." Travis touched Paula's hand, and beamed. "Wait here for the guys. They need a ride."

Paula took out her keys and got behind the wheel. She cranked the AC.

Travis waved before he went inside. He returned to the living room and found Aaron and James sitting on the couch.

"You saved my life out there," Travis said to Aaron and took his hand. "All of ours."

"Who was that guy?"

"A long-time nemesis."

"Glad I could help."

"What took you so long?"

"I was waiting for your call. Like you told me."

"Where did you hide?"

"In the shed. I dozed off, but something woke me up. One of the bags shook all by itself. It creeped me out. Maybe you've got rats. I got the hell out of there." Aaron paused to think. "Then I saw the blaze and came running."

"Just in time," Travis said. He turned to James. "How'd it play out with your mom?"

"She tied my wrists with the belt. I fought at first, but gave up. I knew it wasn't her. Dad raced by and then shot back and brought us inside. My mom turned normal and passed out."

"It's time to forget this day and shift to the future." Travis exhaled and looked at Aaron. "You've got to pick up your car. Paula will take you."

James and Aaron exchanged glances, stood, and followed Travis into the kitchen and out to the driveway. Her Subaru idled and Paula waved from inside. Travis opened the back passenger door and motioned to Aaron.

"You can do better," Travis said and helped Aaron climb in. "Start tonight with Katherine."

Aaron nodded and closed the door.

Travis stood in front of James. *Time to focus on a plan.*

James smiled, opened the passenger door, and climbed in next to his mother.

"First stop, the cemetery," James said. "Next stop, the hospital."

"That's all you need to remember," Travis whispered through the gap of the door before it closed.

Travis stepped back and watched as Paula turned the car around and pulled out of the driveway. No one turned to look. Travis knew already they were free.

He waited until the car climbed a knoll and the taillights disappeared in the dusk.

FORTY-EIGHT

"YOU'RE LOOKING WELL," Travis said as Sorinah emerged from her bedroom. "I'm glad you slept in. The head scarf suits you."

He motioned to the breakfast spread on the table and waited until she settled into a chair.

"I'm still woozy," Sorinah said. "Radu left me with a headache." She poured a cup of coffee from the French press on the table. "So begins a new day."

"Have you petitioned Elisabeta?"

"Yes. Overnight. We can both call the coven home."

"I hope that's possible."

"This time will be different. You return as an elder with a new language to teach. And beyond that, you need the company of witches." Sorinah took a sip from her cup. "You've become confused. Stop toying with mortals."

"Why?"

"I don't like the interventions. You instilled them with impulses to take forward to improve themselves. It's a residue, like my headache."

"I see no harm."

"It is not your place. You are not a god burdened with the well-being of all creation. You are a witch of high order by birthright with the responsibility to fulfill your potential. Busying yourself with the emotional lives of mortals is an unnecessary diversion and, frankly, foolish. You have no mandate to justify your existence."

Travis breathed deeply and paused. "Without the goal of revenge, I have no existence."

"What are you saying?"

"There will be no more conjurings."

"The coven will condone them."

"I needed the power to grow strong enough to fight. There is no need for more."

"You need fuel to survive."

"I can subsist on control alone." Travis locked eyes with Sorinah. "I want to evolve. I no longer see much difference between the hardliners and my own tactics. The distinction was a delusion. My parents sought progress, but the ancestral spell at its core is savage black magic."

"Again, you are confused," Sorinah said. "Killing is pitiless, but fear spun from the spell is erased. It's victimless. Except for mistakes. But already you've learned to avoid them."

"There's something worse."

Sorinah put down her cup. "What?"

"The process is torturous: desecration, conjurings from the grave." Travis exhaled slowly and shook his head before continuing. "The wraiths were in agony, pulled to hell with no warning. The magic does it. My parents never knew."

Sorinah summoned a soft smile. "There was a time of heaven and hell, but I don't think it exists anymore. We are bound to the essence of our origin. Your nature is dark. All magic exacts a price. At least yours is temporary."

Travis looked dour, and his gray-green eyes narrowed into slits.

"I know what I saw, and I made mistakes. I killed Mia. And I liked it. I enjoyed the rush, the same as a hardliner. I never told you. We are not good witches."

"Using fear was never an attempt at goodness. It was a cynical survival strategy to avoid detection. Corpses are investigated and lead to trouble."

"I will find a better way."

"We are descendants of the Devil. Only certain conditions bestow power. We perish without it. You cannot fight your nature."

"I do not wish to fight it but to adapt it."

"To what?"

"To feed from the fear produced by mortals themselves. Plenty exists without need of my contribution. There's no shortage of pain. I will advance my parents' work in ways the ancestors couldn't imagine. The spells are ancient. Desecration was powerful fuel for primitive times. But everything evolves. Fear spawned by humans is still borne of evil. The Devil would approve."

Travis took Sorinah's hands in his own.

"I won't be returning to the coven. At least, not yet. I must test this hypothesis. There is more for me to learn here. The coven will understand and bear witness. They no longer fear my revenge. Elisabeta is open to my research. Radu's sway has ended."

Sorinah considered his words before finding her own.

"Don't lose sight of everything we've worked for. You've grown strong, avenged your parents, and gained the respect of the coven. Perhaps you've already done enough. It is time to sire an heir. That's the way forward. Your bloodline is potent. Let your offspring continue the work. It takes generations."

Travis squeezed her hand.

"I witnessed my parents' torture. Something went wrong. I froze and became an outcast. I didn't know it at the time, but the trauma of the pyre damaged me. I focused only on revenge. I grew stoic, like you."

Travis smiled, then continued softly, "It doesn't bother you, but it bothers me. I think there's something more. I want to feel. We are both allowed to try. There is nothing written against it."

Sorinah smiled and squeezed back.

Already you feel. You just don't recognize it. I take the blame for your isolation. It was all I knew myself. I'll await you in Bucharest.

She paused and touched his cheek.

Once you've come to your senses. Feelings are dangerous.

FORTY-NINE

THE BURLINGTON FREE PRESS ran a front page story with the headline, *"Last Clique Member Crashes Car,"* and termed Rachel's accident and the ongoing investigation of the high school threesome *"mysterious, troubling, and fraught with unanswered questions."*

The article quoted friends and family members who speculated that fear of separation and an uncertain future were the culprits behind the tragic events. A secret, misbegotten pact was suspected. Rachel had granted an interview from her hospital bed but could offer no explanation for losing control or for diving at high speed without a seatbelt. She didn't know where she'd been headed and could only recall a morning visit with her ex-boyfriend. Doctors attributed her vagueness to short-term PTSD and thought her memory might improve over time.

James was interviewed by the local TV station as Rachel's ex and a friend to Mia and Sophia. He refused to believe Rachel's crash could have been intentional. She must have swerved to avoid something and lost control, he said, and yes, sometimes she liked to go fast. There were two speeding tickets to prove it. As for Sophia, he guessed her body would be discovered at some point, the victim of foul play, not suicide. The killer was still at large. And Mia had hung herself on the doorknob accidentally, pretending to be melodramatic on video. Some kind of game or prank gone bad.

Travis waited a few days before mustering the will to visit Paula. It vexed him that he didn't know how she felt. Their night together still filled him with excitement. He'd removed all control, and they'd both luxuriated in what seemed like stolen hours. But the spell contaminated any conclusions because it had initiated the whole thing. *That damn basket of muffins.* He hiked the stagecoach road and realized he had no idea how she might react when she saw him. He wore a fitted blue polo he knew she liked. Maybe it would help.

Travis emerged from the forest and wandered toward her house. He passed the spot where he knew the wraith had terrorized Rachel. A car pulled into the driveway and parked in front of the garage. James climbed out in a fitted button shirt and black jeans. Travis waved and jogged toward him.

"I thought you'd left already," James said and held out his hand.

"Decided to stay on," Travis said. "Came to say hello."

"My mom and Katherine aren't here. They're still at the hospital. I went over early; now they're taking a turn. They like her more than me anyway."

"Who?"

"Rachel. My ex."

"I'm sorry. What happened?"

"Car crash, a freak accident. Slammed through someone's fence in broad daylight."

"Is she OK?"

"Yes. She got lucky with cuts and bruises from the impact. Fence wasn't that strong and slowed her down."

"When can she come home?"

"Probably tomorrow. Physically she's OK, but her memory's sketchy."

"How so?"

"She doesn't remember much about the accident. At first, just snippets. But today she told us she'd been late for work, and was speeding to Old Gold. It seems her memory's coming back as the doctors had hoped. She swears she didn't crash on purpose. She swerved to avoid something, a skunk, I think. She hates the smell. She's sorry for the trouble she's caused."

"That's great news."

James smiled and nodded. "But she's still loopy. When we were alone, she went on a rant about fate. She'd had a theory there's no escaping it. Destiny had come looking for her, but now she's convinced she's free. It didn't get her like Mia and Sophia, her two best friends. She's elated—manic, even. She won't stay in bed. She's desperate to move to campus next week to put everything behind her."

"A fresh start will do her good. I'm sorry about your friends."

"It sucks. And I know they didn't plan it."

"What do you think? I saw you on the news. Anything about the missing girl?"

"That's a murder. They just haven't found the body yet." James took a deep breath and surveyed the lawn. "I found Rachel's cell phone in the grass. Brought it to her in the hospital." James pointed to the yard beyond the driveway. "I was mowing the lawn. I knew it was hers from the case. She thought it was lost in the accident and isn't sure how she could've dropped it. She's not careless."

"Does it work?"

"Yeah. I charged it."

"Did she check it out?" Travis took a step closer. "Find anything unusual?"

"Unusual?"

"Anything from the last week?"

James considered the question. "Last thing I sent her was a pic from the cemetery."

Travis studied James' face.

"I took a selfie with my dad. He'd parked in front of the gates. I'm not sure why." James paused to think. "He couldn't park at my mom's house. She wouldn't let him. He was looking for a place to stay in town. He got a lift to your place. That's my dad. He wanted to spy on you and my mom. His car would have given him away."

"And the photo?"

"First time with my dad in Sussex since the divorce. Rachel knew all about him. She'd hoped things would work out. It was a bad time."

Travis folded his arms and leaned against the car door. "So what's next for you?"

James shifted his gaze to the pavement and then smiled. "Getting college applications together: three in-state, one UMass. They're due in November."

"That's great. Good things will happen. What about your dad?"

"He's coming to visit again in two weeks. He says he wants to do better with me and Katherine. My mom's gonna let him stay at the house this time."

"Show him your applications."

"Yeah, my mom's on top of that, and he gets it now."

"I'm glad."

"Do you want to wait for my mom? She should be back any minute."

"Sure, I'll wait."

Travis helped James unload groceries from his car, and they chatted on the steps until Paula's car pulled into the driveway.

Katherine emerged first and made for the door while punching her cell phone.

"How are you feeling?" Travis asked, and she nodded to acknowledge him sitting there.

"Much better. Back to normal, but I'll still need tests," Katherine answered. "My mom's legit normal too. Please don't get her started." She smirked as she shot up the stairs behind him.

Travis stood and walked toward Paula.

"Stopped by to say hello," he said.

"Nice to see you. I thought you'd already left."

"I decided to stay. Still something to finish up."

"That's good, I guess. I'm not sure what that means."

"Neither do I."

Travis held out his hand, beamed a smile, and they shook as if business partners. He couldn't read what she felt or remembered. Her expression was blank. With no control, already the interaction was complicated.

"Glad to see Katherine's OK," Travis said.

"I'm so relieved. They're puzzled but hopeful. Not finding anything neurological." Paula paused, and they locked eyes. "Probably psychological. And that's on me."

"It was my bad influence. You couldn't help it. I won't interfere again."

"You don't have to worry. It's best we both move on."

"We could try again in a few weeks. This time different, slow with no pressure."

Paula pursed her lips. "It's coming back to me now. I don't like who I was around you. I hurt Katherine, and that outweighs everything. I'm sorry."

"I'm sorry too."

"Seeing you stirs things up. I feel tense. My memory's spotty. Our night together was amazing, but when I dig for more, there's not much else. Except for the muffin visit. And the kitchen fiasco that set off Katherine's psychosis. It's scary, like Alzheimer's. Right now, my heart's racing, and not in a good way. You frighten me. I don't know what's wrong. I can't tell anyone because I can't describe it myself. It's better when I don't see you. Confusion goes away and I feel normal. I recognize none of it matters. Please, don't call again."

"I understand."

Travis nodded and slowly turned. It seemed a long way to the stagecoach road.

He wished he could disappear, but someone might be watching.

FIFTY

ON HIS LAST DAY IN SUSSEX, one solemn task remained. It wasn't a symbol of advancement but an unceremonious marker of regret. Travis now understood the ancestral spell would require more time—and perhaps fall to his heir—to properly develop. His work was but an incremental step that had exposed the magic's dark flaws. Monica and Victor had taught him improvements were essential to elevation. The new focus would be magic that used existing human distress to replenish depleted power. Sorinah was poised to help him in Bucharest; Elisabeta had already installed her as an adjutant.

He collected the bags from the shed, hoisted them onto the back of his truck, and took a last look at the labels.

He drove to the landfill and was directed by a worker to the section for biodegradable waste. He backed his truck up an embankment on the edge of a deep ravine. He remembered when he'd gazed in awe at his parents perched high above the edge of the cholera death pit. It seemed eons ago.

But this day marked the end of a chapter, not the beginning.

Travis mounted the back of the truck and heaved his cargo onto the trash pile. He tried to identify the bags, all that remained of the desecrated graves. But they tumbled down the bank and were soon indistinguishable from the other refuse left to fester.

He drove to the center of town toward the railroad station and crossed the tracks. He parked in front of the cemetery and wandered toward Carol Stilton's grave. He knew its exact location, the spot he had first trained Dylan. He searched for the sod patch but could not discern the edges.

Travis stood in front of the gravestone and studied the inscription.

In Loving Memory of
Beloved Daughter and Sister
CAROL STILTON
Laid to Eternal Rest
April 12, 1949
Aged 20 years
We will cherish and remember you always

But Carol no longer slept eternally beneath the granite headstone. Her remains and picture locket were miles away.

Defiled.

The strange key to the ancestral spell, difficult to marshal. No less dreadful than death itself. At least he knew it now.

The Devil knew it all along.

ACKNOWLEDGMENTS

BRINGING A BOOK FROM concept to creation takes grit, time and perseverance. No part of the process can be rushed, there are no shortcuts. It is a privilege to be able to pursue a dream long ago abandoned for a 33-year magazine industry career. The only reason I was able to complete *The Banished*, my debut novel, was through the patient understanding of my spouse, Mauricio. I am incredibly grateful for his support and encouragement. This book is dedicated to him, with so much love.

I would like to thank the Jericho Writers Club in Oxford, UK for tons of spot-on advice. Through them I secured a manuscript assessment from author Russel McLean that was transformative and led to an overhaul.

I owe a huge debt of gratitude to Julia Houston, an editor in New Orleans. Her careful work on two versions of my manuscript was indispensable, especially during crucial stages when I was operating in a vacuum and desperately needed professional criticism and advice. She identified flaws I never would have seen, and I am very thankful.

Made in the USA
Coppell, TX
20 December 2021

69691896R00236